Song of the Loon

LITTLE SISTER'S CLASSICS

Song of the Loon

RICHARD AMORY

ARSENAL PULP PRESS
Vancouver

ARSENAL PULP PRESS
341 Water Street, Suite 200
Vancouver, BC V6B 1B8
arsenalpulp.com

Movie poster for *Song of the Loon* was provided by the GLBT Historical
Society Archives.

Little Sister's Classics series editor: Mark Macdonald
Editors for the press: Robert Ballantyne and Brian Lam
Text and cover design: Shyla Seller
Little Sister's Classics logo design: Hermant Gohil

Printed and bound in Canada

*This is a work of fiction. Any resemblance of characters to persons
either living or deceased is purely coincidental.*

*Efforts have been made to locate copyright holders of source mate-
rial wherever possible. The publisher welcomes hearing from any
copyright holders of material used in this book who have not been
contacted.*

Library and Archives Canada Cataloguing in Publication:

Amory, Richard

Song of the loon / Richard Amory ; with an introduction
by Michael Bronski.

(Little Sister's Classics)
Originally published: San Diego : Greenleaf Classics, 1966.
ISBN 1-55152-180-6
I. Title. II. Series.
PS3551.M64S66 2005   813'.54   C2005-900473-8

ISBN-13 978-1-55152-180-0

Contents

Preface

Song of the Loon has been out of print for far too long. When it was first published in 1966, it was an unabashedly gay novel with strong characters who discovered, by giving into their newfound desires, personal euphoria rather than the moral hand of judgment and tragedy so common in the gay pulps that came before it. It was a tiny gay Utopia. It was a benchmark.

Escapist, romantic, celebratory, and exhuberant, *Song of the Loon* is presented here as a part of gay history that can now be read in the different light of present-day. This edition has been graced with an extensive and informative introduction by historian Michael Bronski, perhaps the leading authority on the world of gay pulp fiction. We owe our sincere gratitude to the author's son, Cesar Love, for his work in uncovering much of the archival material. Thanks to Dirk Vanden, Larry Townsend, Phil Andros, and the other West Coast gay authors, each of them pioneers in their own right.

We are very pleased to present *Song of the Loon*, by Richard Amory, as part of the Little Sister's Classics. This book is dedicated to his memory.

Mark Macdonald, 2005

Introduction

Michael Bronski

For gay men who came of age from the early 1960s to the mid-1970s – the period immediately before and after the 1969 Stonewall Riots, considered the birth of the Gay Liberation movement – *Song of the Loon*, written by Richard Amory (a pseudonym for Richard Love), was perhaps the preeminent cultural literary icon. Even today, nearly forty years after it first appeared, the book (as well as the film that was based upon it) has a name-recognition that few items of gay male culture ever achieve. As opposed to many works that are now considered "classics," *Song of the Loon* started out as one, and even though it has been essentially out of print for three decades, it retains its resonance and power today.

Song of the Loon is the bucolic tale of men discovering their sexuality and their ability to love other men (as well as themselves), set in a mythical world of trappers and Native Americans in the frontier forests of Oregon in the second half of the nineteenth century. Amory tells the story of Ephraim MacIver, a man fleeing through the dense forests of the Northwest to escape a violent, self-loathing former lover. Through Singing Heron and Bear-who-dreams – Native Americans and members of their Society of the Loon – MacIver matures into a self-loving and self-accepting gay man capable of loving relationships, and able to live within the idealized, outside-of-civilization Loon society. Written in a mock heroic style – consciously miming the great sixteenth-century Spanish pastoral novels such as Jorge de

Montemayor's *Los Siete Libros de la Diana* or Gaspar Gil Polo's *Diana Enamorada* (which was a continuation of Montemayor's earlier book), Amory was precise in naming the inspirations for his work – the original subtitle notes that it is "a gay pastoral in five books and an interlude" and an author's note explicitly states that, especially in the instance of his imagined Native Americans, he has "taken very European characters ... [and] painted them a gay aesthetic red and transplanted them into the American wilderness." *Song of the Loon* was a first: a paperback original soft-core porn novel – more accurately labeled, by today's standards, erotica rather than porn – that didn't merely have literary aspirations; it had actual literary merit.

Even Greenleaf Classics, a publisher not known for its literary impulses, emphasized the novel's high-tone qualities in the jacket copy and described the book as "a mystical blend of elements from Hudson's *Green Mansions*, J. F. Cooper's *Leatherstocking Tales*, and the works of Jean Genet." Forgetting the fact that there is only a vague kernel of truth in this description (there is little of Hudson's late-Victorian sentimentality here, and almost none of Genet's harsh vision of anguished salvation), the reality is that Richard Amory wrote a completely original and dazzling novel that marked a turning point in the evolution of gay literature. But *Song of the Loon* was more than simply literature; it was a cultural milestone as well.

The book was released in 1966, and almost immediately took on a mythic stature in gay male circles. Its publisher, Greenleaf Classics, was based in San Diego, and specialized in paperback original, soft-core heterosexual and homosexual porn. *Song of the Loon* found a willing and receptive audience the moment it was published; it was so popular that in 1967 Richard Amory wrote a sequel, *Song of Aaron*, also published by Greenleaf. It is clear that the author and publisher planned to create a *Loon* trilogy at the time, since the title page of *Song of Aaron* labels it "book two" of "the Loon Songs trilogy." In publishing, popularity breeds productivity, and Greenleaf understood

both the ever-expanding reputation as well as sales potential of *Song of the Loon*. The cover of *Song of Aaron* touts it as "[t]his generation's most eagerly awaited book ... the spectacular sequel to the best selling underground sensation ... *Song of the Loon*." The following year, *Listen, the Loon Sings...* appeared, described on its cover as the "final volume of the sensational Loon Songs trilogy."

Later editions of *Song* make the claim on their cover of "over 100,000 copies sold"; while one should always be wary of sales figures from publishers, it is possible – given Greenleaf's print runs and distribution networks – that sales of the trilogy itself may have reached these proportions. While the exact figures for Greenleaf's print runs and sales are unavailable, we do know that the *Loon* books were so popular that in 1968 Greenleaf published *Fruit of the Loon*, a silly, occasionally amusing parody of the *Loon* books. "Ricardo Armory" is listed as the author of *Fruit of the Loon*, but that is simply part of the parody; Richard Amory had no connection to either its conceptualization or authorship. If the burlesque of *Fruit of the Loon* is a clear nod to the commercial and cultural success of the original books, even more so is the 1970 film version of *Song of the Loon*. Directed by Andrew Herbert, it was the first independently produced, non-pornographic gay male feature to be granted mainstream theatrical release. While it never played top-rung venues, the film – which featured soft-core nudity and displays of affection between its male characters – was booked into theaters in many large American cities and found audiences eager to see how the beloved novel played on the screen.

In the current age of *Will and Grace*, *Queer Eye for the Straight Guy*, and the casual appearance of homosexuality in major Hollywood films, it may be difficult to understand the impact and the importance of *Song of the Loon* not only on gay male culture but on mainstream American culture as well. Richard Amory wrote the book at a vital, and fascinating, moment in twentieth-century American gay history. Not only did this culture affect the writing and the reception

of *Song of the Loon*, the book itself signaled an important shift in a new emerging sense of identity for gay men and their communities in the U.S.

The publication of *Song of the Loon* in 1966 places it firmly at the end of the time period that might be thought of as the first wave of the U.S. gay rights movement. This era began in 1950 when Harry Hay, along with a small group of other men, founded the Mattachine Society, the first major U.S. organization that had as its goal the promotion of justice and equality for homosexuals. During this time, other groups sprang up across the U.S. – Daughters of Bilitis (DOB), Society for Individual Rights (SIR), the Janus Society, among others – which are generally referred to under the umbrella term "homophile." These homophile years essentially ended with the Stonewall Riots in New York's Greenwich Village in June of 1969, giving birth to the modern Gay Liberation movement. With the formation of the Gay Liberation Front (GLF) – a radical political group that took its cues from the new left and other political movements such as the Woman's Liberation Front, the Black Power movement, and the Vietnamese National Liberation Front – the assimilationist politics of the homophile groups were seen by many new gay activists as "old-fashioned" and even self-loathing. The universal cry of the Gay Liberation movement, "Gay is Good," was used as a baseline for how to judge activist politics, personal politics, and all forms of culture.

Historians often make a sharp distinction between the homophile organizations and the Gay Liberation activists, and to a degree, a decisive political break did occur in that summer of 1969. But such historical moments never occur unheralded, without some specters of oncoming change. Indeed, the maxim "Gay is Good" was coined and first used by Mattachine Society activist Frank Kammeny in 1968, an update of "Homosexuality is Good," a phrase he used in a noted 1964 speech. While the Stonewall Riots were a clear result of many late 1960s influences – the direct-action tactics of radical political

groups; the active, rambunctious summer street culture in New York City; the prevalent cultural mind-set of "drugs, sex, and rock and roll"– there is little doubt that its beginnings were also present in some manifestations of homophile politics. I've dwelt on this historical moment at some length here because it completely, and deftly, illustrates the political and social importance of *Song of the Loon*.

Literary critic David Bergman, in his excellent essay "The Cultural Work of Sixties Gay Pulp Fiction,"[1] makes the case that the sexual politics of *Song of the Loon* fall outside of the accepted demarcation line between pre- and post-Stonewall gay sensibility. The overt message of Amory's novel is that only by loving oneself – essentially accepting the fact that "gay is good"– can one ever love other people and be at peace with the world. This was, indeed, the salient message of Gay Liberation. And Richard Amory's genius in the *Loon* novels is that he brought that message (albeit, already articulated by Frank Kammeny to a very small group of politicized homosexuals) to the gay masses – a message they wanted and needed. That he did this years before the Gay Liberation movement began is remarkable and a tribute to the power of art and the imagination.

But *Song of the Loon* did not spring fully formed out of Richard Amory's head, and while the social and political context in which it was written is important, so is the cultural context. Just as there is a perception – a myth, really – that politics before Stonewall was only concerned with adhering to heterosexual social norms, and that post-Stonewall life was all about liberation, there is also a widespread and deeply held-to myth that all gay fiction written before Stonewall was embroiled with self-hatred and ended in suicide, and that post-Stonewall literature is a constant affirmation of the radiance of gay life and gay love.

---

[1] From *The Queer Sixties*. Patricia Juliana Smith, ed. New York: Routledge, 1999.

As with all cultural myths, this is not completely accurate. There is a rich body of American gay male literature that emerged in the post war years. As I illustrate in my anthology *Pulp Friction: Uncovering the Golden Age of Gay Male Pulps*,[2] there were probably close to 300 hardcover novels with central gay male characters and themes published between 1945 and 1969. (The appendix to *Pulp Friction* lists 260 titles, and I am still discovering more.) Many of these cloth-bound titles – on the whole, serious literary works – found a second life in paperback, often with the flamboyantly garish covers that we associate with gay pulp fiction. And along with these books there was a rapidly growing book industry for paperback originals – usually marketed with exploitative or heavily suggestive titles or cover art – that were being published by a host of small, but quickly expanding companies such as Greenleaf, Publisher's Export Co., and Guild Press. While these publishers were not interested in quality literary fiction – indeed, they were almost entirely concerned with acquiring, printing, and then publishing as many titles as the market could bear – they often did attract talented writers who, for various reasons – including overly sexually explicit content or lack of knowledge or contacts in the mainstream publishing world – would not be able to find other publishing venues. So from where did *Song of the Loon* spring? How does it fit into this nexus of gay-themed publishing at the time?

There is no doubt that there was a popular mainstream literary culture in the 1950s and 1960s that allowed for, and even at times promoted, decisively gay-themed novels. There are novels in the 1940s and 1950s that took on daring, provocative gay themes and found a readership: Richard Brooks's *The Brick Foxhole* (1945) gave a startling critique of how American masculinity led to violent homophobia (and racism); Thomas Hal Phillips' *The Bitterweed Path* (1949) looked

---

[2] Bronski, Michael. *Pulp Friction: Uncovering the Golden Age of Gay Male Pulps*. New York: St. Martin's Griffin, 2003.

at a complicated erotic relationship between a father and son and a third man; Paul Goodman's *Parents Day* (1951) examined the relationship of a married man with a student at a private school; Gerald Tesch's *Never the Same Again* (1956) was a sympathetic account of an affair between a thirteen-year-old boy and a thirty-year-old man; and Lonnie Coleman's *Sam* (1959) observed the problem of a middle-aged gay professional man looking for love in New York. Even in the 1950s, Americans could read more sexually explicit gay-themed material. Allen Ginsberg's groundbreaking poem *Howl* was published (along with other works) in 1956; *Chicago Review* published portions of William Burroughs' *Naked Lunch* in 1959; John Rechy's *City of Night* was a bestseller in 1963, the year that the English translation of Jean Genet's *Our Lady of the Flowers* become a cult novel for the intelligentsia; and in 1964, Hubert Selby's *Last Exit to Brooklyn* became a literary *cause célèbre*.

At the same time as mainstream publishing was promoting – and in some cases, such as Selby's *Last Exit*, possibly even exploiting – gay male themes, the smaller, paperback original companies were promoting something of a revolution. While many of these companies had been releasing heterosexual-themed books since 1963 or 1964, titles with gay content were relatively few until 1966. Guild Press, based in Washington, D.C., published two books by Alexander Goodman – *The Soft Spot* in 1964, and *A Sliver of Flesh* in 1965 – but for the most part, it wasn't until two years later that gay male-themed books flooded the market, including *Song of the Loon*.

The co-existence of these two very different publishing markets raises an interesting question: could Richard Amory have published *Song of the Loon* with a more mainstream publisher? Amory's novel is so much a part of the fabric and history of gay pulp publishing that it is difficult to think of it as anything other than what it is. On the face of it – given the overt sexual content of the novel – a chance at mainstream publishing seems unlikely. Yet, when examined more

closely, it is not out of the question. Certainly Rechy's *City of Night* and Selby's *Last Exit to Brooklyn* are far more explicit in their depiction of sexual activity. And while it might be argued that these two novels give a distinctly downbeat, if not completely negative, view of gay male culture – as opposed to the sunny optimism of *Song of the Loon* – it is also true that novels such as Coleman's *Sam* and even Richard Meeker's *Better Angel* (1933) showed that mainstream publishing was capable of promoting (albeit, infrequently) gay novels with happy endings. Even the fact that Amory's ambitious literary aspirations – the rewriting of classic sixteenth-century Spanish pastorals – may not have been held against it. *The Evergreen Review* and its publisher Grove Press, as well as Olympia Press, were always interested in quirky literary experiments and were in the forefront of publishing exciting new writing. While the bulk of this writing was concerned with heterosexual relationships and activities, there were important exceptions: *The Evergreen Review* first published Rechy's and Selby's writing; and Olympia Press' Travelers Companion series published Burroughs' *Naked Lunch* and *The Ticket that Exploded*, William Talsman's *The Gaudy Image*, and Parker Tyler and Charles Henri Ford's notorious underground classic *The Young and the Evil*, as well as Jean Cocteau's *The White Paper*, Oscar Wilde's *Teleny*, and the highly sexual, long suppressed *Black Diaries* of Irish revolutionary Roger Casement. They were also not adverse to publishing quirky items such as Akbar del Piombo's collage graphic novel *Fuzz Against Junk*.

It is not impossible to think that Richard Amory's quirky, well-written and original *Song of the Loon* might have found a home at *The Evergreen Review*, Grove Press, or the Traveler's Companion series in 1965 when he had completed it. In fact, in 1971, Amory did publish *Frost* with the Other Traveler series, an imprint of Traveler's Companion. So why did he decide to publish *Song of the Loon* with Greenleaf Classics?

We have no answers, but there are some clues. Because of the popularity of *Song of the Loon* Amory was interviewed in gay publications including *The Advocate* and *Vector* (the publishing arm of SIR [Society for Individual Rights]), and frequently wrote essays on literature, gay publishing, and politics for these publications as well. With a few exceptions, Amory seems to dislike much of what has been published in the mainstream on gay themes. In an interview in *Vector*, he posits that the gay novel is "already an identifiable genre ... with roots going back to the nineteenth century if not further. (I don't think that the *Satyricon* counts)." But his major complaints were with more recent books published by mainstream publishers:

> I'm no expert on the gay novel (there is room here for
> a serious study), but it seems to be that up until now,
> we've had two main types of books, neither of which is
> much to my liking. First there is what I call the "Closet
> Queen Novel," a dishonest put-on wherein the es-
> sentially gay characters are disguised as heterosexuals.
> These things are much older than *Who's Afraid of Vir-
> ginia Woolf* and probably much more common than the
> straight world would like to believe.

After naming a varied assortment of works and authors who fit into the category – the thirteenth-century *Le Queste del Saint Graal*; the works of Tennessee Williams; Mason Hoffenberg and Terry Southern's *Candy* (for its "perverse cleverly disguised misogyny"); "at least two popular writers of westerns, one very good and one very bad, both deceased"; as well as *Virginia Woolf* playwright Edward Albee – Amory cites his second complaint.

> The next wave is what I call the Gay Grotesque. This
> is the whole tiresome series of novels from *Finistère*
> to *Myra Breckinridge*, also written for a straight pub-
> lic in which the hero is either killed off at the end or

straightened out, or else he is so ridiculous or repulsive that he allowed to live on in a hell of the author's making.

Amory's complaints are fascinating, but curious. It is true that there always has been criticism – from both gay readers as well as conservative heterosexuals – about the "closeting" of what-might-be-read as gay characters by some homosexual writers. (In 1961, *New York Times* theater critic Howard Taubman created a minor sensation and panic when he wrote a piece entitled "Not What It Seems: Homosexual Motifs Get Heterosexual Guide," in which he accused writers like William Inge, Edward Albee, and Tennessee Williams – none of whom he actually named – as misrepresenting their gay content in order to fool a straight audience.) In the *Vector* interview, Amory seemed to be arguing for a more distinctly out and proud gay culture. But his complaints about *Finistère* and *Myra Breckinridge* feel off the mark. In other writings, Amory complained about the idea of the gay "problem novel" – and certainly Fritz Peters' *Finistère*, as well as many of the fine books from the 1950s and even the early 1960s – James Barr's *Quatrefoil* (1950), Russell Thacher's *The Tender Age* (1954), James Yaffe's *Nothing But the Night* (1957) – might fall into this category. This is all rather odd, since if there is one thing we can see in many of Amory's writings about literature, it is that he was a careful, smart, and observant reader. Surely he must have understood that *Finistère* is as much about homophobia as it was about a "gay grotesque" (given the fact that the "grotesque" character is a destructive closeted gay man who attempts to molest his stepson) – and certainly that Gore Vidal's *Myra Breckinridge* is a full-fledged attack on heterosexual America, not an attack on homosexuality.

Amory's critique of *Finistère* is also curious after one reads the positive, extraordinarily insightful review he wrote in the April 1972 issue of *Vector* of Charles Jackson's 1944 novel *The Fall of Valor*, about a

married man who discovers his sexuality when he is suddenly attracted to a heterosexually identified marine. *The Fall of Valor* hardly
ends happily – its protagonist is badly beaten by the man he loves
– so it surely can be (mis)read as a "grotesque." But the key to much
of Amory's writing on literature – and perhaps the key to *Song of the
Loon* – is that he was eager, even demanding for psychological truth
in writing. In the early 1970s, Amory wrote two pieces for *Vector*
explicating Mark Twain's work – a long, smart analysis of *Tom Sawyer*
("Richard Amory reads Tom Sawyer"), and a larger examination, entitled "Mark Twain, Too," of some of Twain's other novels, including
The Prince and the Pauper and *Pudd'nhead Wilson*. In them, he came
to the conclusion that Mark Twain had homosexual desires, if not
encounters. While these observations feel dated now – his reliance
on psychoanalysis was not as sophisticated as it might be today – his
investigation into the subtext of these books was original and invigo-
rating for the time. But one of his main concerns was that Twain was
not being truthful to himself, a complaint that he also made against
Somerset Maugham in a long *Vector* piece in which he castigated the
author for concealing his homosexuality behind heterosexual situations. Throughout much of Amory's writings on literature, one re-
curring theme is crystal clear: he demanded that homosexual authors
be truthful to their own gayness. This was, apparently for Amory, an
impossibility for almost anyone who chose to write for, and be com-
promised by, the mainstream.

It is probably safe to say that Richard Amory published *Song of the
Loon* with Greenleaf Classics, at least in part, because he saw this
house – and some of the other smaller paperback original publishers
that were now catering to a gay male market – as the closest option
to a "gay publisher" that was available. In his *Vector* interview, Amory
shared his vision for the gay novel of the future: "I would like to see,
and I think it's coming, a genre written by gay authors, for a strictly
gay audience, no holds barred, telling it like it is, or should be, *and put
out by a gay publisher*." There are two observations to be made here.

The first is that Amory experienced real problems with Greenleaf Classics. Not surprisingly, being a money-making company with no overt commitment to literature, art, or sexual politics, and certainly not to a gay culture or gay community (except as a source of revenue), Greenleaf produced books as quickly and as cheaply as possible – not the best situation for authors who cared about their work. In this interview, and several other writings, Amory happily enumerated every problem he had endured at Greenleaf: bad, sloppy, and politically insensitive editing; title changes without his permission; a refusal to honor his contracts or to send him royalty statements; and – at the heart of it – a refusal to take him seriously as a writer. Without a doubt, all of this is true; Dirk Vanden – another immensely talented gay writer who published with Greenleaf – had many of the same complaints. And why should it have been otherwise? These were writers with a vision of a new community and a new literature, and they were dealing with a publishing house that shared none of these same concerns.

But what is equally important to note is that in the interview, Amory was articulating a vision – granted, following the Stonewall Riots – in which he postulates an independent gay culture that was not held hostage by, or indebted to, the larger heterosexual culture. This was a tremendously revolutionary idea for the time – in accordance not only with the politics of the Gay Liberation movement, but with the desire for cultural autonomy that was also evident in the Women's Liberation movement, the Black Power movement, and other nationalist and identity politics movements. This is what, in part, made *Song of the Loon* so vital, and so original and meaningful in comparison to the other erotica and soft-core porn titles being published by Greenleaf and other paperback original publishers at the time.

It would be easy to sketch a sharply dichotomized picture of the state of (non-mainstream) gay literature at the time of Stonewall in which pioneers such as Richard Amory and Dirk Vanden were being exploited by publishing houses such as Greenleaf. While there is no doubt that these writers – indeed, probably most of the writers who worked with these houses – were underpaid, not given fair contracts, and often not treated with even minimal respect, there is a larger, and far more interesting, framework that also bears critical examination.

While Richard Amory and Dirk Vanden certainly have valid and well-articulated complaints against Greenleaf, we see a differing point of view in articles written by Larry Townsend during this period. By 1970, Townsend had published twelve novels with Greenleaf – including the now classic *Kiss of Leather* – and was then making his living as a full-time writer. In the April 1970 issue of *Vector*, Townsend penned a response to an interview with Dirk Vanden that had appeared in the previous month's issue, in which Vanden had complained that Greenleaf was only interested in acquiring and publishing novels with a high degree of sexual content, as well as offering the standard criticisms of their economic disregard of their authors. In his response, provocatively entitled "In Defense of 'Exploiters'," Townsend gave his version of Greenleaf's side of the story:

> The first fact we can't ignore is that publishing is one
> hell of a rough business. When the *Saturday Evening
> Post* can't make it … well, face it, fellas – it ain't no bed
> of roses. Greenleaf, like every other successful business
> in this country – is run for one reason and one reason
> only. That long green – the break by which we live and
> buy our beers. And in the gay market, who determines
> what sells and does not sell? You! If you are more apt
> to buy a lurid title, that's what the publisher (gay or
> straight) is going to put out. If you buy stories with sex
> in every chapter over stories with a lighter saturation
> of "hots," what do you expect Greenleaf or any other
> house to publish? Anything that is produced and mar-
> keted in any art field is – and must be – a compromise

between the product the artist would like to produce
and the product the publisher, studio, gallery, agent or
what-have-you is able to profitably sell. However un-
fortunate this may be, it is very much a fact of life.

With Greenleaf I have found an outlet that will print
what I write, allowing me a great latitude in subject
matter so long as I slant the stories into their market.
And this market is sex. Still, whether publishers like
Greenleaf intend it or not, they are helping us to establish a core of working writers and (albeit of "porno,"
by current standards) a core of literature where a great
many ideas are finding the light of exposure to a large
reading audience. Sexual? Of course! We are a highly
sexual subculture.

Now accepting this, what is the answer for a writer like
Dirk Vanden – or Larry Townsend? I want to write
and I want to see my stories in print. I can either adapt
(some will read "prostitute") my art to this market,
thereby making a living at it; or I can take a regular
job, sweating my ass off at night in front of the type-
writer, producing things that will make a lovely pile of
unpublished manuscripts on a shelf in my den. I choose
to go the Greenleaf route. Nor is it quite as bad a route
as one might think from Dirk's disgruntled evaluation.
He was not patient enough.

Townsend continued pragmatically:

And let me add one final word – a plea if you will:
The gay market is changing. Greenleaf Classics, like
any other publisher who puts material into it, is aware
of the situation. They are upgrading the standards of

their line by more careful selection of stories, vastly improving editing, and more careful proofreading of the finished products. The crap that hit the stands a year ago is no longer being bought. (Published maybe, but only to clear out the backlogs.) Writers like Richard Amory, Jeff Lawton, Peter Tuesday Hughes, Carl Driver, Dirk and (I hope) myself are selling. If we keep our stuff on a higher literary level, we will continue to sell. This is how it should be – whether we sell to a publisher who is straight or otherwise. But in the long run, the future of this market rests with you dear readers! If you buy the crap, they are going to keep publishing it. And that is going to make it tougher for the good writers to produce what they want to produce – and what I think most of you want to read.

I have quoted Townsend at some length here because I think his piece sits in fascinating juxtaposition to the complaints of Vanden and Amory. It isn't that one side is correct and the other wrong – they are both, to varying degrees, right – but that it gives us a window into the gay literary world of the early 1970s. What we see is a classic political conflict between the pragmatists and the idealists, between those who have made the choice to be patient and encourage change in increments, and those who have a vision of the future and can't wait for it to happen. As Larry Townsend wrote of Dirk Vanden: "He was not patient enough." But what we also see here is a wonderful, engaged, sometimes angry, very public conversation. It is about many things: art and capitalism, the nature of community, the burden of responsibility, the authority of the author and the power of the reader. But most of all, it is a discussion about the state and the future of gay male writing.

No matter where each of these men stand – and there are a series of overlapping positions that each of them take – it is clear that they all care passionately about the relationship between gay men, the gay community, and literature. This is, I believe, a new discussion that is taking place; it is a discussion that has never before happened on this ground and on these terms. Beginning in the 1940s, a large, diverse, growing body of literature with gay male themes was being published by mainstream houses; there is no doubt that many men who grew up and came out before Stonewall were familiar with it. And certainly many men loved these books – they were important to them, and meaningful in a way that nothing else at the time could have been. And indeed, many of these books were written by gay men, with an insider's perspective, and are quite good – some, even great. But for all of their worth, they were, by the mid-1960s, seen as relics of a bygone homosexual world that was being left behind as gay men and their communities moved forward.

But what we have seen so far here are the words and the ideas of gay male writers. What about their readers? What did they want? In an angry column published in the May 1973 *Vector*, Douglas Dean – who wrote twelve novels for Greenleaf Classics between 1969 and 1971 – took a dim view of the contemporary gay male readership. After complaining about the state of the mainstream gay male novel – he singled out *The City and the Pillar*, *The Sling and the Arrow*, *City of Night*, and *The Lord Won't Mind* – as dealing with "highly neurotic types in extreme, melodramatic situations," and noted that "straight readers gobbled these books up, because that's how they want to think of us … [and] gay readers went right along for the buggy ride." And then he came to his real criticism:

> Why is it though that we don't have more honest gay novels and short stories? It is my contention that the reason for this, in the final analysis, may be found in the attitude of the gay readers themselves.

> Most gay readers do not want "good" gay literature,

they couldn't care less about novels and short stories
that are honestly written. What they want is, for the
most part, crap – and that's why the publishers go on
giving it to them. That's why the "fuck" books, ground
out by some publishers in the way that a butcher grinds
out hamburger, are good sellers, and its also why a
writer who tries to elevate the tone of the gay paperback novel is doomed to a certain and never ending
battle.

Dean ended his column by noting that "at the moment many gay
writers are at the crossroads of their careers as writers of fiction.
Should we continue when so few publishers are willing to take a
chance on a quiet style of writing in this field when the reading public
who cares for it is so limited?"

Dean didn't mention *Song of the Loon* – his only reference points
mentioned were a non-literary novel entitled *Clint Wins His Letter*
and the novels of James Colton, the pseudonym of Joseph Hansen
– but it is probably safe to assume that Amory's novel would not have
fit into his definition of "'good' gay literature." Dean is looking for
emotional and psychological honesty in the realm of realistic narra-
tive. This is not *Song of the Loon*.

The enormous popularity of Richard Amory's novels are predicated
upon their being, in essence, homoerotic fantasies of freedom. It is
certainly possible to do an analysis of Amory's antecedents and his
uses of classic tropes and themes in American literature – for example, his use of the specific American pastoral is resonant of Walt
Whitman and the paintings and photographs of Thomas Eakins; his
concept of freedom residing outside of the "civilized" realm of the
urban reminds us not only of Mark Twain, but Melville and Cooper; and certainly his conceptualization of the "noble savage" can be
traced back to Aphra Behn's 1678 novel *Oroonoko*. But these are all

the literary trappings that display one clear message – that "gay is good."

It may be only possible to understand how important *Song of the Loon* was to its readership by seeing it clearly as a rejection of the many "problem novels" that preceded it in the 1940s, 1950s, and early 1960s. Those books – no matter how well they were written, no matter how anti-homophobic many of them were – never had the luxury of *not* being problem novels. It was simply impossible in the pre-Stonewall era. Even Douglas Dean's novels and stories – as well-written and psychologically astute as they are – were, on some level, still problem novels. Richard Amory's genius was that he anticipated – by three years – the fullness of the freedom that Stonewall and the Gay Liberation movement would offer gay people across America. In Amory's vision, and in his historical context, that freedom was necessarily a fantasy, and had to be set in the idyllic past. But the irony here is that despite its nineteenth-century setting, *Song of the Loon* is not an escape into a fantasy of the past, but a journey into the possibilities of the future. It is a message that is still needed, and applicable, today.

Song of the Loon

The author wishes it clearly understood that he has, un-fortunately, never known or heard of a single Indian even remotely resembling, for instance, Singing Heron or Tlaso-hkah or Bear-who-dreams. He has taken certain very European characters from the novels of Jorge De Montemayor and Gaspar Gil Polo, painted them a gay aesthetic red, and transplanted them to the American wilderness. Anyone who wishes to read other intentions into these characterizations is willfully misunderstanding the nature of the pastoral genre, and is fervently urged not to do so. The same might be said of those who love to point out anachronisms and factual im-probabilities.

Book One

A brilliant day; the high May sun streamed through the Douglas firs, glanced from their pale green needles into pools of air, tangibly blue. Darker green, the waters of the Umpqua fell in tiny crystals from the paddle – the waves from the canoe sighed in the shadows of white alders and lacey vine maples. A pair of jays screamed high in the tree tops, then streaked far into the woods, crying hoarsely.

The sunlight turned the man's hair to new copper; shirtless, his deeply-muscled shoulders stretched and tightened as he paddled, formed knots and hollows across his back. His chest hair gleamed with sweat, and the thin line of hair down his belly, widening below the navel, was flattened against his undulating muscles. He paused. The jays returned, still screaming.

Another sound reached him, from upstream, a thin sound, and hollow; then it stopped, and began again. He started paddling, silently gliding across the still pools near the bank. At a bend in the river he paused again.

Perhaps fifty yards upstream was an Indian, leaning carelessly against a fallen tree, playing a wooden flute. He also was shirtless, and his black hair, unbound, fell past his shoulders. Broad, smooth chest: lithe, narrow waist, as supple as a willow tree.

The white man paddled closer, listening to the strange music. The Indian saw him then, but continued playing. As the canoe neared the shore he stopped and laid his flute on the ground. They gazed at each other in silence. When the canoe touched the river bank the Indian rose; his eyes, like chips of obsidian, rested on the white man.

He pulled the canoe onto the sand. "You are Ephraim MacIver," he said calmly.

"Yes," said the white man, rising; he pulled on a shirt, leaving it unbuttoned, and stepped onto the shore. "How did you know my name?"

"Astoria is not far. And you have been slow." The Indian sat down again and picked up his flute.

"There have been difficulties," said Ephraim. He pulled the canoe farther up on the bank and started to unload it.

"Not here," said the Indian. "I will take you to a cabin upstream. We must hide the canoe."

"Now?" said Ephraim.

"If you wish." The Indian stood again, and took the paddle. He pointed to the middle of the canoe where he wished Ephraim to sit, shoved off, and climbed in gracefully. "Face me," he said, "so that we may talk." And when Ephraim turned around carefully to face him: "What sort of difficulties?" he asked.

Ephraim stared at the Indian's long, smoothly muscled arms, at the sinews flexing as he paddled. "Do you know the man at Salem who calls himself Mr. Calvin? The Indians call him Thunder-in-the-Pines."

"Ah, yes," said the Indian. "I know him well. He taught me to speak English."

"You went to his school then?"

"Yes. For many years, until I ran away." He paused. "His ways are not my ways."

"He knows me," said Ephraim. "I was forced to hide."

"That is bad. Very bad."

"He hasn't followed me, however. I waited along the Siuslaw for eight days, in hiding, to see if he was following, but he lost my trail. He thinks that I either went south along the Willamette, or west, perhaps up the MacKenzie. He won't find me."

"Perhaps not, but he never forgets." The Indian paddled a while in silence, frowning. "My English name was Daniel. It is a name that

Mr. Calvin gave to make me Christian, so I put Daniel aside when I ran away, and became Indian again. My Indian name is Singing Heron."

❧

He beached the canoe in a clump of white alders and they pulled it far from the river, hiding it in a windfall. With great care they removed all traces of their landing from the river bank. "If Mr. Calvin passes, he will perhaps be fooled," the Indian murmured, "but I think Mr. Calvin is far away." He smiled at Ephraim for the first time, showing strong, even teeth.

The cabin was a lean-to of branches and bark; one side was protected by skins. Ephraim lay down on the grass to rest, eyes half-closed, head propped on one arm. With his other hand he lazily fluffed the sweat-flattened hair on his chest. Singing Heron took up his flute again and played a long, slow Indian melody, watching Ephraim. Then he stopped.

"Did the old man from Astoria – the man who is called Ixtlil Cuauhtli – did he give you a sign?"

"Yes," said Ephraim. He leaned on one elbow and reached into his pocket. "Here it is."

It was a leather pouch. Singing Heron opened it carefully and looked inside. "The sign of the loon," he said, and gave it back to Ephraim.

"You are the first to see it," said Ephraim.

Singing Heron took his flute again and played another slender, drifting tune that curled like smoke among the trees. When he finished, he gazed at Ephraim. "You are very beautiful," he said softly.

Ephraim breathed deeper and shut his eyes. "And so are you," he replied. "You are a very handsome person."

They lay in silence, listening to the jays. Finally Singing Heron stood up. "That is good," he said. "We will eat now, and then go to the river." He went into the shelter and brought out two cooked rabbits, still warm, and parched corn and dried fruit. "I cooked these this morning," he said, "thinking that you might come today. And I was right – you have come." He glanced at Ephraim with warmly dark eyes, and began to cut up the rabbits.

"Tell me," Singing Heron said when they had sat on the ground to eat, "how did you meet Ixtlil Cuauhtli?"

Ephraim thought for a long time before answering, wondering how much he was expected to say. Finally he murmured, "He found me, on the beach, on the sand. I was sick –"

Singing Heron gazed thoughtfully at Ephraim. "He took you to his cabin?" he asked.

"Yes," Ephraim answered. "He was very kind to me."

"Why were you sick on the sand?" Singing Heron asked softly.

Again, Ephraim thought carefully before answering, wanting to tell the whole story, yet not daring to trust his questioner. He breathed a deep sigh, and answered haltingly. "I had been following a friend – a friend of mine I had known in the East. We had gone to San Francisco together, and suddenly he disappeared, and I managed to follow him by ship to Astoria, and there I lost him completely –" He stopped in confusion and reached for the parched corn.

Singing Heron chewed on a rabbit leg and waited silently for Ephraim to continue.

"I – I was desperately unhappy, and I lost my head, and got into trouble, and they left me on the beach where Ixtlil Cuauhtli found me. I was – delirious for a long time, and the old man listened, and he talked to me, and cured me. Now I must go to the wise man, the medicine man of the painted cave." He faltered, and fell silent.

Singing Heron leaned back and gazed away into the depths of the forest. His face was calm. "The man you were looking for – was he your lover?"

Ephraim's head spun around in fright, and he stared at the Indian's profile. Singing Heron's eyes were hidden from view, and Ephraim looked at the ground in embarrassment.

"Yes," he answered bitterly, "but I no longer think of him. He is gone, and has no more power over me."

"I am beginning to understand," the Indian murmured. "Such things happen very often among – other people." His head turned slightly, and his gaze fell on Ephraim's outstretched legs. "It is a strange way, a cruel way. Did you love him, Ephraim?"

Ephraim grinned wryly. "Yes, I think so," he said. "Perhaps in my own way. But he was dishonest to himself, and to me, and he never spoke of love; often, he spoke of hatred, and said many cruel things."

"How strange," the Indian mused, "that he should not speak of love to you." His fingertips touched the back of Ephraim's hand, lightly, tentatively.

Ephraim's fingers curled inward, instinctively, and his hand trembled. He sat up, heart pounding, and looked away. Then, suddenly, he wished he had lain still.

Singing Heron's soft, melodious voice came from behind him. "I am sorry. I did not mean to frighten you."

Ephraim bent his head and drew random lines in the earth. "No – it was my fault. I didn't expect it – there's nothing wrong. I should have trusted you." He turned around and looked into Singing Heron's enigmatic eyes. "I am very sorry," he said, and leaned back again.

Hesitantly, almost fearfully, he reached out to touch the Indian's shining hair, at the temple. "The old man from Astoria told me," he whispered, "that many men were not like Montgomery."

Singing Heron drew closer, languidly; his cheek brushed against Ephraim's shoulder, then his lips. "Was that your lover's name?"

"Yes." Softly, he touched the Indian's forehead with his lips.

"A very sad man."

"Sad, and unhappy –"

Suddenly Singing Heron sat up and gazed down at Ephraim. "Let us not speak of him," he said.

"No. We don't have to. He is forgotten."

Singing Heron smiled and stood up. "Come," he said, and Ephraim rose to follow him.

The Indian's strong legs glided through the underbrush, past clumps of currant blossoms and purple asters – his powerful back rose from hard, muscular buttocks; his shoulders were broad and graceful.

At a clearing near the river he stopped.

Breathing deeply, Ephraim watched the Indian remove his moccasins.

"Ixtlil Cuauhtli is a very wise man," Singing Heron said. "I have known him for many years; it was he who brought me to the Way of the Loon." He turned to face Ephraim and untied a cord around his waist; his leather leggings fell to the ground and he stepped out of them, naked, waiting for Ephraim to undress. The hair at the base of his belly glinted in the slanting rays of the sun; his long and heavily veined penis was downward hanging but lengthened slowly; his testicles hung heavily against dark thighs.

Ephraim's voice caught; he swallowed and unbuttoned his shirt. With an effort to control his voice, he said, "The old man told me many things I shall never forget." His shirt fell to the ground and he stooped to unlace his boots. "He told me that the lover I am seeking is rare among men; one who walks proudly and with strength in the sun, who draws strength from the earth, as do the cedar and the Douglas fir; one who can love others because he can love himself." He looked at Singing Heron.

The Indian was watching him calmly, unconcerned with his own slowly rising cock.

Ephraim stood up and began to unbutton his breeches. He hesitated, knowing that his cock was swollen. The breeches hung at his hips below the silky, copper-shining hair of his lower belly. Quickly, he pulled his breeches off and threw them on the ground by his boots.

Singing Heron gazed casually at Ephraim's cock, thick and muscular like an oak tree. "There are such men," he murmured, "and you will know many of them soon." Then he turned and walked toward the river, glancing back at Ephraim; when Ephraim caught up to him, the Indian touched his hand, and lightly caressed his shoulder.

Ephraim was blinded with excitement and shyness; the Indian's gently swinging cock was a blur in the corner of his eye.

At the river's edge, Singing Heron stopped; then like a golden flash he dived into the water. Ephraim stood on the bank and watched the Indian swim to a rock on the far side. When he turned, smiling, beckoning, Ephraim dived in, and swam to the mysterious form, glowing palely under the water.

Carelessly, Ephraim climbed onto the rock and sat down; Singing Heron remained in the water, long hair floating languidly about his shoulders. He touched Ephraim's ankle, drying in the sun, and delicately passed his fingertips over the golden hair of Ephraim's calf.

"You are as the old man said," he breathed. "Like the sunlight of an April noon."

Ephraim blushed and turned away. "You have talked to Ixtlil Cuauhtli about me?" he asked.

Singing Heron pulled himself up on the rock and sat facing Ephraim, leaning on one elbow. "Ixtlil Cuauhtli sent a message to Bear-who-dreams about you, a month ago, before you left. I was at the painted cave when it arrived. We all know of your coming."

With veiled eyes, Ephraim glanced at the Indian's naked body stretched out on the rock, at the long cock lying carelessly across a heavily muscled thigh. "I am glad that I came this way," he whispered, and looked at Singing Heron's eyes.

"I, too, am happy," the Indian answered softly, "and we shall make love, I think. Do you wish to?"

Ephraim's voice caught; "Yes," he muttered, almost inaudibly. "You are beautiful and gentle, and strong –"

Singing Heron smiled slowly, and stood up, and offered his hand to Ephraim. In an instant they were off the rock, into the current, laughing, chasing, splashing, wrestling, teasing. Their bodies met and pulled apart, fingers, lips, thighs, seeking, yearning, caressing.

Finally Singing Heron pulled away, laughing, and stood on the shore. He turned and walked back to the clearing, and Ephraim followed. Silently the picked up their clothes and followed the path back to the cabin, side by side, glancing at each other, drying their bodies in the patches of sunlight.

When they reached the cabin Singing Heron spread a blanket on the ground and lay down, leaning on one elbow. Ephraim sat before him, gazing at the Indian's smooth, powerful body, at the muscles of his belly, the brown, strong thighs. Then he too lay down, on his back, and reached over to touch the Indian's face.

They embraced, suddenly, fiercely; the Indian's lips sought Ephraim's body – his chest, belly, thighs – then gently, he kissed Ephraim's swollen, trembling penis with his lips.

Ephraim felt the slow, rhythmic pressure, the incredible caress of the tongue; all sensation flowed into his cock, gathered unbearably, culminated, strained for release. In the agony of pleasure, his loins tensed and thrust upward; his body arched, belly hair glinting in the sunlight, chest muscles knotted, then broke and fell with a wrenching moan.

Panting, he pulled the Indian up beside him, and then sat up.

Singing Heron's vibrant, pulsating cock rose straight from his crotch. Ephraim stared in wonder at its dark strength, at the testicles hanging loosely between strong thighs. He leaned over and touched the head of the Indian's cock with his tongue; it glistened in the sunlight, smooth as a flower petal, soft on his lips.

Singing Heron thrust gently upward; his belly hair touched Ephraim's lips, and he writhed, muscles taut, and threw his legs far apart. His testicles hung down to the blanket. The base of his cock was hard and powerful on Ephraim's lips. He burst with overpowering urgency, quivering tensely, in aching gasps.

They lay embraced in the sun until the shadows of the Douglas firs fell across their brown and white interlocking bodies. Singing Heron arose first, and picked up his leggings. Ephraim, watching him, said, "Don't get dressed –" A smile crossed the Indian's face, and he leaned down to touch the other man's cheek. Haltingly, Ephraim whispered, "You are better this way – handsome, and free –"

"Ah, my lover," sighed the Indian. "I will do as you wish, for that is our way." He caressed the coppery hair. "You are one who has lived too long with cruelty, one who needs to know the way of kindness and love, one who needs to know our way. And your heart is good." He straightened up. "I will build a fire, for soon the evening will come –"

Ephraim watched the naked Indian as he chopped wood with great, swinging axe-blows, watched the interplay of muscles on his back, his buttocks, his chest; watched the heavy cock swinging as he walked. He remembered Montgomery, who had first taken him in a drunken frenzy, who could offer his love only when witless with liquor, and who woke up screaming curses in the middle of the night.

Singing Heron was stooping, blowing on the coals of the banked fire. Ephraim marveled – Montgomery seldom showed himself naked unless he meant to taunt his lover. Singing Heron's nakedness, however, was a gift, offered smilingly.

Montgomery's ugly phrases crawled through Ephraim's mind and he sat up, frowning. The Indian glanced at him fleetingly, then resumed his fire-building. "Are you troubled, Ephraim?" he asked.

"Just by ugly memories, from a long time ago. But when I look at you, they go away."

They smiled. "That is good," said Singing Heron.

A cool breeze caught the smoke from the campfire and riffled the Indian's long, straight hair. He smiled apologetically, and picked up his leggings. "For now," he said, and pulled them on. Ephraim was happy at the implied promise, and picked up his own breeches.

"A man as handsome as you," Ephraim whispered, "should feel good when he walks naked for he gives much pleasure to others."

Singing Heron laughed. "That is our way," he said.

They cooked a supper of salmon and corn meal, with coffee from Ephraim's supplies. After eating, they sat close to one another, staring into the campfire. The poor-will's cry pierced the night, and an owl glided softly through the trees. Ephraim laid his hand on the Indian's knee, and they moved closer to the fire. "The old man in Astoria," Ephraim whispered, "said that I should go to the wise man who is called Bear-who-dreams. He said that this man will tell me many things, and cure my sadness –"

"Yes, that is true," said the Indian. "Bear-who-dreams knows many things; he will know your soul, and make it known to you. And if your path is lonely, he will bring you a partner. But it seldom happens that we are lonely."

"And do you have a partner?"

"Yes, I have a partner. He has gone down the Willamette, and will return soon. He is a white man, a trapper; Mr. Calvin does not know him."

Ephraim sat up suddenly, frowning. "I don't understand," he blurted. "What if he comes and finds me? If you have a partner, why did you – why did you make love to me?"

"Ah," said the Indian softly. "You suffer from the white man's disease, the proud man's disease, the sickness of the Missionary way. It is called jealousy, but sometimes I think it is called selfishness." He sighed. "If I love one man, can I not love another at the same time? If one man has filled my heart with love, can I not share it with another? If I make love to you, that does not mean that I love another less. I do not want to own you as I would a puppy – that isn't love, Ephraim."

"I still don't understand. It doesn't seem right." Ephraim was vaguely depressed.

"You will understand, in time," said the Indian quietly. "When you understand love, when you know love in your heart, then you will understand."

Ephraim leaned back again, resting his head on Singing Heron's chest, and the Indian continued. "Only one man has ever tried to own me, as he owned his house, his pony, his dogs: that man was Mr. Calvin. He wanted to own my soul, so that he could destroy it. He wanted me to hate myself, my body, just as he hated himself and his body. That is the Missionary way – the way of hatred. That is not love; it is not our way."

"Just the same –"

"Be patient, my love! Let me tell you – I love you deeply; my heart is filled with you! Do you think that I will stop loving you when you continue your journey up the river? No, Ephraim: I will love you always; and you, I think, will love me always. We will come together again, many times – you will come gliding down the river like today, filled with love, searching for me, and we will play in the water and kiss on the sand. Or I will seek you out wherever you are, call to you from the woods, and you will come – we will take off our clothes and run through the woods laughing and naked, and our bodies will meet in the mossy shadows, and we will make love as we did today. And your partner, and mine, will be happy, don't you think?"

"How strange!" Ephraim murmured. "Do you really love me?"

"Ephraim, Ephraim! Has no one ever loved you?"

"I'm not sure," Ephraim sighed. "Certainly not in this way."

Singing Heron fell into silence, stroking Ephraim's forehead, staring into the fire. He started to speak several times, but thought better of it; finally he said, "Mr. Calvin is a very dangerous man, I think. Would this Montgomery you have spoken of be likely to become friends with such a man?"

"A friend, no. But he also is dangerous, and filled with fear and hatred."

"Might he have harmed you if you had found him?"

"Quite possibly," Ephraim whispered.

Singing Heron leaned forward to stir the embers. "Think back," he said. "Before you got sick in Astoria, what was the last trace you had had of Montgomery?"

"At that time," replied Ephraim slowly, "my only clue was from an old river hand who thought he had seen a man like Montgomery on the Willamette, heading south."

"Another thing. How did Mr. Calvin learn about you?"

"I don't know. He has never really seen me, although Ixtlil Cuauhtli pointed him out to me once in Astoria. But he knows of me, I am sure. I traveled only at night, and slept during the day, well hidden – and one morning I saw him riding down the wagon trail, south of Salem. He stopped a settler, and I could hear them. He mentioned my name, described me, and added something about my being a criminal."

"Could Montgomery have told him?"

"It's entirely possible."

Singing Heron stood up. "That is very bad. But let us sleep now – we will think again in the morning."

Ephraim stood up and followed the Indian into the cabin. Singing Heron undressed and spread blankets on the floor. The moonlight fell on him in the doorway; his cock hardened slowly as he watched Ephraim pull off his clothes. Ephraim could feel a warm roll of love and desire swell through his body, into his genitals.

Singing Heron lay down on the blankets, on his back. "Come to me, my love," he whispered.

Ephraim knelt, and touched Singing Heron's standing organ gently, wonderingly, and then he kissed it, went down, hungry to have this man's body in his. He made love slowly, delighting in the Indian's mounting passion, the writhing hips, the moans of pleasure. And the final passionate thrust, when the Indian's furious love overflowed. 'Into me, into me, oh, God!' Ephraim thought.

He sat up, filled with an indefinable sense of beauty, contemplating the slowly relaxing body in the moonlight.

Singing Heron pulled Ephraim down and they kissed. "Come to me –" he whispered, and in a half-reclining position, he kissed Ephraim's belly, his thigh, until Ephraim could wait no longer. Insistently, he gave a thrust, and Singing Heron took him in, past the strong, firm lips; Ephraim stared transfixed at the handsome angular jaw, and remembering the Indian swaying in the moonlight, he exploded, burning darkly into the Indian.

Silently, they got under the blankets. With the Indian's arm across his chest, Ephraim drifted off to sleep. His dreams echoed the poor-will's call, and he dreamed in the Way of the Loon.

$$\approx$$

The morning sun lay in motionless bars in the doorway when Ephraim awoke; only the fog moved, hung in opalescent wisps in the sunlight. He was alone. Singing Heron had left. Pulling on pants and a shirt, he peered out of the cabin into a white world – the trees were flat shadows hung from a sky like an abalone shell; the ground was pale, and the branches were a brilliant gray.

The dew was icy on his bare feet as he followed instinctively the trail to the clearing.

At the clearing's edge he stopped. In the center was Singing Heron, facing east, away from Ephraim; standing straight, arms loose at his sides. His hair was parted and braided. He wore only a loin cloth; in the fog, his body was a dark silhouette.

Singing Heron knew that Ephraim was there, but he didn't turn. His voice rolled clearly, sharply, in the mists, in a song.

> Spirit of the Northern sky
> spirit of the winter snow
> walk with me in peacefulness
> walk with me in winter calm
> my heart will be a winter bud
> my heart will be a patient seed
> dreaming in the snow.
>
> Spirit in the Eastern sky
> spirit of the rising sun
> spirit of the April rain
> walk with me in hopefulness
> walk with me in eagerness
> my heart will be a nesting bird

my loins will be a rushing stream
my step will quicken in the woods –

Spirit of the Western sky
spirit of the setting sun
spirit of October leaves
walk with me in thoughtfulness
walk with me the inner way
my voice will be a falling leaf
my thoughts will be a flying seed
my heart will be a flying bird.

Spirit of the Southern sky
spirit of the summer sun
spirit of the golden day
walk with me in fullness
walk with me in summer heat
I will be the ripened corn
I will be the Douglas fir
I will be the great river
All things will be good in me.

The Indian turned and walked to Ephraim, smiling warmly. Ephraim
felt a powerful surge in his chest, a physical quickening of the heart,
a desire to reach out and hold –

They took hands and went back along the path.

"Good morning," said Singing Heron. "Did you sleep well?"

"Yes – yes," said Ephraim. He was suddenly shy. This man knew
so much –

"Is your heart filled with love?"

"Oh, yes –" That was what he had wanted to say, but had been
afraid –

"And so is mine," said the Indian, touching him lightly on the
shoulder.

– afraid of reaching out, afraid of meeting coldness.

≈

After breakfast, Singing Heron announced, "Today I will show you how I catch fish. It is very easy."

"Fine. I would like to go."

"I want you with me so that I can talk and sing to you."

Ephraim didn't know what to say, and remained silent and confused.

"Do you sing?" asked Singing Heron.

"Yes, sometimes –"

"I mean the songs that come from you."

"Maybe I know some songs, if I can remember them –"

"No. You must make them up yourself. You do not sing songs of your own making?"

"Well, no –" Ephraim was puzzled. Make up songs?

"You must learn."

Ephraim thought for a long time. The songs he knew were hymns, or joking songs, or bad songs. "If you teach me a tune, I'll try to make up the words. But I can't make up a tune."

"Ah! You don't need music to have a song."

"You mean poetry, then."

"It is all the same," the Indian said simply.

They went back to the canoe and carried it to the river. Ephraim sat in front this time, paddling; Singing Heron sat behind, steering with his own paddle, and they sped silently through the water and the thick mist, aware only of their canoe and of the fleeting gray shadows along the bank.

Singing Heron slowed the canoe to a glide, and reaching over, lifted up a fish trap made of saplings. There was a trout inside, struggling violently; a silver creature in silvery air. He slipped it into a leather bag reset the trap, and they continued down the river.

Behind him, Ephraim could hear the Indian's low voice whispering a melody –

> You came up the river
>> chest shining
>> arms flashing
>
> Gliding up the river
>> shoulders gleaming
>> muscles dancing
>
> Up to the riverside
>> trembling voice
>> troubled eyes
>
> You sorrowed on the riverside
> You trembled in the shadows
> Your heart fled like the red deer
> You walked with fear and shyness.
>
> We met in the waters
>> our hands met
>> our lips touched
>
> And swimming in the sunlight
>> gleaming thighs
>> copper hair
>
> I wondered at your kinship
>> golden skin
>> radiant heart
>
> The sun betrayed your secret
> Told me of your kinship
> Oh, Brother of the Sun!

Ephraim was stunned. He stopped paddling and turned around. "Did you make that up?"

"Ah, yes, Sun-brother."

He gazed at the Indian for a long time, deeply pleased, not

knowing what to say. "It was very nice," he said finally, and resumed paddling.

"It is from the heart."

Ephraim was confused, almost overwhelmed. He didn't know what to make of it. Was it flattery? Montgomery needed and craved flattery, and took childish delight in compliments; yet somehow he never seemed to believe them. This could not be the same, Ephraim thought, for Singing Heron was a man, not a child.

Turning, he flashed a thoughtful smile at the Indian, and resolved to compose a poem of his own, however awkward.

The morning passed in dreamy vagueness and Ephraim's mind wandered, floated without direction among the many details of their closed-in world – a jay flashing suddenly before them, then lost in the mist; droplets of dew on a Douglas fir like watery beads, and the pale green ripples of the river spreading from his paddle, losing themselves in the deeper shadows of the river bank, beneath a laurel tree.

When he could, he gazed at Singing Heron, lazily, and pensively. The Indian's nose was arched, almost hooked; it was high and narrow, ending in strongly flaring nostrils. His mouth was wide, strong, well-defined; when he smiled, it was a kind smile, open, and knowing. The muscles of his shoulders swelled intricately; in repose, they were smooth and rounded; in motion, they were corded like rope. The cords and tendons played in and out swiftly, a vivid, sudden dance, always changing. He gazed for a long time at the Indian's belly – the part not covered by the loin cloth. Below the navel there was a gentle, soft swelling, disappearing beneath the cloth: at the point where his belly met the thigh, the skin was somewhat lighter, and a few hairs spread outward.

Singing Heron caught Ephraim's gaze, and finally he laughed, saying, "Do you want me to take it off?" He pointed to the loin cloth.

Ephraim lowered his eyes in confusion. "No – no. I was just admiring you." He looked up, smiling nervously.

"That is good. I like to be admired. It is a way of making love."

"You're not embarrassed?"

"Why should I be embarrassed? If it gives you pleasure, I am happy. You are making love to me with your eyes, and I feel it like a caress."

True, Ephraim thought. That was what the Indian had meant the night before, when he chopped wood naked –

Singing Heron murmured, with a smile in his eyes, "I, too, enjoy making love with my eyes. You are beautiful to see –"

Ephraim felt his shirt and pants; completely covered from his neck to his feet, he wondered at his own thoughtlessness. He took off the shirt suddenly, and ran his fingers through the hair of his chest, but hesitated at the breeches, knowing that he had no loin cloth. 'What the devil?' he thought, and pointed to a sandy clearing on the edge of the river.

They beached the canoe. He jumped out and pulled off his breeches, enjoying the cool air on his backside and penis, vaguely afraid that he would get an erection. 'Let it happen,' he thought.

Singing Heron was watching him, admiringly, his eyes frankly fixed on Ephraim's genitals. Their eyes met and they laughed; suddenly Ephraim was proud of himself, of his body, of his free, heavy penis, of the mass of coppery hair on his belly. The Indian leaped out of the canoe and untied his loin cloth, throwing it in the canoe; his long, veined penis swung free. They stood apart, staring at each other for a moment. Ephraim's chest swelled. Touching his own penis, he knew that it was lengthening, hardening –

"Come," said the Indian. "I have enough fish for now. Let us go back to the cabin." He stepped back into the canoe. "Face me. I will paddle."

Ephraim rolled up his pants and shirt and sat on them, facing the Indian, gazing at the handsome face, the strong, muscular body, the thick, black belly hair. Singing Heron's cock rested between his thighs.

Ephraim looked at his own body – the glistening hair on his legs, his own white thighs. His now-relaxed penis was hidden from the

Indian's view – unconsciously hidden, so he spread his legs slightly and his testicles fell to the clothing underneath. His penis arched over and downward, touching the floor of the canoe.

Singing Heron was watching him intently. Ephraim looked at the Indian's eyes – black eyes, half closed – at his lips, parted in the trace of a smile. Ephraim was intensely pleased by the Indian's gaze, excited, and wished to please him more. He touched his penis and it began to lengthen, to rise, hesitantly at first. Then in a rush of force it stood upright, fiercely proud, swaying slightly with the motion of the canoe.

The mist was clearing, and in patches the sunlight poured down on his white skin and on Singing Heron as they drifted downstream. The Indian paddled languidly; his penis was standing up in the air, surprisingly, almost like a separate being, long and hard, reaching far out before him. Ephraim, as if dozing, reclined backward, his cock gleaming in the sunlight.

"I love you," Ephraim whispered.

"I love you, Sun-brother."

When they reached the clearing near the cabin, Singing Heron pulled from the water a brightly painted stick, curiously notched. "Ah," he said, "we are going to have a visitor." He tossed the stick back into the current.

"What does that mean?" asked Ephraim.

"It is a message sent from upstream. When someone is planning a journey down to the coast, he throws perhaps five of these sticks into the river the day before he starts. Those downstream will know he is coming."

"Who is it?"

"It is, I think, a young man from Eagle Camp. An Indian. He is looking for love, but he is not ready yet for a partner. It is a play journey."

Ephraim was vaguely annoyed. "Will he stop here?"

"Oh, certainly. But he will not come between us."

As they pulled the canoe up on the bank and hid it, Singing Heron continued his explanation. "Among our people, many young men make such journeys – especially in the springtime, when the heart is restless. When they are perhaps twenty, they make fewer journeys, but they may still do so as they wish. I myself made a journey last summer – upstream, to visit some of our people in the mountains. In this way we are closer together. But this young man will know that I am occupied with you and you with me; he will see it in our eyes, and it will not bother him, because there are many others –"

As they were preparing the fish at the cabin, a long cry pierced the woods. Singing Heron answered – a series of shrill, clear hoots. "He has come," he said, and silently tied on his loin cloth. Realizing suddenly that he was naked, Ephraim pulled on his breeches, relieved, and wondering at his relief.

A young man burst into the clearing, smiling radiantly – a slender Indian, perhaps seventeen, lacking the fullness of mature manhood, yet beginning to show the promise of handsomeness. The two Indians greeted each other simply and happily. Singing Heron turned to Ephraim. "This is John, from Eagle Camp. John is his English name, but he changes his Indian name every year."

"And you are Ephraim MacIver," said the youth. "You are as handsome as they say you are."

Ephraim smiled. "Who says I'm handsome?"

"Ah!" John laughed. "We know many things. Bear-who-dreams is very wise."

The young man's overflowing spirits were contagious. As they ate, he talked of his journey, laughing and singing, and Ephraim forgot his annoyance at the intrusion. "There is a young man on the coast that I must visit – Ah, he is beautiful! His body is like the morning sky, and his spirit is like mist from the sea. When I think of him I laugh with joy and longing. And another on the Siuslaw, as strong and graceful as an elk – we will make love in the moonlight and sing until dawn. Ah! He sent me a message, saying, 'when the columbines bloom –' They will not bloom until the moon is full again, but I saw one in a dream, dancing gently in the wind, delicate and lovely – his heart had spoken to me softly in the night, carried on the wings of a poor-will, or perhaps by the gray owl. And I met another of our people three days' journey upstream, an older man, very wise in the ways of love. He turned my soul into a raging fire with his secrets. Ah! The world is filled with much beauty –"

"Perhaps," said Singing Heron with a sly grin, "with so many lovers, you will not see your friend on the Siuslaw until the vine-maples are red –"

John's eyes widened, then he laughed. "Oh, no – I will call to him in the night, and he will come to me."

"Perhaps by that time, you will be like the cornstalk in August or September –"

John laughed again and lay back on the ground, spreading his arms and shouting to the sky, "How could that be, if I am so full of love? There is no end to it, I tell you!" He sat up suddenly. "Singing Heron, if you were not so busy, I would show you!"

"Get away, you young rabbit. I have no time for you."

They both laughed, a friendly laugh, and teasing. But John frowned suddenly. "I was told to be very careful along the coast and on the Siuslaw."

"Why?" asked Singing Heron.

"Mr. Calvin has left the Mission, and is heading south along the Willamette."

"Bah!" said Singing Heron. "He has lost the trail. He thinks I am far to the east, in the Great Mountains. And as for Ephraim, he has lost that trail, too."

"There is another man with him – very blond –"

Singing Heron's eyes flicked in Ephraim's direction, and

Ephraim nodded imperceptibly.

"– who met him five days' journey south of the Mission."

"Where are they now?"

"No one knows. We have lost them. Bear-who-dreams is awake far into the night, and sings many prayers. He is afraid of Mr. Calvin, and of the yellow-haired stranger; but I told him not to worry, for they are probably lovers." John laughed, and sat up. "If they are not lovers, then they are looking for someone like me, and I would gladly lie with both of them."

Singing Heron did not smile. "That is a very silly notion. You must be careful."

John became suddenly serious. "Have you not known," he asked, "many men who conceal their desires for love, who keep them cruelly hidden beneath an ugly mask?" He pulled anxiously at the grass, twisting the blades in his fingers.

Singing Heron asked softly, "How do you know what is under a mask? How do you know when a man is wearing a mask at all?"

John's voice was intense. "I am not as silly and emptyheaded as you think. Let me tell you. Do you remember the trip I made to the rendezvous near Fort Boise last month? It was thought best that I go with my cousin Blue Wolf, for he is wise in the ways of other people and could protect me from danger. Since we are parallel cousins – my father and his are brothers – we did not go as lovers, following the laws of our tribe, although other tribes have different laws concerning cousins. Some day I shall ask Bear-who-dreams about that, although I know what he will say – that it is all the same, whether I follow the customs of one tribe or those of another, and that the way of the heart can be followed among all men, so long as the heart is good. Anyway, we went not as lovers but as brothers, sharing the same adventures, and it was delightful. Sometimes we shared the same lovers, even; but usually not, for there were many handsome young men who were eager to know the Way of the Loon.

"Ah, but Fort Boise was different! There were many trappers, many traders from the eastern plains and rivers, many thieves, and many who would kill. We stayed among the Indians, outside the fort. My cousin cautioned me to be quiet like the wood-mouse, to observe everything and to say nothing. Before long I noticed an Indian there – I will not name his tribe – who attracted my attention because of his boasting and loud, profane words. In the councils he said many harsh things, many cruel jokes about the Loon Society. He said that we stole young warriors' souls by witchcraft and made them unfit for battle, that we performed unspeakable acts of sorcery, and that we wasted our lives in idle dreaming.

"He did not know that Blue Wolf and I were followers of the loon, nor did we tell him. I was angry at his stupid, profane lies, and wanted to speak out against him in the council ring, but my cousin told me to be silent. 'Wait,' he told me, 'and you will see something very interesting.' I waited, and closed my ears to the boaster's vicious talk.

"We had been at the encampment for five days when one night I was awakened by a stranger in my tent. His hand was on my mouth so that I could not call out. With his other hand he – but I will not say what he was trying to do, for his intentions made the act evil.

"I struggled to free myself, and finally he released me and sat on the other side of the tent. 'Who are you, and what do you want?' I asked. Of course, it was the boaster, the liar, the one who had blackened the Loon Society.

"'I want you to do such-and-such,' he said.

"'You are mistaken,' I replied. 'I don't know why you want me to do that.'

"'I will pay you,' he said.

"'You are again mistaken,' I said. 'I do not make love for money. That is worse than slavery. And I could not make love to you anyway, for you do not know the nature of love.'

"He said, 'What I want you to do will take only a few minutes, and then it will be over, and you can forget it, and you will be much richer tomorrow.'

"'What you want me to do,' I replied, 'is to lower myself, to make myself something less than a man – a tiny animal without pride. I will not sell my pride and decency.'

"We argued for a short while in this way, and then I left, for I could see that he was stubborn and might try to overpower me again. As I left, he said that he knew that I followed the Way of the Loon. He cursed me, saying, 'Vile loon-man, I know you – offering yourself shamelessly for fox and beaver pelt, and then pretending ignorance when you have become rich.'

"I disappeared into the darkness, leaving him there in my tent. I found my cousin by the river bank, where he was sleeping, and told him my story. We talked until dawn, wondering what to do, for Blue Wolf was quite frightened, and grave and serious. Finally we decided to pack and leave that morning. I helped him gather his supplies and pack them into the canoe, but when we returned to my tent, we were seized and bound by a band of men and dragged into the council te-pee, where many of the most important old men were gathered. We were thrown into the center of the ring, and unbound. I watched my cousin, who sat silently waiting, and did as he did.

"Then the boaster stood before the council and made a speech. 'This man,' he said, pointing at me, 'is a member of the Loon Society, and has tried to corrupt me. He followed me into the woods and tried to capture my soul by sorcery; but I know more sorcery than he, and was able to resist him. I accuse him of sorcery.'

"The chiefs questioned him. 'Did he do anything else?'

"'No.'

"'Did he steal from you?'

"'I am not sure. I have lost many pelts at this encampment, but I have not spoken of it because I had no proof as to who is the thief.'

"'What was the nature of his sorcery?' they asked, and he told a long, fantastic tale of how I had made God's-eyes to make him lose his senses and had assumed the form of a beautiful, sleeping witch, whom he had pursued until he saw the witch-mark on her forehead. The men from that tribe tell many tales about a witch luring unwary men to their deaths.

"Finally the chiefs turned to me, and asked for my story.

"I thought silently for many minutes before I replied.

"'I follow the Way of the Loon,' I said. 'That is true. But everything else he says is false. Among my people, we do not make God's-eyes. We do not know how, nor do we need them. We do not need sorcery to find happiness.'

"An old chief from the mountains said that this was true; that the people along the coast did not know the spells of the boaster's people.

"Then I said, 'We do not turn ourselves into witches or even dress as witches, as do some men from other tribes, who have some of our ways but do not belong to our society. We do not have berdaches, for we do not need to be a berdache or to dress as a witch. We were born as men, and never pretend to be otherwise. That is our way.'

"Again I stopped, and again they declared that I had spoken the truth.

"Then I said, 'I am a young man. Many have said that I am handsome, and that may be true, for I have never had difficulty in finding another handsome man to share my blanket. Since this is so, I do not need to beg favors of an unwilling man. If I were forced to beg, it would mean that I am ugly, either in my body or in spirit, and without pride. You who are sitting here cannot judge my spirit, but judge my body. Do you believe that I would have to beg?' Here I was frightened, for the boaster was indeed a handsome man.

"'It is as he says,' they decided, and I was relieved.

"Then I thought long and hard. Should I tell them what had really happened in my tent? I decided that I had already said enough to save myself, and that the boaster had woven his fantastic tale merely to protected himself, for he was afraid that I would speak out and mock him. If I told the true story, I decided, he would have to take even greater revenge on me and perhaps kill me. So I spoke again. 'I think this man has had a bad dream. I do not know the meaning of his dream, nor do I think he knows. Perhaps a medicine man can tell the meaning, but it was not I who appeared to him in the form of a witch, for I do not desire him.'

"I stopped again, and the chiefs conferred. Then I said, 'You may search my belongings and those of my cousin. You will finding nothing belonging to this man among them. Nor will you find any articles of witchcraft or of sorcery, for we do not know of such things.' Then I sat down.

"Blue Wolf and I waited in the council circle for a long time while they searched our belongings. At midday the braves returned, saying that I had spoken the truth – that nowhere in our camp were skins, or white man's money, or God's-eyes, or articles of sorcery.

"Then a chief rose and addressed the boaster. 'The council has decided,' he said, 'that you have indeed had a medicine dream. The meaning of this dream is not wholly clear, but some parts of it are known to us. You must make peace with the Loon Society, or you will meet your death in one way or another. The witch is not of the Loon Society, but she wants your death; you must purify yourself; you must change the mind of the beautiful witch who would capture your soul. Seek the council of the wise men of your tribe. There are wise men on the coast who know more than all of us about these matters. Above all, go in peace, for you are in danger of losing your soul.'

"The boaster covered his head with a blanket in fear and perhaps in shame. I have not seen him since, for my cousin and I left the following day."

Singing Heron sighed, and smiled bitterly. "You behaved very intelligently with great wisdom. I would not have done differently. You were especially wise in not telling the council what really happened, for as you say, the boaster might have killed you. And what does this man look like? I suspect that we may see him this summer. If he followed the advice of the chiefs in council, he went to his tribe for purification, and then, perhaps – perhaps if he is a wise man – he will come to see Bear-who-dreams."

"He is a handsome man," said John, "and very strong. There is a scar on his chest, right here –" he drew a line on his own chest, above the right nipple "and another one here –" indicating his belly, well below the navel.

Singing Heron grinned slyly. "How do you know that?"

"Ah!" John laughed. "He was naked in my tent, and there was enough light. Even though I would not have him, I noticed such a scar." He sighed. "In the midst of great danger, I think I desired him." He rose to leave. "I think of him often."

Ephraim and Singing Heron rose also, and the three men walked to the river. Singing Heron caught Ephraim's hand, casually caressed his back, as if John weren't there. With a sense of shock, Ephraim realized that it didn't matter whether John was there or not, and he returned the caress.

The young Indian climbed into his canoe and with a happy, adolescent grin, disappeared down the river.

Still watching the canoe, Singing Heron pulled off his leggings and turned naked to Ephraim. With both hands, slowly, languorously, he clutched his penis; it was stiff and hard and huge, far longer than the breadth of his two hands.

Ephraim sat down and stared. Desire surged through him in warm, rolling waves; his mouth was dry, and he trembled. He unbuttoned his breeches, fumbling at the buttonholes, and stopped. The Indian stared at Ephraim's belly, at the mass of coppery hair that sprang from the opening.

Singing Heron stooped to touch the hair with his fingers, his lips, and then looked up, into Ephraim's eyes. "Take them off," he said, and the two stood up. Singing Heron, arms folded across his chest, stared intently as Ephraim lowered his breeches.

Ephraim's already erect penis leaped outward when it was freed. Then, turning, Singing Heron led Ephraim into the woods. The powerful muscles of the Indian's buttocks flexed rhythmically as he walked. The hair in the cleft dividing the muscled swells was shiny black and mysteriously inviting; the muscles rolled as he strode along the path, smoothly, with soft firmness; his thighs were like columns, and his calves swelled with each step.

On a sun-dappled patch of moss beneath a giant Douglas fir,

the Indian lay down on his back, hips twisting, penis thrusting high. Ephraim fell onto him with a moan. "I love you," he whispered. "I love you!" And the Indian clutched him around his waist, and they rolled over, frantically, wildly thrusting, clutching, straining –

Ephraim felt the Indian's warm, moist, almost raspy tongue, all the way down, nose buried in the coppery hair. He twisted around and pulled the Indian's hips upward, and took him as far as he could. His hands explored the Indian's backside as the warmth in his belly grew – explored down the cleft, rubbing the hair, and touched the anus softly. Singing Heron tensed, spread his legs, and suddenly Ephraim felt a finger thrust into his own anus, bringing a sharp electric shock of pleasure. Seconds later the unbearable sweetness in him burst out, a dazzling explosion of warmth and pleasure.

That night, curled up in blankets and Singing Heron's arms, Ephraim whispered into the dark brown ear:

> Wrapped in the fog of the ocean
> cold in the night of aloneness
> searching for the mouth of the river
> lost and alone then I wept –
>
> I glided like smoke on the waters
> the silvery sun slowly rising
> glowed through the mist of the morning
> crystalline glistening world –
>
> The mist disappeared in the sunlight
> curling away through the forest
> emerald leaves in the shadows
> shadowy leaves in the sunlight
>
> Then you standing tall in the morning
> strong as the redwood and proudly
> patterns of shadows upon you

shadows of love in your eyes

Wisdom of centuries in you
darkness of lust in your body,
mystery, loveliness, magic,
singing to me in the sunlight –

Singing Heron sat up. In the darkness, Ephraim could tell that he smiled. He touched Ephraim's forehead and murmured softly, "I will remember it, Sun-brother; it is very lovely, from your heart."

࿊

In the morning, Ephraim awoke to find Singing Heron sitting beside him. He saw that it was late, and sat up suddenly; then he smiled at the Indian.

Singing Heron brought warm tea from the leaves of the mountain laurel, and they drank peacefully.

"Ephraim, my love," the Indian began softly, "you must go soon to see Bear-who-dreams."

Ephraim's heart skipped, and fell. "So soon?" he whispered.

"He will be waiting anxiously; you have until the next full moon."

Ephraim swallowed. "That is three weeks away," he said.

Singing Heron was silent; his eyes were anguished.

"I can be there in five days," Ephraim added.

"I do not want you to go, my love, but you must, for you will never be at peace until you have seen the wise man."

"I am at peace now, for I love you," Ephraim answered. His throat began to ache.

"No, Ephraim," came the gentle reply. "You love me, but you are not at peace. You must be rid of the shade that haunts you."

"When I am with you, it is gone!" Ephraim cried.

"Ah, Sun-brother," the Indian sighed, "I wish that what you say were true. If there were no one but you and I on the river –" His voice trailed off into silence.

Ephraim lay back and covered his eyes. "Your partner?" he asked.

"Perhaps," answered the soft voice. "But also the many lovers you will know in your journey up the river." He paused, searching for words. "You must not think, Sun-brother, that I am the only person who will love you."

"I can imagine no other happiness," Ephraim murmured hoarsely.

"That is because you are new to our way, my love." He paused again. "But, Ephraim, if, at the end of the summer –"

Ephraim interrupted: "If your circumstances change, do you think that you and I could be partners?"

He opened his eyes. Singing Heron was staring out the doorway. "I do not know, Ephraim. My circumstances are likely to change, but you must know our way, and you must have known love from many people."

Ephraim reached out and touched the Indian. "You are all the love I want; my soul can hold no more."

Singing Heron's eyes were sad, and glistening. "You are making it very difficult for me," he said. "I have told you the truth; please ask no me no more." He leaned close, and his warm breath caressed Ephraim's ear. "Know that you have touched me, Sun-brother, in ways that no one has done before."

Ephraim reached out and pulled Singing Heron to him, and they made love slowly, gently; Ephraim filled his soul with the mysteriously beautiful body, and gave of himself violently, and his throat ached with sadness.

෧

He made his preparations for leaving with a sense of falling into nothingness.

On the river bank, Singing Heron touched a tear in Ephraim's eye, then touched his own eyelash with the still wet fingertip. "I will not forget our love," he whispered.

"I shall love you always," Ephraim choked. "I leave you here with my love, with my heart. I do not wish to go!" Blindly, he turned, leaped into the canoe and started upriver, staring straight ahead, seeing only the brilliant ripples of the Umpqua.

Far behind, he heard the sad, distant melody of a flute.

Book Two

While struggling savagely up the river, Ephraim's mind was a chaos of thoughts and emotions: love, despair, hope, and fear. Confused and sick, he made camp that night in a clump of incense-cedars, and tossed fitfully throughout the night. The next morning he awoke to a distasteful dampness on his blankets – the fog again, cold and wet, bringing out the smell of wool in the blankets. He felt shriveled inside, lost and alone again. Listlessly he pushed on, upstream, hoping the sun would come out, seeing Singing Heron's body in the vague shapes floating in the mist, calling to mind the bronze flash of the Indian's thigh striding through the forest.

He cried out in anguish, his voice piercing the fog with hollow sharpness, and he doubled over in the canoe. The jays screamed in reply.

After many minutes had passed, Ephraim realized that he was drifting downstream, and resumed paddling.

On the third day, he found an abandoned lean-to near the river, and decided to make camp there, in spite of the fact that it was only noon. His appetite returned, and he ate ravenously, like a wolf. The fog had lifted, and he spread his blankets in the sun to dry.

He lay down to sun himself, and began to think more calmly of the future. Perhaps the mysterious Bear-who-dreams would be able to help him. Perhaps, he allowed himself to think, there would be another like Singing Heron –

He left it at that, and drifted off to sleep.

When he awoke, stretching languorously, there was a stranger in the clearing – seated on a log, watching him, calmly smoking a pipe.

A white man, huge, with a long, deep-brown beard, quizzical blue eyes, the trace of a smile.

Ephraim sat up, startled.

"Have a nice nap?" The man's voice was deep and rumbling, with echoes of summer thunder.

"Yes, thank you." Ephraim stood up, nervously, then sat down again.

The other smiled. "My name is Cyrus Wheelwright." Standing up, he offered a huge, hairy hand.

Ephraim shook the hand and mumbled, "Very pleased to meet you."

"Coming from the coast?"

"Yes," said Ephraim, "I found this shelter and decided to stay here, to dry out –"

"Going any place in particular?"

"No – no place in particular," Ephraim answered slowly, hoping the other would ask nothing more.

Cyrus' bushy eyebrows arched, but he smiled. "I have a deer over there on my mule. I just shot it. If you help me skin and clean it, we'll have venison for supper."

"Good – I'll be glad to help," Ephraim said, relieved. Apparently this Cyrus was satisfied with vague answers.

Cyrus didn't really need the help. He carried the carcass easily over one shoulder, and worked with a swiftness and precision that Ephraim had to admire. As they worked, the huge man talked, telling of his trip to Fort Vancouver to trade the skins from a winter's trapping for supplies – powder, soap, lead, new traps. He mentioned the Mission on the Willamette, and his blue eyes darted to Ephraim, who continued working, hoping his nervousness wasn't noticeable.

Cyrus fell silent. But as they were stringing up the haunches of venison on a cedar bough, he said quietly, "You didn't tell me your name. It is Ephraim MacIver, I believe."

Ephraim started, uncontrollably, and didn't answer, pretending to examine a small cut on his finger.

Cyrus was watching him. He continued, "You needn't worry. Look at this." Unbuttoning his shirt, he pulled out a small object strung on a length of rawhide around his neck, almost lost in the thick hair of his chest. Ephraim took the object in trembling fingers – a bird, carved in stone. "The loon," said Cyrus.

Ephraim looked quickly into the other's eyes, then back at the loon. He let it fall against Cyrus' chest, then turned away, unsettled in his mind.

"Don't be frightened," Cyrus said. "You haven't an enemy within a hundred miles – yet. But I'll tell you what I know later on. Go get cleaned up now, if you'd like; I have a few more things to do here, and then I'll be down at the river with you."

Ephraim looked at his hands, his shirt and breeches – they were filthy from cleaning the deer. Still nervous, he chanced a smile at Cyrus, then walked quickly to the river.

He took off his clothes and pinned them under a heavy rock in the middle of the current, knowing they would be washed clean before nightfall. Then he splashed lazily in a deep pool, closing his mind to all thoughts, all questions, concentrating on the coolness flowing across his body.

Floating face up, he looked over to the bank to see Cyrus, naked, wading cautiously over the slippery rocks near the shore. In confusion, Ephraim dived under the water, but the image was engraved on his mind. The man was Herculean – immense chest and shoulders, hairy –

Ephraim came up for air, not daring to look back at the man; but the vision, the sheer sculpturesque quality of his body filled his mind. Involuntarily, he turned and floated on his back, gazing at Cyrus, who was soaping himself unconcernedly.

"Soap," he was saying, "is one of the few luxuries that I like to have. I try to bring enough to last all year."

Ephraim watched him, fascinated. The man's cock matched the rest of his body: enormous; fully the length of his enormous hand. He had the testicles of a bull. The thick mass of hair on his belly and chest contrasted warmly with this white skin.

"Here –" he called, "take this," and tossed the soap to Ephraim. Catching it, Ephraim swam closer to the shore and stood up. Cyrus, he noted, appraised him calmly, openly. Ephraim knew himself to be handsome and well built, and was glad. An anticipatory fever began to warm his body.

Cyrus, however, still seemed unconcerned. He dived into the water to rinse off, washed his hair and beard carefully, then sat on a rock in the sun to dry himself. He occasionally glanced at Ephraim, but mostly just gazed dreamily and absently in Ephraim's general direction.

Finally Ephraim finished, and waded up to the rock with the soap. "Here," he said. "And thank you. I haven't used any in weeks." Cyrus smiled, but didn't move to take the soap, so Ephraim laid it on the rock beside him. Then he sat down to dry in the sun, on the same rock, a short distance from Cyrus, and turned slightly away from him. Suddenly he remembered his clothes, but decided to leave them where they were.

A few minutes later, not entirely dry, he got up and walked back to the lean-to to find a fresh change of clothes. He was just buttoning his shirt when Cyrus returned from the river, fully dressed.

They set about making a fire and cooking supper – silently, efficiently. Ephraim could help at this, and before long they were lying back before the fire, bellies full, and Cyrus was contentedly filling his pipe. He had a handsome-ugly face with a strong, crooked nose; but it was a pleasant face, and profoundly kind.

Cyrus spoke as he was lighting his pipe. "You sure lost Mr. Calvin and that fellow Montgomery for good. I met them going back northward from the MacKenzie; they didn't seem to know where to start looking next. I said I'd keep an eye out for you." He grinned slyly.

"I came down the Siuslaw and around by the coast."

"You met Singing Heron then?"

Ephraim started. "Yes. I stayed there for several days."

"Good. And you are in love with him?"

Ephraim was silent.

"Well, no need to answer that. I'm sure he was in love with you also." After a pause in which Ephraim's heart turned over, Cyrus continued. "That is our way. And I am his partner, as I suppose you have already guessed."

"Yes," Ephraim said weakly, "I was beginning to guess –"

"Don't worry about what I think you're worrying about," Cyrus added softly, "for I understand Singing Heron, and I'm not unhappy when he loves another. Do you find that hard to grasp, hard to accept?"

Ephraim laid a forearm over his eyes and talked into darkness. "I don't understand it at all. I would certainly be unhappy. I am unhappy now."

"Why?" Cyrus asked. "Is it my presence that makes you unhappy?"

"Not that exactly," Ephraim mumbled. "It's more the fact that he should have a partner at all."

"Ah, Ephraim," Cyrus breathed. "I know how you think, for I am a white man too. But in the Loon Society it is not that way; who am I to say that Singing Heron shouldn't love whomever he pleases? I am not his master, nor is he mine; love is equality, not slavery."

Ephraim closed his eyes tightly, fumbling for words. "Then these partnerships," he said, "must be very loose and casual."

Cyrus laughed softly. "They are sometimes extremely fleeting, which doesn't mean – believe me – that they can't be as lovely as a hummingbird's flight across a hillside of flowers –"

"It's so terribly different –" Ephraim murmured.

Cyrus stared at the slanting rays of gold that poured through the forest and flowed through his thick beard. His blue eyes squinted in the sunlight. "Yes, beautifully different. Only a few of us know, really deeply, the meaning of those words." He paused. "As an example: Do you want to make love to me now, as a for-instance?"

Ephraim rolled away, turning his back on Cyrus. His heart

pounded; he was afraid, awake; pained. In a strained voice he answered, "I don't want to make love to anybody just as an example, as a for-instance."

Behind him he heard a sudden movement, a sigh. Then close to his ear, "Ephraim, I didn't mean it that way. Please understand."

"I'm sorry," whispered Ephraim, still facing away.

"But do you? I'm asking you."

Ephraim thought bitterly of Montgomery, who always forced him to admit his own desire, while admitting nothing himself. He decided to make the issue clear since it was, after all, a white man he was dealing with. "Do you want me?" he asked. "I must know."

A huge hand was on his hip. He felt the prickle of a beard on his neck. "Oh, yes! My God yes, I want you. Couldn't you tell?"

"I'm not used to your ways. I have very often been mistaken in the past." He rolled over, face up. "Yes, I want you very much – very much, if you want me."

The luxuriantly-bearded face was inches above his own. Gently, their lips touched; Ephraim knew the deeply exciting feeling of a dense, masculine beard on his face.

"Ah, yes, how I wanted you!" whispered Cyrus. "From the time I first saw you, lying asleep – your sad, sensitive face! And from the time I saw you naked in the river – beautifully naked, white and perfect as an ancient god, strong, graceful –" His hand was on Ephraim's belly, almost spanning it. "I want to see you again as you were in the river – see you and adore you –" He caressed Ephraim's cheek with rough and callused fingers, began to unbutton his shirt.

Ephraim stood up; Cyrus remained on the ground, watching with fever in his eyes. With his eyes on Cyrus, Ephraim unbuttoned the shirt, pulled it out of his breeches and tugged at a sleeve. Cyrus was watching his every movement intently. First one sleeve, then another; then he dropped the shirt to the ground and took a deep breath. There was a growing bulk in Cyrus' breeches.

Ephraim's knees and ankles trembled. Deliberately he unbuckled his belt and unfastened the top button of his breeches. Slowly he unbuttoned the breeches completely, then quickly dropped them to the ground. His cock lengthened in a rushing fullness as he watched Cyrus' eyes.

"Just stand there; let me look at you," Cyrus muttered hoarsely.

Ephraim stood without moving, enjoying the intensely sweet pain of anticipation, bathing himself in the other man's eager stare.

Cyrus stood up. Ephraim could hardly believe the bulk, the sheer length in the man's breeches. "Shall I?" he said.

Ephraim smiled tightly. "Yes, do," he said. Nervously, hastily, Cyrus tore off his shirt and breeches.

"God," breathed Ephraim.

"It is yours to do with as you wish," Cyrus whispered. Staring at Ephraim, he continued, "I am glad that I excite you, for I wish to make love to you, kiss you wherever I wish, take your penis in my mouth and drain your love from you, because you are beautiful and handsome."

Ephraim answered slowly: "I want you to do that – and now I want to look at you, to enjoy the sight of you –"

They stood silent, unmoving. Ephraim filled his eyes. The other man's cock was perhaps twice as long as when he had seen it before, at the river; thick, heavy, standing straight out from his body.

Then a desire struck him to touch Cyrus' broad, deeply-muscled chest, to run his fingers through the thick mass of silky hair, down his belly, down to the hair that stood like a deep, soft bed on his groin.

He held out his hand to Cyrus; Cyrus took it and they walked slowly to the shelter.

Ephraim couldn't take his eyes from the huge organ swaying outward before them. Noting this, Cyrus touched it and repeated, "It is yours to do with as you wish."

"It is beautiful," muttered Ephraim. He touched it lightly – the head swelled and rose slightly.

"Now tell me what you want me to do," said Cyrus. Ephraim looked at him in surprise. Cyrus explained hastily, "I would like you to begin, to take the initiative. That is why – I have been waiting for you to indicate something all day: approval, or attraction – Don't be afraid; just tell me; then later, when I know how you feel about me –"

Ephraim's chest swelled, and he lost his shyness in a headlong rush of desire. "Lie down," he said, and Cyrus lay down. "Spread your legs –" Ephraim knelt between the muscular, hairy thighs; the other man's penis loomed enormously before him. Cyrus propped himself up on his elbows, blue eyes staring.

Ephraim glanced at Cyrus' eyes and said, "I want you to watch –" and took the huge, swaying penis in both hands. "The center of all things," he breathed.

"I love you," said Cyrus.

Ephraim bent forward and kissed the head, took just that into his mouth, fingers exploring behind, in the hairy cleft of the other man's buttocks.

Then he straightened up. "Lie back –" he said, and stretched himself along the length of the other man's body; Cyrus' chest and belly hair crackled against his skin: He kissed the eyes, lips, bearded cheek, ran his hands down the hard, swelling arms and chest to the thick hair at the base of his belly. There was a warming sweetness in his own body, and he rolled off, panting, and stood up. Then he lay down in the opposite direction, with his head on Cyrus' hips, and with a quick twist Cyrus was on him, unbearably warm and sweet, rapidly, the pressure –

A flashing kaleidoscope of images as Cyrus pulled all the warmth of his being into his mouth – the brown, silky belly hair at his hips, the curve of a white, hairy thigh under his head, Cyrus' beard bristling against his belly, and he let go – Cyrus tensed, frenzied, eager, harder, faster –

Ephraim rolled away, sighing, eyes shut. He opened them to see Cyrus standing over him like a centaur. Ephraim sat up and took the head in his mouth, and the huge organ burst into him hotly, chokingly.

Cyrus crumpled to the ground, moaning, "My God, my God

–" and Ephraim helped him onto the blankets and covered the great naked body. Lying beside him, he whispered, "I love you."

Cyrus encircled him with a massive arm and cradled his head on his bristling chest. "You're wonderful," he whispered. "So fine, so perfect, so powerful. You are beautiful, with a classic beauty –"

"Your sheer strength," Ephraim said, "is beautiful. It astounds me. It excites me."

"Many people don't think so."

Ephraim raised his head. "How could they think otherwise?"

"Mere strength, Ephraim, is not beauty. And it frightens many people."

"I am not frightened. I love the sight of you, the feel of you –" He laid his head down, rubbing his cheek against the bristling chest.

Cyrus tightened his arm and then relaxed again. His bicep was a great lump at Ephraim's shoulder. "Love me, my child, and I will be beautiful."

They dropped off into a deep slumber.

In the morning Ephraim awoke first, and rose to start the fire. Coming back into the shelter, he stood gazing for several minutes at Cyrus, half covered by the blankets. On an impulse, he dropped to his knees beside the sleeping form, moved by a desire to explore this body again. "It is yours to do with as you wish," Cyrus had said; Ephraim put a hand on the broad, muscular chest, running his fingers through the thick, silky hair.

The blue eyes opened; his head lifted. "Lie back –" Ephraim said softly. Cyrus lay back but kept his eyes on Ephraim, smiling dreamily. Slowly pulling the blankets down, Ephraim uncovered the naked belly down to its base, followed with his fingers the pattern of deep brown hair, then pulled the blanket to one side. The great penis, still limp, lay heavily between Cyrus' thighs. Then, remembering Cyrus' pleasure in seeing, Ephraim widened his legs so that Cyrus could

see his already erect, stiff-standing penis. He kissed Cyrus linger-
ingly on the mouth, then bent down and took as much of him as he
could in his mouth – at first slowly, then more insistently, lovingly,
intently fondling the heavy, loose testicles. Cyrus came, gently, freely,
enormously; he flowed in long, swollen spasms, with a deep groan of
pleasure.

Ephraim looked up. The man was peacefully relaxed, breathing
deeply, eyes closed. He covered him again and willed his own erection down.

He picked up his breeches, but again impulsively, threw them
down. "Perhaps I shall go naked today," he said, and at the idea a new
pounding began in his penis, but he went to the river to bring water,
and made himself think of other things.

While the water was heating, an idea occurred to him. He slipped
stealthily back into the shelter and gathered up Cyrus' clothes, then
hid them in the forest a short distance from the camp. On his way
back he picked two fragrant myrtle leaves, which he dropped into the
now boiling water. Finding two cups, and sugar, he brought the tea
into the shelter and set a cup beside Cyrus, then sat down on a corner
of the blanket at Cyrus' feet.

Cyrus opened his eyes slowly, yawned, and smiled blissfully.

"Good morning," Ephraim said.

Cyrus sat up languidly, still smiling, and touched Ephraim gently
on the cheek with his rough fingers. "You're real. I wasn't dreaming." He leaned back and discovered the tea. "You're too good to be
true."

They sipped the tea silently, content to watch each other, smiling
foolishly when their glances met. Ephraim had difficulty controlling
himself as he watched the momentary flexing of the huge biceps,
the interplay of rolling muscles on chest and belly, and when he felt
Cyrus' gaze fall like a caress on his own body, his penis and coppery
belly hair. But he took the cups when they were finished and went
down to the river to wash them, walking stiff-legged, knowing Cyrus
was following him with sharp blue eyes.

While at the river he retrieved the clothing that had been washed clean in the river's current, wrung it out, and spread it on a rock to dry in the brilliant morning sun.

Coming back, he saw Cyrus standing before the shelter like a beautiful stallion, looking perplexed.

"Where did I leave my clothes last night?" he called.

"You left them inside," answered Ephraim, "but I hid them elsewhere."

Cyrus' eyes widened; then he laughed – a low, pleased rumble. "You demon!" he chuckled. "Playing tricks on me." He walked around, kicking at leaves on the ground, rubbing his thighs. "Very well. If that's the way you want it, that's the way it will be. You're a demon, but an adorable one." He caught Ephraim in an embrace, and they kissed – very hard, but not insistently.

After breakfast, Cyrus went off to tend to the mules, and came back carrying two bows; one was quite large – five feet or more in length. "Would you like to learn to shoot one of these?" he asked. "Or do you already know?"

"I'm afraid I know nothing about them," said Ephraim.

"You should learn. It's a real mistake to rely exclusively on rifles out here – a bow and arrow is quiet, and you never run out of powder. Come. I'll show you something about it."

They picked their way carefully through the forest to a clearing, Cyrus leading the way. "I made both of these myself," he called over his shoulder. "Around here you'll find an occasional yew tree for the bow – but these aren't Indian-style bows, and I use steel arrowheads. Here. I'll show you how to do it –" He took the larger bow and fitted an arrow to the thong. "That tree –" he indicated, and drew his arm back. The powerful shoulder muscles knotted and the arrow flew in a blur to the tree, where it hit with a thonk and struck, quivering from the impact.

Ephraim took the smaller bow, and with Cyrus standing close behind him, arms reaching around to direct his grip and aim, shot at the same tree. The arrow hit, slightly lower than the other.

"Very good!" Cyrus' hand fell on Ephraim's shoulder.

"Just luck," Ephraim said, smiling and pleased. Cyrus' beard brushed his shoulder, and he could feel his chest hair against his back; his great cock brushed momentarily against Ephraim's buttocks.

Cyrus stepped back. "Try again."

Ephraim tried several times more, but hit the tree only once. Cyrus trotted off to retrieve the arrows; the flesh of his backside quivered as he ran – a surprisingly soft quiver that filled Ephraim with unknowable urges. Coming back, Cyrus' cock swung high, almost wildly, as he trotted. Ephraim stared openly; Cyrus merely smiled as he picked up his bow again.

The sun glinted on the fine, soft hair of his backside as his shoulders strained at the bow. Ephraim reached out to touch, softly caressing the downy hair, the soft skin, and the arrow sped – wide of the mark. Cyrus stood still. Ephraim explored further, down and into the cleft, fingers probing; then, pushed by the same mysterious urges, not knowing what else to do, he knelt and kissed – first the soft skin, then the cleft. He probed –

In a blind agony he flung himself on the ground, on his back. "Take me –" he cried. Cyrus stared at him pensively for a few brief seconds, then came down on Ephraim, taking the whole of him hungrily, rapturously –

They spent the remainder of the morning, target-shooting. Ephraim's skill improved gradually, but still left much to be desired. He found that it was much more exacting and tiring than he had expected. Both men were dripping with sweat at midday. Ephraim's desire had been somewhat blunted, but the vision of the naked Herculean giant was still pleasant and exciting; they stared at each other frankly, smiling foolishly, and caressed each other casually as the desire to do so arose.

In the afternoon they went to the river again and bathed, and swam, and wrestled in the water. Afterward, they sat on the same flat rock to dry in the sun; Ephraim laid his head on the other man's lap and closed his eyes.

"I have a poem for you," he said.

"Really? I'd like to hear it."

With his eyes still closed, Ephraim softly spoke his poem:

> Your smile the mountain wind, an azure cry,
>> and granite shoulders jutting shining clean –
>> your chest the rolling hills where April green
>> has turned to gold beneath the August sky;
> A sinuous river, lazy rippling sigh,
>> in dappled shadows rolling rapture seen,
>> a river slow and deep or swift and lean
>> and curving down to meet the forest's eye;
> An ancient cedar standing wildly free
>> and nobly crowned above the forest floor –
>> volumnar muscle, gnarled Olympian Zeus;
> Profoundly rooted; deep beneath the tree
>> from lithic masses vital river pour
>> volcanic magma straining darkly loose –

"My God," said Cyrus, "I didn't know you composed poetry."

"I never tried, until recently –"

"It's very flattering. I'm touched."

"It's how I feel about you."

"I love you, Ephraim."

"Yes, and I love you."

Cyrus caressed Ephraim's forehead for a long while, staring silently across the river. Finally he mused aloud, "It's interesting that you should compose lyric poetry. I could have guessed, of course. I have always loved poetry, but more the epic than anything else. When I first read the Iliad – I'll never forget the experience. I think it was then that I first came to some knowledge about myself. Achilles and Patroclus – epic lovers – how I welcomed them!"

He paused, staring down at Ephraim. "I must tell you some things about myself – some things I've never told to anyone. I'm telling you because you are perhaps the first person I've met in several years who has the background to understand what I have to say. Or at least I think you will understand – I gather from several indications that you're from the East, and that you've been exposed to a certain amount of learning. Also that you're intelligent.

"Anyway. A number of years ago, when I was a student filled with Greek and Latin, I fell in love with a young man named Roderick, likewise a student. He returned my love, although he was many things that I was not – handsome, graceful, witty, and well-to-do. I wasn't poor, only by comparison to him. At any rate, he returned my love, and returned it sincerely. The differences in our characters were never in the beginning the cause of difficulties; on the contrary, we seemed to stabilize each other. He could always point out to me when my seriousness bordered on pomposity, and I was able to restrain his more irresponsible flights of fancy.

"We did everything together: reading – Homer, Plato, Petronius, Montaigne; hunting, which I loved, and mixing in society, which I came to hate and despise with a passion, but which became, as time went on, Roderick's true element. The theatre, the salons, the concert halls; the elegant chatter and refined manners; endless throngs of gentlemen interminably imposing their conventions on us, when all I wanted was to be alone with my lover.

"But he enjoyed it, very obviously, and I was in a continual state of despair. 'If he truly loves me,' I thought, 'how can he bear to divide his attentions so outrageously?' At first, being certain of his love, I could formulate no answer to my question. I would watch him, seated on a brocade-backed chair in one of the many hateful drawing rooms, holding a demitasse of coffee, engaged in long, animated conversations with one gentleman or another, and I would burn with rage. It was even worse if the other was young and handsome, and it wasn't long before the inevitable possibility wormed its way into my mind: he was either tiring of me or was looking for another lover, or both.

"I confronted him with my suspicions one night after a particularly trying evening. 'Don't be ridiculous,' he said, in a kind of mixture of scorn and outraged honor. 'If I were interested in anybody else, you would have known long before now.'

"This answer had a certain logic to it, but was far from being a satisfactory – particularly since his behavior didn't change a bit.

"Out of desperation, I hit upon a plan. In the same city lived a doctor who was an old friend of mine but not of my lover's, and I took him into my confidence. He was quite sympathetic, but raised some grave objections as to the wisdom of my scheme, saying that I was like the skater who jumped hard on the ice to see if it would break. In the end, however, on the basis of our long-standing friendship, I obligated him to follow through with my plan.

"This doctor, I should say, was still young, and certainly hand-some. He was also a cultivated gentleman, and entirely at ease among people. I introduced him to Roderick, and gradually succeeded in leaving them alone in each other's company as often as possible. My object was, of course, to see if my lover could be lured away from me – to test his loyalty and affection.

"It soon got to be my custom to meet the doctor either in his lodgings or in a tavern close by to discuss the progress of my scheme; we analyzed Roderick's every reaction, discussed the affair at great length, and often went on to talk of other things – love, constancy, the Greek ideal, literature and so on. The tavern where we met often engaged a string quartet, whose music was both a distraction to me and a sensual background to my feelings.

"On one of these nights, when the heat of the day continued long after sundown – in August, as I recall – we sat drinking ale until late in the evening. There were fireflies flickering in the darkness, the quartet was playing something by Mozart, and I grew bored with the incessant analysis of my lover's behavior. The doctor suggested that we go to his lodgings, where, he said, it was cooler. Since I was not sleepy and was really quite warm, I agreed. When we arrived, he made himself comfortable by removing most of his clothes, and I did the same. You can probably guess what happened. I don't know whether it was the music, the ale, the fireflies, his handsomeness or my own desire, but we made love. I wish I could say that I rejected the whole affair immediately afterward out of a deep-seated sense of moral rectitude, but I can't, for our love-making was certainly enjoyable, both tender and passionate, and came to be the customary ending of our evenings together.

"On one of these evenings, to my utter horror, Roderick burst in on us at a time when there could be no mistake as to our activities, and the scene that followed was filled with verbal and emotional pyrotechnics, to say the least. Roderick played the part of the aggrieved, faithful lover, the doctor kept an embarrassed silence, and I, stupidly, tried to defend myself in an essentially indefensible position. One question led to another, and either because of my simplicity or Roderick's astuteness, the whole plot came to light, and our relationship to an end. I changed lodgings the following day, and saw Roderick only twice thereafter, and that from a distance.

"Furthermore, the doctor's efforts on my behalf bore fruit. I learned later that he and Roderick had become lovers, after a fashion. I say 'after a fashion' because, although they lived together, each, as I understood, felt free to make love to whomever he chose.

"As for myself, it dawned on me one day that Roderick had guessed my intentions and activities long before the final scene, and had chosen to use them as an excuse to be rid of me, having decided that I would never allow him the freedom he desired, even though I would surely claim that freedom for myself. And perhaps he was tired of me. At any rate, after several months of agony and suffering had passed, I awoke one morning filled with eagerness and joy, as if a burden had been lifted from my back. I was able to laugh at my blind mistakes, and above all, I was free of the poisoned love for Roderick, half love and half hate, that had blackened my life for almost a year. Everything was right again; life was again beautiful, and I reveled in the intense joy of pure freedom to do what I chose to do, unhampered by sick anxieties. On that wave of self-confidence I left the East and after much wandering, here I am, with Ephraim MacIver resting his head on my naked lap."

His rough hands caressed Ephraim's cheek. "And now," he said, in a changed tone of voice, "I think we had better be getting back to the shelter in a hurry, because that is the fifth danger-stick I've seen in the past half-hour." His arm pointed to the river.

"Where?" asked Ephraim, raising his head and squinting into the sunlight.

"Over there. See it?"

Ephraim followed his pointing finger. Floating in the current, almost invisible, was a half-peeled stick perhaps six inches long.

"I see it. What does it mean?"

"It means we have about an hour, I judge, to clean up our tracks and make ourselves scarce before some very dangerous people come down the river. Two of them, according to those sticks, and unless I'm seriously mistaken, one of them is your old friend."

He wrapped his arms more tightly around Ephraim, bent his head to Ephraim's ear. "We'll have to get some clothes on, although I hate to take away the obvious visual pleasure you derive from my na-kedness." His hand passed down Ephraim's side to his hip and thigh. "And I myself hate to give up the painful sweetness of watching you, my love, naked and glowing in the sunlight." His lips touched Ephraim's cheek; his beard prickled on Ephraim's shoulder.

"Either we go now," whispered Ephraim, "or you will have to make love to me, and we'll be caught in the act –"

Cyrus straightened up, smiling. "Yes. There's no great hurry, but we mustn't waste time either." They stood, and Cyrus looked around him – at the rock, the river bank, the little path up to the shelter. "Go get dressed," he said, "and bring my clothes halfway down the path; wait for me there. I'll be done here in about five minutes."

Ephraim trotted off, wondering at Cyrus' cool alertness. The danger-sticks had been floating down the river for an hour or more, yet he had neither mentioned them nor let them worry him. And Ephraim was sure that he himself wouldn't have seen them at all; not in a thousand years. He dressed quickly, found Cyrus' clothes and hurried down the path. Through the trees he could see Cyrus' naked body by the river bank, carefully obliterating their tracks in the wet sand with two pointed stones.

Desire welled up in Ephraim's throat again as he watched the heavily muscled buttocks and thighs as Cyrus stooped in the sand and backed up the trail, brushing after himself with the branch. When he had come to where Ephraim was standing, Ephraim seized him around the waist from behind, kissing the voluptuously curved back, reaching down his hairy belly to the cock – long, thick, soft – and Cyrus laughed, straightening up. Ephraim blushed and gave him his clothes.

"Tonight, my love," Cyrus whispered as he pulled on his breeches. Hastily he jerked on his boots and laced them; still buttoning his shirt, he set off through the forest, motioning to Ephraim to follow.

A minute later, Cyrus dropped to his belly and Ephraim did likewise; slowly they inched forward; Cyrus stopped, then motioned Ephraim up beside him. They were on a low, rocky bluff overlooking the river, not twenty yards from where they had been swimming. Cyrus wrapped an arm around Ephraim's shoulder; they drew closer and settled down to wait and watch.

Ephraim quickly tired of staring at the river. His attention wandered – to the brilliant blue and scarlet dragonflies dancing over the water, to the lacelike shadows of the ferns above his head, and to the rhythm of Cyrus' deep, slow breathing. Cyrus turned and brushed Ephraim's ear with his lips, half-smiling, wriggling his belly so that it rested against Ephraim's backside, and pressed his thigh between his legs. Ephraim flexed his buttock, and felt Cyrus' hardening penis.

"Perhaps," Cyrus whispered, "I could entertain you with a poem that has been composing itself in my mind since this morning."

"You too compose poetry?"

Cyrus grinned. "When suitably inspired." He thrust with his hips; Ephraim felt the enormous cock hard against his backside.

"Go ahead," Ephraim whispered, smiling. "I am anxious to hear your feelings –"

Cyrus spoke:

Lie down, my love, upon the grass
　　Your love has pierced me to the quick
For winters come, but winters pass.

Together we will hold a class
　　To teach you every lover's trick
Lie down, my love, upon the grass.

In loving struggle we'll amass
　　A store of pleasure, warm and slick,
For winters come, but winters pass.

Then I'll caress your lovely ass
　　And gently tongue and warmly lick
Lie down, my love, upon the grass.

Your swollen penis will surpass
　　An oaken bough, both strong and thick
For winters come, but winters pass.

I'll kiss your belly's hairy mass
　　And press my lips upon your prick
Lie down, my love, upon the grass,
For winters come, but winters pass.

Ephraim smiled again. "Soon –" he whispered.

Then Cyrus turned his attention back to the river. Following Cyrus' gaze, his slightly lifted head, Ephraim looked down to the river bank. There was a stag, stepping delicately in the sand that Cyrus had so carefully cleared of tracks. Cyrus seemed pleased. "Those tracks he's making would fool even an Indian, which mine wouldn't have." The stag lowered its head to the water, then sprang upward in a wild, disjointed leap, and came down, floundering, in the shallow water. Simultaneously Ephraim heard the ringing crack of a rifle. Cyrus ducked his head and pressed down tightly on Ephraim.

"Got him!" he heard. Looking down, he saw a canoe, with two white men in it. The man in front was Montgomery, holding a rifle. Ephraim nodded slightly to Cyrus' questioning look, and hardly dared to breathe, conscious of a shiver that rose from his spine to his scalp.

The canoe glided to the shallows, where the stag lay, oozing brilliant scarlet into the gently rippling river, Montgomery leaped out, splashing noisily, and dragged the buck onto the sand. The other man, dressed completely in black, beached the canoe carefully and stepped onto the shore with precise, controlled steps, hardly glancing at Montgomery.

"Calvin," whispered Cyrus. Ephraim grimaced, and studied the man intently.

Without a word, Mr. Calvin began to skin the hindquarters of the deer, while Montgomery watched.

"Pretty good shot, huh?" Montgomery said.

Mr. Calvin nodded.

Montgomery cleaned and reloaded his rifle, then amused himself by throwing rocks into the river. "Why don't we make camp here?" he asked. "Then we won't have to pack the whole carcass with us."

Mr. Calvin lifted his head, staring at Montgomery almost blankly, and Montgomery sat down with an exasperated sigh. Mr. Calvin lowered his head again and continued working. Finally he said, "It's three hours till nightfall. We will take only the hindquarters with us."

"And leave the rest here?"

Mr. Calvin replied in a flat, calm voice. "We can't eat it all before it spoils."

Montgomery resumed his rock-throwing.

Ephraim studied his former friend, searching for signs of change, for clues to his thinking. Montgomery had a five-day growth of beard, but that was fitting – though handsome and vain, he was often slovenly. His clothes were filthy, but worn with a certain careless grace that was not unattractive. The back of his head, his full lips and his beautiful fingers portrayed the same deceptive weakness, danger-ous when misunderstood. The cold, metallic denial was still there – in his eyes, and in the arrogant tilt of a shoulder.

Mr. Calvin was quite different. He had a wiry black beard, neatly trimmed; his shirt and trousers were clean, and he even managed to keep them clean while skinning the deer. His body was medium-sized and compact. He never wasted a movement, never looked up, never spoke unless spoken to. Ephraim would learn nothing from the man's expressionless face, but guessed somehow that he was an intense person, filled with pride. He remembered the brief glimpse he had had of Mr. Calvin in Astoria, and again along the Willamette – the tensely controlled expression, the stiff, erect, precise walk.

Mr. Calvin loaded the haunches of venison into the canoe and waited for Montgomery to shove off and jump in. 'A strange pair,' Ephraim thought. 'Calvin does all the work. Montgomery amuses himself shooting deer and throwing rocks, and they seem to get along just fine. I'll bet Calvin thinks he's in charge –'

In a swirl of blood-colored water they slipped into the current and were gone. Cyrus waited a full minute before wriggling forward, then cautiously stood on all fours, peering intently downriver. He turned back quietly and whispered to Ephraim. "I think they're gone, but they may have noticed something suspicious. There's a bend in the river where it loops back about a half-mile down, if you remember; we can make it there before they do, and see if they're re-ally going on downstream." He set off again through the forest, with Ephraim following.

After a steep climb they came onto the top of a small ridge which gave a full view of the river far below. They hid in a thicket of dog-wood and laurel, although there was little likelihood of their being seen at such a distance. After waiting wordlessly for a few minutes, Ephraim saw the canoe below, its occupants both paddling, speeding down with the current.

"They're gone," breathed Cyrus, and he rolled over on his side, propping himself with one elbow. He looked at Ephraim and grinned slyly. "Are you sorry?"

"What do you mean?" said Ephraim, confused. "Oh! About Montgomery being gone?" He laughed drily. "That is very amusing indeed. Actually, I hadn't thought about it – I spent so much time searching for him, and now that I do catch sight of him, I hide for my life. Ironic, isn't it?"

"You're sure it's all over?"

Ephraim nodded emphatically. "Very sure. Suddenly, when I saw him, I was frightened, and repulsed. No, it's completely over, and has been for months."

"Good," said Cyrus standing up. "And now we have several things to do to warn our friends downstream."

He pulled out a jackknife and began to cut laurel branches. "You can help me – cut about ten, between an inch and a half-inch thick, and six or eight inches long. We have to make some more danger-sticks." While cutting he explained. "They said they'd camp at sundown: I reckon that's about two hours from now, likely less. We'll let these go in the river as soon as we're finished, and they'll float right by them in the night, probably reaching Singing Heron by about this time day after tomorrow – in plenty of time. Just in case he doesn't see any of those that we saw, which he probably will."

"Oh," said Ephraim. "I hadn't thought of that." He started cutting twigs. "But won't a lot of them get snagged here and there?"

"Some of them will, to be sure. But you'd be surprised at how many get through."

"And won't Calvin and Montgomery see them?"

Cyrus grinned. "If I'm any judge of character, they'll both miss them entirely. Even if they see one or two, they won't know what they mean."

"That Calvin is surely a peculiar-looking type," said Ephraim. "Is this enough?"

"Yes, that's plenty. Let's go back to camp and peel them there. But tell me what you thought of Calvin, how you size him up. I've spent a lot of time trying to figure that man out, and I think I've finally got him nailed down, although the Indians around here don't agree with me at all. I think that's because they simply can't comprehend how such a man as Calvin can possibly exist. But tell me your impressions."

They scrambled down the hillside, and Ephraim thought. "Well, first, he seemed nearsighted, as if he needed glasses." Cyrus didn't answer, so he continued. "I mean, he has a rather blank stare – as if he really doesn't see what he's looking at –"

"The Indians say he's one of the best rifle shots in the Territory. But I think you saw something that I've noticed too, in a different way. Go on; you're very observant."

Ephraim began absently to pick the small, lavender, daisy-like flowers that bloomed in the spaces between the firs. "Well, then this blankness is connected with something else. When Montgomery suggested that they camp there for the night – there wasn't anything really wrong with the suggestion, from their standpoint anyway, but it took a whole minute for it even to sink in on Calvin. And then he didn't argue back; he just stated very simply what they were going to do. He didn't really even consider the suggestion."

"You're right," said Cyrus.

"And then, you noticed how he did all the real work while Montgomery played around, and he didn't even get dirty? I don't see how he did it."

Cyrus laughed. "Long practice," he said.

"And I'll tell you something else," continued Ephraim. "Mr. Calvin thinks he's in charge of the outfit, but he really isn't. I'd bet my last cent, if I had one, that Montgomery doesn't give two whoops for whatever it is that Calvin thinks he's doing. Ultimately, Montgomery is pursuing his own goals, and Mr. Calvin is just tagging along."

"How's that?" asked Cyrus, startled. "I thought he was looking for you."

Ephraim frowned. "I don't understand that. The more I think of it, the less sense it makes. But whether he is or isn't, the point is that he's quite likely not looking for me, really. He could be looking for gold –" Cyrus' eyes widened. "Really, I mean it; or he could be, and this is quite possible, figuring out what our Mr. Calvin has that's of use to him, and how to get his hands on it. Or maybe all these things at once. But he's not simple-minded as he appears. Believe me, his mind is working all the time."

"Very interesting," Cyrus mused. "Tell me more."

"What probably happened," Ephraim continued, "is that Montgomery did a lot of talking around Astoria and Fort Vancouver. He knew I was following, and wanted to set a trap for me. And the reason he wanted to do this, I think –" Ephraim paused. "I think he wanted to set a trap for me because I had pointed out the truth to him, and he was finally beginning to understand, and felt deeply humiliated. Anyway, Calvin must have gotten wind of Montgomery's stories – they were probably true enough, as far as they went – and sought out Montgomery and talked him into this search. But let me tell you, as soon as Montgomery figured out what Calvin's mind is like, his own mind started working. Mr. Calvin had better watch out, for if there's one thing Montgomery will spend a lot of time and real effort on, it's figuring out how to make life easy for himself."

"Wait a minute," laughed Cyrus. "Let me add something. You said Montgomery was possibly trying to set a trap for you. What kind of trap? Do you mean something like telling the trappers and traders up in Astoria about your love for him, if that's the right word, and then hoping that they'd finish you off?" He began to grin.

"Something like that, yes. As I said, he didn't have to invent much." Ephraim suddenly felt wretched, deeply ashamed of his whole affair with Montgomery.

Cyrus laughed, whooping in rumbling booms until he staggered. "Those lions," he finally said, "are already half of them Christians, and most of the rest are beginning to meow in a way that sounds like the catechism. But," he continued more seriously, "their jungle heritage comes out in them every once in a while. I agree with you – if Montgomery is a Vancouver lion, Calvin had better watch out."

Ephraim frowned. "I don't understand," he said. "Montgomery a lion?"

"Wait," Cyrus interrupted. "Let me tell you a few things about Mr. Calvin. As you said, he's as blind as a bat – but in other ways. Ostensibly, he's here operating a mission to bring the white man's civilization to the Indians, which is a silly idea; but actually, the only thing Calvin thinks about, talks about, and even literally sees, is the Loon Society. He sees it everywhere. But the fact is, Mr. Calvin is fighting his own sin."

"Calvin too?" Ephraim said. "That's Montgomery's story."

Cyrus nodded, grinning.

They arrived at the shelter, and Cyrus squatted on his heels and began to peel bark in narrow, lengthwise strips from the twigs they had cut. Ephraim set himself to do likewise, following Cyrus' example. The bearded man's massive, hairy hands worked with agility and sureness; the crotch of his breeches pulled tightly over the genital mass within, a fist-sized bulge. Ephraim's mouth went momentarily dry.

"I'm as sure of this as I am of my own name," continued Cyrus. "Now, I've seen Mr. Calvin only about five times in my life, but it happens that last summer I caught him in the most revealing situation imaginable. I was going up the Willamette trail with my mules when I heard voices over in the river. I tied my mules and went to investigate. First I saw Calvin, sitting on a bank overlooking the river. Down below, unaware of Calvin's presence, was a group of Indian boys bathing. Neither Calvin nor the Indians had heard my approach, so I hid myself and observed the whole scene at my leisure. There were about five boys, from about fifteen to twenty years of age – all naked, all handsome, all having a good time just splashing around. And then Calvin – watching them like a lynx, hidden in a clump of willows. At first I thought he was simply spying for further evidence regarding what he calls sin, but then I watched his hand, on his genitals – a spasmodic clutching, and then he must have come. When he left shortly thereafter, he passed within ten feet of me, absolutely glassy-eyed, in a trance. I don't really think the poor man knew what he'd done."

"I don't see how that's possible," Ephraim murmured, shocked and rather embarrassed.

"I don't either," said Cyrus, shrugging his shoulders. "But it's the only way I can explain it."

As he finished the last stick, Cyrus stood up and squinted at the sun, now a fiery glimmer through the trees, close to the horizon. "Let's go down and toss these into the river; the sun will set in another half-hour." Ephraim followed the great strides down to the river bank and watched as Cyrus threw the sticks one by one into the current.

"The Indians have developed quite a system of communicating downriver with these sticks, something you should learn about as soon as possible."

"I've already seen one other kind," said Ephraim. "It was painted orange, with notches cut in it."

Cyrus' blue eyes turned momentarily to Ephraim. He smiled. "That was a love-journey stick. Who had sent it?"

"A young Indian named John. He was going downstream to visit several friends." Ephraim shifted uncomfortably. Somehow the thought of Singing Heron now, in Cyrus' presence, made him feel vaguely guilty.

Cyrus was still smiling, but it was a set, fixed smile. "Ah, yes – I know the young man. If what I hear is correct, there will be many songs of tender lamentation sung in his home camp while he is gone. A very nice fellow, and most eagerly sought-after." Cyrus paused, staring broodingly at the water. "As you will be," he added.

Ephraim fixed his eyes on the ground. In spite of the compliment, he was embarrassed.

A minute passed in silence. Then Ephraim cleared his throat. "Tell me about the other kinds of sticks."

Cyrus glanced at him again, then back at the river. "A blue stick with a spiral groove is the summons to a formal council at the lodge of Bear-who-dreams. Ordinarily they take place in the spring. You just missed one. A yellow stick with lengthwise grooves is an invitation to a feast; they call them game-sticks, and they're usually sent in the summer. In fact, I'm surprised that you haven't seen any game-sticks yet, because they're preparing now for a feast at Eagle Camp.

"And now, Ephraim," he continued, throwing the last danger-stick into the water, "we have to figure out what to do with the remains of that carcass." Cyrus pointed to the half-skinned deer a short distance away, left by Montgomery and Mr. Calvin, and rubbed his hands on the seat of his breeches. "What I'd like to do is cut off a good-sized chunk and cook it tonight, so that we can dine tomorrow courtesy of our friends. But the remains should be dragged across the river, so that we won't be bothered by varmints like a stray bear or two all night long." He pulled out his knife, and Ephraim watched as he cut into the forequarters.

"I'll take the rest across the river when you're through," Ephraim offered.

"That will be fine. I'll get supper ready meanwhile. I'd just swim it across, there's no reason to bring out the canoe."

When Cyrus had finished and gone, Ephraim stripped quickly and seized the remains of the buck by the antlers. Picking his way among the rocks of the river bank and dragging as much of the carcass as possible behind him, Ephraim wondered at the accuracy of Montgomery's marksmanship.

He shivered slightly, for the water was cold in the twilight, and towed the heavy carcass clumsily across the river. On the return trip he hurried, swimming freely and strongly, and then threw the remainder of the carcass into the swift-flowing current, grimacing with distaste. Then he dived in to rinse off his body thoroughly, left the river, and picked his way back to his clothes.

While hopping first on one foot and then the other to dry off and to keep warm, he spotted the lavender flowers in his shirt pocket, where he had absently put them. Smiling to himself, he took them out and began to braid a flower chain, making a complete circle, and hung it on a branch. He smiled again as he pulled on his breeches.

Looking up, he saw Cyrus standing in the shadows, watching. "I brought you a blanket," he said softly. "It's getting cold." He wrapped the blanket around Ephraim's shoulders.

Taking the flower chaplet, Ephraim placed it on Cyrus' head. "For your thoughtfulness, I crown you king of the wood."

Cyrus seized Ephraim's hand and brought it to his lips. "A king who is beginning to love you very much, very much," he replied more softly still. He leaned down and kissed Ephraim's forehead, his eyes; in the half-twilight, Ephraim could see a new tautness on Cyrus' cheek, a troubled expression about his eyes. "Come," he said. "I have something to eat." He held the blanket around Ephraim's shoulders as they walked silently back to camp.

Cyrus had buried the venison in a pit and had covered it with hot stones and coals from the fire. "It will be cooked through by morning," he said, and served Ephraim cold pemmican, wild berries, and slices of cold venison from the previous day. Like Cyrus, Ephraim ate with his fingers and a knife, from long habit almost totally indifferent to the food he was eating.

Cyrus stared moodily and silently into the low fire. Once he removed the chaplet, studied it carefully, and replaced it.

His silence increased Ephraim's uneasiness; he moved closer, and sat next to the other man, pulling his big arm about his shoulders and slipping the hand inside his shirt as if for warmth. Cyrus pulled Ephraim's head down to his chest and held him, tightly, silently.

When Cyrus got up to add more wood to the fire, Ephraim broke the long silence. "I think I should be leaving tomorrow." He was uncertain, almost fearful.

Cyrus' head swung around, his eyes wide. "So soon?" he cried.

Ephraim hardly knew what to say. "It's – I mean, I should be upriver as soon as possible, and I think you're expected downstream."

Somehow this was the wrong thing to say; it was false to his own feelings. On the other hand, he didn't know with any certainty how he really did feel, or what the right thing to do was regardless of his feelings. His confusion showed in his voice as he added, "Actually, I don't know what to do, but I think I must see Bear-who-dreams right away."

Cyrus sat down again and pulled him close, encircling his body with great arms, holding his head against his chest. "I know that, my love," he whispered, "but I want so badly to know you more, so I can hold you, caress you, talk to you, give you my love, all the time, every day –" His voice trailed off.

Ephraim opened his mouth to speak, but it was gently covered with a great hand. "I know what you are wondering, my love, and I am wondering many things too. Let me just talk for a while, then you tell me how you feel." He took a deep breath. "First of all, I love you, from the inside in a way that makes me tremble. You've shaken me down to my roots. When I see you standing almost thoughtlessly naked with the sunlight in your belly hair, your cock hanging free in the sunlight, your lithe, classic hips and thighs walking unconcerned through the forest, I hunger for you. And you have a way of letting everything you feel show on your face, telling me more about what you think and feel than what you actually say. Thus I know how much I excite you – how you feel when you see me naked, or even dressed. You were excited by the tightness of my breeches this afternoon when I was kneeling before you, weren't you? I know, because you blushed. You make me feel beautiful, Ephraim."

"You are beauti –" A hand covered his mouth.

"Be still, my love, and listen. I want you to be my partner, so that we can –"

"But –"

"Hush, my love. So that we can love each other in ways that you are only vaguely aware of – ways that will discover dimensions of love that only you and I, I think, can understand." He lifted his head and stared into the fire. Ephraim remained silent, confused, feeling only a turmoil of emotions.

"If you wish to be my partner, I will tell Singing Heron and he will understand." He paused. "You must believe me when I say this, for you have no way of knowing, really knowing, how things are. Summer is the hunting season, Ephraim, and many changes occur before the leaves fall."

Ephraim concentrated on the chest hair beneath his fingers; combing, stroking, twining, exploring the deeply curved muscle, the nipple –

Cyrus groped behind himself for his pipe, filled it, and held a long twig over the fire.

When he had lit the pipe, he asked, "Do you like to smoke?"

"Yes, sometimes."

"Would you like to share my pipe?"

"Yes, thank you." He sat up and took the pipe, inhaling cautiously. He handed it back to Cyrus but stayed sitting up. The smoke made him feel lightheaded.

Cyrus continued. "Would it make any sense to you if I said that I love Singing Heron as he loves me, and that we will continue to love each other, in this way, regardless of what you and I decide to do? And yet in spite of that, I love you, Ephraim, in a way that brings me close to tears sometimes – twice today without your knowing it." He paused again. "There are many things I could say about my love for you and for Singing Heron that you probably want to know, since you are a white man and so new to the Way of the Loon, but I can't say them, simply because they are unsayable in our language: unsayable in any words that would be fair to the ideas we are dealing with."

Ephraim borrowed the pipe again and inhaled. He sat forward, elbows on his knees, facing away from Cyrus. "What you are trying to avoid is any comparison between myself and Singing Heron," he said softly. "I'm not asking for a comparison at all, because I find myself in something of the same situation." The pipe went out, and he lit it again. "As a matter of fact, Cyrus, what you are trying to avoid is any comparison possible. I sense, with my heart, why such a comparison would be useless and perhaps even unfair; it has never occurred to me to compare you, for instance, to anybody."

He handed the pipe back to Cyrus, glancing briefly at his eyes. They were widened, almost pleading, and Cyrus quickly looked back into the fire. "It's quite paradoxical, isn't it?" Ephraim continued. "And you must know something else. You are right in seeing my excitement with you; you stir my feelings in ways that I haven't words for describing. Yes, your cock, your hairiness, your massiveness – but also some other things: your kindness, thoughtfulness; your concern. I do love you, Cyrus –"

"Wait –" Cyrus interrupted, placed a hand on Ephraim's shoulder. "Understand, my love, that I'm not asking you to decide now. Go to Bear-who-dreams; make love to many others this summer; but send me a message in August. We must work during September and October to prepare for the winter. I must know before the first frost." He shook his head suddenly. "But if you called me in December, I would come, Ephraim. I may seek you out anyway, regardless of your circumstances –" His voice had sunk to a whisper, a pleading urgency.

Ephraim turned and stared into the other's eyes for a long minute; the dancing firelight lit their frightened wideness. He stood up quickly, and in a single movement slid his breeches to the ground and kicked them into the shadows. "Undress, my love," he whispered, unable to say more for the dryness in his throat. He stood with his back to the fire, hands clasped behind him, feeling the warmth on his buttocks, the warm rush of excitement into his penis.

Slowly, Cyrus' hand moved down the front of his shirt, unbuttoning as he went; the opening across his chest bared a dark, soft mat. His eyes moved up Ephraim's body to his face, their glances crossed, and Ephraim caught sight, fleetingly, of a tightly controlled deepness, a sensitivity that shocked him. He knelt and took the bearded face in his hands, staring into Cyrus' eyes, trying to discover the meaning of what he saw. But the eyelids closed, the lips murmured something he couldn't understand. He pulled Cyrus' head against his chest, stroking his hair and beard; touched his lips to his forehead, aware of the deep emotional breathing.

When he stood up again, there was a faint glistening in the other man's eyes as he pulled off his shirt, then his head lowered as he unlaced his boots and kicked them off. When Cyrus stood up, bare-footed, bare-chested, to unbuckle his belt, he was smiling, tightly at first, then more broadly as his fingers undid the buckle. He said, "I feel wonderful now, this minute – as big and free as the wind, watch-ing you watching me as I'm about to take off my breeches."

As each button was undone, more of the muscular belly showed. The mass of hair curled outward from the opening more thickly as he unbuttoned further; then he bent over and, standing first on one leg and then the other, yanked off the breeches. He straightened up, hands on his hips, still smiling; his cock dangled heavily, half swollen, lengthening, rising in swaying jerks. Ephraim came closer and their cocks touched momentarily, then touched again as they rose, thick-ened, pulsated. The veins on Cyrus' cock were as thick as those on his arm, twining like ivy around a tree trunk.

Ephraim turned and found the blanket he had worn, and spread it on the ground in the firelight. Cyrus knelt, then lay down on the blanket, gently pulling Ephraim with him, on top of him; they kissed, rolling hips languorously, thrusting, grinding belly against belly, hair crackling –

Ephraim felt a calloused hand moving down the grooves of his spine. He flexed his buttocks in anticipation; the hand caressed softly, the roughness prickling against his sensitive skin. He flexed again, hoping – not knowing what – that a strong finger would reach down, and in, hard. But the hand moved back up his spine, restlessly, and stopped at his waist.

He became suddenly aware of the enormous bulk pressing against his belly – Cyrus' cock – and rose to his hands and knees. The unbelievable organ lay on Cyrus' belly, reaching up to his na-vel. Swiftly, Ephraim kissed first the bearded chin, the throat, chest, nipples; then, with his tongue, touched the wildly hairy navel and the tip of the cock. A rolling thrust answered, but he brushed his lips down, under, to the testicles resting, hanging loosely down to the blanket; he held the cock in one hand – it filled his palm, warm, hard

– and gripped hard, moving the skin up, down – the thrusting became more insistent – Cyrus' back arched, thighs spread, and Ephraim went down on his cock and thrust a finger behind the testicles, into the anus, hard, all the way, and was answered by a choking, frenzied thrust as the cock swelled on his tongue, his throat, a bulbous, frantic thing; then the taste, and again, and again, until it softened and he could hold it all, down to the base, his nose buried in the belly hair, lips circling the base of this great, mysterious thing. The lean hips twisted as he rubbed his forehead on Cyrus' belly, tightened his lips, moved his tongue; then gently, his head was lifted by two huge hands and he released the cock and it fell heavily, wetly, down to the blanket. He was panting.

They rested for a long time, side by side, until Cyrus' breathing became deeper, more even; but Ephraim was still warmly anxious, alert, restless; his cock pressed insistently against Cyrus' thigh, and his hand moved over the muscular body, curved, undulating and hard. Finally Cyrus turned on his side and Ephraim strained his body against him. Cyrus was smiling beatifically.

He slid his hand down Ephraim's back again, caressing softly, touching, probing gently; then he touched the anus and Ephraim widened his thighs in a sudden jerk. Cyrus, surprised, pushed his finger tentatively, then shifted his body onto his knees between Ephraim's thighs. In a single flash of warm, sharp sensation, Ephraim felt the mouth on his cock, warm and pressing, the beard prickling against his thighs – and the finger thrust, long and powerful. He arched, strained, clutched, lived wholly in the warm sweetness gathering force, pivoting wildly on an axis at the center of his being, strangely, oddly off center, reaching up to his vitals as the finger whirled up his anus, then the sweetness snapped, and it was the big man's mouth, tongue, teeth, the sweetness surging into the center of the earth, down, down into black oblivion –

Eyes tightly closed, Ephraim clasped the life-defining body to himself. Just before he drifted off to sleep, he was vaguely aware of Cyrus' voice, whispering, "My beautiful lover, you and I both want to make love in another fashion – you are ready to give, and I to receive you, but, oh! my love, I do not want to cause you pain. I am ready to give of myself, but can you receive me?"

Ephraim slept late; he awoke to a thickly foggy, chilly world. Cyrus had risen long before, and was packing his gear. His face was troubled, but he worked calmly and resolutely, saddling and loading the mules. Together they finished packing Ephraim's canoe, and ate their breakfast in silence. Finally, at noon, the fog began to break up into thin patches, and the sun shone through on the river as Ephraim made ready to leave.

Cyrus took his hand and kissed it, held it tightly, looking down as he spoke. "Ephraim," he said, "two days upstream is Eagle Camp, where a small group of Loon Society members are spending the summer. There you will find an Indian named Tlasohkah, a friend of mine who has taught me many things. I am very fond of him, as you will be also: Learn from him, and remember that his way of making love can also be my way; that as you make love to him, so you may make love to me."

He looked briefly into Ephraim's eyes, noting their questioning, their confusion. Ephraim only half understood, and willfully refused to pursue the hints any farther in his own mind. Cyrus continued, haltingly. "Tlasohkah is – the only person who has been able, and willing – to accommodate my, to be perfectly frank, rather embarrassingly cumbersome organ – in another way of making love, Ephraim: my organ in his body; that is, up his backside." He paused, then continued quickly. "And of course I learned the strange pleasure of accommodating him."

Ephraim understood, and stammered without thinking, "And if I were able and willing to receive you in the same way?"

Cyrus' eyes burned with such intensity that Ephraim had to look down. Finally Cyrus looked away, saying in a trembling rumble,

"Don't think of that now, my love – think only of giving your love to me." He paused again to control his breath, swallowing, and then continued more calmly. "I think it is fortunate that you are leaving me now, without having loved me in this way, for the desire for such an experience will bring you back to me." He steadied the canoe and indicated to Ephraim that it was time to leave.

He shoved the canoe into midstream, wading in after until the water was above his knees. "Good-bye, my love; my heart goes with you." His face was somber, and stricken with sadness.

"Good-bye, Cyrus," whispered Ephraim. "I will write to you in August, before the leaves turn." He struggled to find a way of saying something more, of giving Cyrus some assurance – of what? He wasn't certain himself. "And – I love you, Cyrus – deeply and surely –" He tried to think of something else to say, but couldn't.

Finally he turned away and began paddling upstream, aware of the huge, muscular form in the river behind him; at the bend in the river he turned back to look, and saw Cyrus still standing knee-deep in the river.

They waved, and then he shot onward, around the bend.

Interlude

The river narrowed as Ephraim continued upstream, and he passed through occasional stretches of rapids where the canoe had to be guided with extreme caution. His strength and skill had increased greatly, and he enjoyed the challenge of swift, white water, daring to think of the possibility of being dashed against a rock and overturned, and not really caring.

He camped that night in a grove of ponderosas, and awoke singing, feeling intensely beautiful. He packed quickly and ate, feeling somehow like the huge pine above him, as if the pine were inside him, giving him strength and beauty. He caressed its rough, unyielding surface, stretched his arms, trying to encircle the enormous trunk, pressed his face and lips against the bark and closed his eyes. His penis began, strangely, to stir and thicken as he pushed his belly against the tree, and he remained thus for a length of time, unthinking, aware only of the live, woody texture against his hands and cheek, and of the slowly growing pleasure in his cock. Then he dropped his arms and returned to the river, where his canoe lay in readiness for the day's journey.

Slowly, tentatively, as he paddled in rhythmic thrusts, he allowed his thoughts to return to Cyrus – to Cyrus' last words before his departure. He was quite sure now that he understood Cyrus correctly, and he began to explore, warily, his own desires and urges, and to picture in his mind the act itself. A vivid image struck him – of the Herculean body, thighs spread, the muscular buttocks and dark, hairy cleft yielding to his own pressure; and he knew, in a flash of desire, that this was what he wanted. His heart pounded and again his cock began to stir – yes, the buttocks, yes, the ass, yes, – and he pushed the image from his mind in empty frustration.

In a minute, however, his thoughts returned to Cyrus. He fleetingly reviewed certain other images that sprang to mind, especially the tenseness in Cyrus' face that morning, and his stricken, wide-eyed look of surprise the night before, when he had learned of Ephraim's departure: But Cyrus can wait, he decided finally. He will wait, quite probably, and meanwhile – this Indian – what was his name? – who will teach me –

Suddenly the river broadened, came pouring and combing at him over a wide, shallow, rocky bed. The canoe scraped gravel, and he berated himself for not having heard the rapids, for not having noticed the white water ahead. The canoe drifted back downstream, and he allowed it to beach on the gravelly shore.

He jumped out and pulled it entirely out of the water, wondering what to do. He pulled off his boots and waded part way out into the rapids, seeing immediately that there was no channel deep enough for a canoe, although the rapids were not particularly dangerous. The only solution, he decided, was to unload the canoe, carry his pack past the rapids, come back, and somehow either drag the canoe overland or float it up the rapids.

As he began to unload, he saw a moccasined foot out of the corner of his eye, perhaps two yards behind him. He whirled around, startled.

The Indian watched him without a trace of expression – on his face or even in his bearing – and Ephraim had no idea how he had gotten there.

"Come with me," said the Indian. "My canoe is upstream. Help me carry it down here, and I will help you."

Ephraim smiled, relieved. "Of course. That will save a lot of time."

The Indian turned and led the way silently over a grassy knoll to the place where he had left his canoe.

They heaved the canoe onto their shoulders, provisions and all, and returned downstream by the same route, the Indian still leading. Then, without pausing to rest or speak, they carried Ephraim's canoe upstream. Although the Indian didn't seem tired, Ephraim noted the quivering muscles of his back, and his sweat-glistening thighs and calves. He was the same height as Ephraim, but perhaps a few pounds lighter – wiry, and darkly, broodingly handsome. His breechclout and moccasins were worked with a beaded design that Ephraim had never seen – he certainly wasn't from the coast; probably from the mountains or even possibly, from the central plains. But the face puzzled Ephraim: his expression was not unfriendly, but – carefully controlled, Ephraim decided. It was as if he were working very hard to force every muscle into a masklike calm, and hadn't quite succeeded. Occasionally, a darting movement of his eyes or a quick jerk at the corner of his mouth revealed a nervousness, a feeling-state that wasn't meant to be seen. Ephraim guessed that the emotions the Indian was hiding were not pleasant.

They lowered the canoe with grunts of relief onto the shore, and the Indian fell on the ground to rest, closing his eyes. He seemed, suddenly, very tired. Ephraim brought a jug of water and some venison from his canoe and offered it; the Indian drank, but shook his head at the food. He lay back again, shading his eyes with a forearm, and Ephraim sat beside him, warily curious about this strange, intense man, and tentatively conscious of his bronzed, wiry, half-naked handsomeness.

With his eyes still covered, the Indian asked, "You are Ephraim MacIver, are you not?"

Ephraim was beginning to get used to being known by every stranger he met. He paused briefly before replying. Then he said slowly, flatly, "Yes, I am."

The Indian's shaded eyes cast a quick glance at Ephraim, then he closed them again. "I know your name because I have been to see Bear-who-dreams; he has spoken of your coming, although he has never seen you. My name was Tsi-nokha, which in my tongue means Storm-at-dawning. I am looking for an Indian whose name is perhaps John."

Ephraim paused to untangle this strange statement, and studied the Indian's flat, hard belly: each muscle was shadowed distinctly, the bones of his narrow hips protruded slightly above the cord of his breechclout – and of course the tip of a scar showed on his lower belly, white against the brown skin, leading down and under the narrow beaded flap.

"Why are you looking for this Indian named John?" Ephraim began.

Tsi-nokha's eyes bore into him as he spoke. "He has stolen my soul," he said, and closed his eyes again. His mouth twitched. Ephraim noted the deep hollow of his cheek, the strong, square chin, slightly cleft, and the arched nose. "I know," continued Tsi-nokha, "that Bear-who-dreams says it is not witchcraft, as the medicine men in my tribe have said: Bear-who-dreams was very angry with me, and we talked for many days. He says that my sickness is love." Tsi-nokha sat up. "I do not know. Perhaps he is right." He picked a stalk of grass and chewed it, glaring across the river. "Bear-who-dreams says many strange things." He fell into a taut silence.

"Why do you say your name was Tsi-nokha?" asked Ephraim. "Why don't you have a name now?"

"Because my name was stolen with my soul," the Indian snapped. "John has it. He is keeping it. I have no name."

Ephraim stared again at the Indian, who was now facing partly away from him. "But what shall I call you?" he asked softly.

The Indian shrugged his shoulders angrily. "I don't know," he spat out. Then he turned completely away, still chewing the stalk of grass.

Ephraim was at a loss for something to say. Finally he asked, "Would you like me to give you a name?"

The Indian turned around and gazed levelly at Ephraim. Then

he lay down again, shading his eyes as before. "As you wish," he said. His fingers moved restlessly over one hipbone, his belly, then lay flat on the ground.

"I will think about it," said Ephraim. "Before I leave, I will give you another name."

The Indian drew a deep breath. After a slight pause, he said carefully, "That would be very nice. I need a name – a temporary one, until I get my real one back."

"I will think of a name, then," said Ephraim, "and I hope you will like it."

The Indian continued rapidly. "Bear-who-dreams has sent me on a medicine journey. He says that I have not really lost my soul, that John does not have it, that I don't know the real words for my sickness. Perhaps this is so, but I do not think he has the real words either. I do not understand his words. In my tribe, there is a real word for my sickness, but I will not tell it to you, because it is ugly. Bear-who-dreams says that my word is not the right one, which is good, because if my word is right, I would have to dress differently, act differently, and – But I won't tell you anything more about my – their – way. But, if Bear-who-dreams is right, why do I have my people's medicine visions at night? Sometimes it is a witch, and sometimes – not. Sometimes my visions are as Bear-who-dreams says they must be. But only twice. And I have forgotten them." His mouth was a hard line.

Ephraim touched the Indian's hand with a fingertip. "I think," he said softly, "that Bear-who-dreams is right: that the Way of the Loon is the right way."

Tsi-nokha said nothing. His hand quivered, but he didn't move it.

Ephraim moved his fingertips up to the wrist, now resting three fingers lightly, aware of the strong pulse. Tsi-nokha lay perfectly still.

"Surely," Ephraim continued, "there is no need to dress differently, to act in another way. I have never been anything but what

I am; nor do I wish to act, or dress, or talk, or think in any other fashion –"

His palm rested on Tsi-nokha's forearm, then on his bicep. "Names cannot really change what we are," he whispered. "We are what we are, and words –"

With a sudden, savage snarl, the Indian leaped to his feet and fell upon Ephraim, knocking him flat, straining to pin his arms to the ground. In a flash of surprise and fear, Ephraim struggled, thrust, arched, threw the Indian off, and rose to one knee. The Indian rushed again, but Ephraim was ready. They rolled on the grass, grunting, straining; arms and legs slashing for a hold.

Ephraim felt the Indian weakening. In a frightened surge of strength, he locked an arm under the Indian's shoulder and kicked, catching his leg, and flipped him onto the ground and pinned his arms. Tsi-nokha kicked and twisted, writhed like a whip, but Ephraim stayed on top. Finally the Indian went completely limp, breathing heavily, head turned to one side.

Ephraim glared down, panting and sweating. The Indian remained motionless, except for his heaving chest, the throbbing pulse in his neck.

"What's the idea?" Ephraim growled, teeth clenched, furious.

The Indian didn't answer. Ephraim jabbed his chest with a knee, lowered his face to within inches of the Indian's and roared, "What's –?" but changed his mind, and straightened up a bit. He glowered at the Indian's averted face, and slowly his anger began to ebb.

"All right. No more fighting?" he barked.

Tsi-nokha didn't answer. Ephraim jabbed him more sharply with his knee and lowered his face again. "I beat you. No more fighting," he shouted.

The Indian's mouth twisted. "No more," he whispered, with a bare trace of a snarl.

Ephraim tensed, sprang free, and faced the Indian in a half-crouch, prepared for a new attack. But Tsi-nokha only sat up, hunched over, and rubbed his wrists. Ephraim waited until he was certain that Tsi-nokha would remain peaceful, then sat down, still keeping a wary eye on him.

Looking down, Tsi-nokha muttered in a strange, flat voice, "You won. You may take me."

Ephraim answered, "I don't understand."

"It is the custom of my people. Take me now, as you wish, but quickly –"

Ephraim comprehended, but he stood up and walked away. "I'm not interested," he said flatly over his shoulder. He sat down again a short distance away staring into the river. The surprise and fright had smothered completely his previous excitement.

He thought of leaving, but a soft noise from behind made him spin around, crouching. Tsi-nokha, however, had only come to sit down. "I did not hear you," he said.

"I said I wasn't interested," Ephraim repeated. "You frightened me. You made me angry. That isn't our way."

Tsi-nokha lay back, shading his eyes again. "I do not understand," he said, "but it is as Bear-who-dreams said it would be."

Ephraim stared absently across the river at a pair of orioles flashing through the trees; a buzzard wheeled in lazy circles far in the distance. He thought again of leaving, but remained seated out of inertia, and perhaps from a last tiny prickle of curiosity.

"Tell me," Tsi-nokha said after a long silence, "how you would begin again – your way – if you were still interested." Then he added, "I must know."

"Why do you have to know?" Ephraim asked.

"I want my name back. And besides, I must know."

Ephraim glanced at the Indian's face – the same twitch at the corner of his mouth, the same hard-set jaw. He leaned back on one elbow. "No more fighting?" he asked.

"No, but – that was my people's way. It is the only way I know. There are other ways, but they are just as bad. I must know your way." Nervously, the Indian cocked the leg on Ephraim's side, hiding his loin cloth from sight; his hand lay clenched at his side.

Ephraim mused, unsmiling. "Well, I know now that what I did before, when I touched your hand, didn't tell you what I was thinking. So, if I were to begin again, I might do several things. I might, for instance, tell you that you are very handsome, very handsome." He glanced at Tsi-nokha, whose face was like a mask.

"Words," the Indian said.

"I am telling you what I might do. But I never say things that I don't feel or don't believe."

"Or," he continued, "I might do several other things. I don't know. Perhaps I would kiss you – very gently, on the cheek – lightly, just a brush. Or I might, perhaps, undress and go swimming, to let you know that I was inviting your interest. But –" He plucked a stem of grass and began to chew it absently, and leaned close to Tsi-nokha, without touching him. "But since I know you better now, I would never do any of those things unless I were given some sign, some indication that you were also interested in making love."

He watched Tsi-nokha's face intently, having decided that if the Indian gave him no sign of acceptance, of wanting his love, he would leave as quickly as courtesy allowed.

Suddenly he wanted a sign very badly – a chance to hold and comfort this strange, beautiful man. But there was no sign; only a quivering about the Indian's half-parted lips.

Tsi-nokha's black eyes darted to Ephraim's face, then closed; his chest rose and fell in irregular shudders, but he said nothing.

Ephraim thought, 'He has to know that he wants me, and admit it, and tell me –' He straightened up and rose to one knee, still watching the Indian, resolved to leave.

Slowly, then, the Indian straightened the cocked leg until it lay flat; Ephraim guessed that Tsi-nokha's eyes were barely open, just enough to see. The Indian's loin cloth was arched, had risen far above his hips; he cocked the far leg and opened his eyes a bit more; his lips were still half-parted. Ephraim stared at the strained loin cloth, then into Tsi-nokha's eyes. Softly, he asked, "Is this a sign that you want me?"

The Indian licked his lips and answered hoarsely. "Yes. Do you want me now?"

"Ah, yes," whispered Ephraim, leaning closer.

"You want me just – for nothing, but myself only?"

"Yes, yes –"

"Tell me why. This is very strange –"

"Because you are very handsome," Ephraim breathed haltingly, urgently. "Your face – the high nose of a proud man, a strong man, and your eyes so black, so swift, that tell of the battle within you; your lips, trembling with your unhappiness – I want to touch your face, your eyes, your lips, to make you calm again, at peace, filled with the joy of life. So handsome, so fierce, proud – My lovely one. I was struck with your beauty when I first saw you. I trembled; I made a mistake." He leaned closer, still without touching the Indian. "I am telling the truth, and probably nobody has ever told you these things. Do they make you happier?"

Tsi-nokha waited for two deep breaths before sighing his barely audible reply. "Yes –" he murmured.

"You must know these things. I would like to fill your soul with the knowledge of your own beauty." He touched the Indian's ear with his lips, then leaned back slightly to study his reaction. The hips moved restlessly, the loin cloth rose unsteadily –

Tsi-nokha lay almost rigid, watching Ephraim. Finally he whispered in the same hoarse voice, "What – other things did you say you were going to do?"

Ephraim touched the Indian's cheek with his fingers, caressed his eyes, brought his lips close to his face. "You are so beautiful, my love. I will show you in another way how you affect me." He stood up, and passed his hand over his fully erect cock, tightly outlined his breeches. Quickly he pulled them off and stood looking down, legs wide-planted, caressing his rigid cock, enjoying the feel of it, then he dropped his hands.

Tsi-nokha's eyes widened as he rose to one elbow, staring in wonderment at Ephraim's golden bronze hair, at his pink, swelling cock, at his testicles hanging loosely between his thighs. With a quick twist he untied his loin cloth, and his own pulsating cock sprang outward.

They gazed at each other briefly; the Indian's cock was a strange, unexpected contrast to his lithe, narrow hips and belly – it was wide, full, mauve-headed and sharply rounded.

Making an effort to restrain his eagerness, Ephraim slowly lowered himself onto Tsi-nokha, lying full length atop him, cradling the Indian's shoulders in his hands. Tsi-nokha lay back rigid and unmoving except for a tremor in his breathing. Ephraim kissed his eyes gently, touched his lips with his tongue, then forced his tongue into the Indian's mouth, exploring, probing. The Indian's tongue met his, tentatively, hesitatingly.

Ephraim whispered, "Relax, my love, and accept me. I want to give you pleasure, for I love you – so handsome, so sad –"

The trembling in the Indian's rigid body increased. Ephraim rose to his knees and caressed the dark body, strongly, with both hands, then touched a nipple with his tongue, playing with it; he nipped lightly, pressed his mouth down hard, nipping, tonguing – The Indian began to roll from side to side in voluptuous pleasure.

Quickly, Ephraim placed himself between Tsi-nokha's thighs and kissed the base of his cock, fondling the testicles in one hand, and when the Indian's hips began to thrust in sensual agony he took him in his mouth.

Tsi-nokha was surprised, and lifted his head to watch as Ephraim's head rose and drove down, warmly, tightly circling – then Tsi-nokha let his head fall back, and he arched upward in an impassioned thrust, off the ground again and again, hard; then he held the upward thrust, crying out, trembling violently, and he came, twisting, and came, thrusting, bursting: Ephraim was aghast and excited by the sheer strength and duration of the Indian's orgasm.

Tsi-nokha's hips fell, and he lay panting; Ephraim lay by his side and enclosed the heaving body in his arms, holding the Indian's head against his own chest, caressing the naked back, lightly kissing his ear, his high cheekbone, his forehead. Slowly the Indian grew more calm.

"Are you happier, my love?" Ephraim whispered.

Tsi-nokha opened his eyes and touched Ephraim's chest with his lips. "Oh, yes –" he murmured. He struggled to say more, but couldn't, and fell silent. Finally, in a very low voice, he said, "I want to do the same thing to you, but it is not my custom. But would you think I was strange, or weak, if I did to you what you have just done to me?"

"Do you think I am strange or weak?" asked Ephraim.

"No," Tsi-nokha said vehemently. "You are strong and powerful, and yet your are gentle –"

"Kiss me; explore my body with your hands and your tongue: make love to me, and you are still a man, my love, just as I am still a man."

Tsi-nokha stood up and looked at the sky silently for a full minute, his face intense and drawn. Then he looked down at Ephraim. His hand was on his cock; amazingly, it was lengthening again. "All right," he said. "I will do what you say, because I want to. This will be out of my life, out of time; I will be someone else within myself." He looked at the sky again. "Perhaps it is my real self. And I will kiss you because I want to; I will touch your body with my tongue, I will feel your body with my hands, because it excites me, because it is beautiful – and I will take your cock in my mouth, for it will give me pleasure to do so. I tell you now that I want to!"

He looked down at Ephraim. "Do you hear me?" His voice rose to a roar. "Do you think I am not a man for that? Look at me!" He held his cock in both hands, and shouted. "I say this and I am still a man! I came into you, and you are still a man."

His voice fell, and he knelt beside Ephraim, passing his fingers through the hair on his chest. "I have not slept for many days, and I will do what I please, because it – I am out of time, unconnected with the past and future, and I can say that I love your man's body, that the sight of your prick, the touch of your lips, the sound of your words send the blood racing and pounding through my body."

His hand moved down Ephraim's belly to the thick hair at the base of his cock, luxuriously exploring, feeling, combing with his fingers. Then he fell on Ephraim in a crude, furious frenzy, kissing, licking, biting, probing, experiencing every muscle, every hidden recess: mouth, armpits, navel, thighs, testicles, anus: They rolled over and over on the grass. At one point Ephraim found himself on top of the face-down Indian; he ground his belly against Tsi-nokha's buttocks, his cock between his legs, and was answered with a frenzied flexion of the Indian's buttocks. He grasped him, rolling over, and pulled his head down onto his nearly exploding body, thrust into his mouth; Tsi-nokha came down on it eagerly, clumsily, and Ephraim's being centered on the tongue that was pulling him outward.

They lay for several minutes. Ephraim stroked the Indian's back, his buttocks; voluntarily, Tsi-nokha extended his tongue into Ephraim's mouth, with a low, shuddering moan of pleasure, and kissed his eyes, his forehead.

Then he jumped to his feet, facing away from Ephraim, speaking over his shoulder. "Am I now," he asked, "not a man?"

Ephraim sat up. "Turn around," he said.

Tsi-nokha turned.

Ephraim said harshly, "Look at yourself." He touched the Indian's testicles. Tsi-nokha watched his hand as he pulled the testicles forward, stroked the cock. "Look at yourself. You ask me if you are a man?" He stood up and grasped his own genitals with both hands, asking, "Do I look like anything else?" He dropped his hands and stared nakedly into the Indian's eyes. "Yes, you are a man – proud, fierce, brave, strong; you have always been and always will be a man. And I love you – as a man, because you are a man. Do you understand that?"

Tsi-nokha's face was ashen.

Suddenly Ephraim laughed. "But you are worrying about the wrong things, don't you see? And I'm wasting my time. I should be telling you how much I love you, how beautiful you are –" He threw an arm around Tsi-nokha's shoulder. "Come," he said. "Let us bathe in the river and look at each other, and touch each other, and I will tell you of my love for you, and you will accept me with joy in your heart. We'll play our own game, by our own rules – by whichever rules happen to please us. Don't you see? Our rules, not somebody else's."

"You're not serious then."

"Serious?" Ephraim laughed. "Of course I'm serious. All games are played seriously."

They began walking slowly toward the river. Tsi-nokha was frowning. "I received this wound," he said, "this scar, in a game." He pointed to the scar at the base of his belly.

"I don't think I'd like to play that game," Ephraim said. "Nor do I have to."

At the river's edge, Tsi-nokha turned to Ephraim. "I think that you are very wise. Perhaps, instead of my being out of time, I should be in time with myself, and begin to play your game by your rules. I shall have to try it, and think about it."

Ephraim smiled and waded into the river. The water was shallow, but deep enough to rinse off the dust and sweat. He splashed himself until he was cooler and refreshed, then stood on the bank in the sunlight. Tsi-nokha stood knee-deep in the water, watching him; his black belly-hair glistened, sprinkled with tiny drops of water. Ephraim gazed at the Indian's still half-erect cock, smiling, wondering if he was still interested in making love. He touched his own cock, and it began to lengthen.

"Let us say," the Indian began, "that I may stare at you."

"Oh, yes," Ephraim replied. "I like that rule. Stare at me." He planted his feet wide apart.

"Good," said Tsi-nokha, coming out of the water. "And let us say that I may touch you."

"Yes. Whatever you wish. As much as you want."

Tsi-nokha drew near, and with the fingers of one hand he explored Ephraim's body, lightly, pensively, almost wonderingly.

Ephraim spread his legs further and bent over so that the Indian could look at and touch his anus. Tsi-nokha's cock was full-length again.

"And let us say that I can ask you to make love to me as you did before, and that you can answer 'yes' if you wish."

Ephraim laughed, and for the first time a trace of a smile passed across the Indian's face. "All right," Ephraim said, "ask me."

"Will you make love to me as you did before?"

"Yes, I will, with great pleasure," answered Ephraim. "Lie down."

The Indian lay down, with his hands clasped behind his head. "Watch me if you wish," Ephraim said. "And spread your legs." He stared at the bronzed body on the ground, the wide-spread legs, at Tsi-nokha's face which was perfectly impassive. "Do you like this game?" he asked.

"Yes, I like this game," Tsi-nokha replied.

Ephraim smiled. "I do too." Then he knelt between the Indian's thighs, moving his head up and down at once – deliberately, purposely.

Tsi-nokha was in no hurry, and Ephraim took the time to savor the experience, enjoying the feel of the head, the thick roundness on his lips. He set a slow pace at first, moving faster as the Indian's hips began to writhe and tense; then, sensing that the Indian was about to come, he thrust a finger up his anus: Tsi-nokha cried out and came in quick jerking spasms.

Ephraim smiled to himself as he got up. Tsi-nokha lay as if dead. It's about time, he thought wryly. Or is he insatiable?

He waded into the water to rinse himself off again. When he returned, the Indian was lying in the same place, unmoving. Slowly Tsi-nokha opened his eyes, and struggled to his feet. He smiled weakly. Slowly and silently they walked back to their clothes, and got dressed.

"Yes," the Indian began, staring vacantly into space, "I think you are very wise." He looked at Ephraim. "And perhaps I love you. I do not know. Do you think I love you?"

"Oh, yes; probably you do. And I love you very much," Ephraim answered.

"Give me a name, then."

"All right. Your name is Amatus Sum."

The Indian looked puzzled. "What does that mean?"

"I won't tell you," Ephraim said, "but when you can change your name to 'Ambam' you will be at peace with yourself."

Tsi-nokha nodded.

"I must go now," Ephraim said, "so I will tell you that the young man you are seeking is downriver, possibly on the coast, and that he thinks of you often."

Amatus Sum's eyes widened in surprise, but Ephraim turned and led him back to his canoe, closing the subject. Amatus Sum watched him sadly as he pushed the canoe into the water. "Farewell, my friend," he said. "You have given me peace."

"Farewell, Amatus Sum, my love; I will see you again, and we will play the same beautiful games."

Amatus Sum smiled. "And I will be more rested then, and stronger, and we can play more often – all day, many times."

"Impossible!" Ephraim laughed. "But I will take care to see that I, too, am fully rested. I will see nobody for a week ahead of time."

Amatus Sum laughed. "Do you promise?"

"Ah, yes, my love. And you are very beautiful when you smile and laugh. It makes me happy."

"And you, Ephraim, walk in handsomeness always."

"Farewell, Amatus Sum."

"Farewell, my friend, and perhaps my love."

They waved, smiling, and Ephraim pushed onward.

Book Three

For the rest of that afternoon and the following day, Ephraim paddled slowly but steadily up the increasingly narrow, increasingly rapid river. It was becoming obvious that soon he would have to leave the canoe and travel overland to the cave of Bear-who-dreams; the directions given by the old Indian at Astoria had been specific enough, but Ephraim was concerned now lest he lose his way. Ixtlil Cuauhtli had said he would have no trouble finding a guide when he left the river, but none had appeared. Ephraim had assumed that Eagle Camp, mentioned by both Singing Heron and Cyrus, could be easily found, but now he wasn't sure. Perhaps he would miss it altogether.

He dismissed the thought from his mind, and began to think instead of Amatus Sum. He felt warmly pleased with himself, knowing that he would meet the Indian again, and that their next meeting would be one of pure, frenetic love-making. He smiled to himself, thinking of it, remembering the dark, lithe body, the intense, darkly handsome face, the almost constantly erect penis. There will be time for everything, he thought. We will do everything. We will roll on the grass for hours, coming, and coming again, until we are exhausted.

On the morning of the third day he decided to leave the canoe, having spent several hours of fruitless battle against rocks, shallows, and rapids. Actually, his progress had been very slow for over a day, but he had continued upriver simply because he enjoyed the struggle, enjoyed the new strength in his arms and shoulders. It was pleasant to realize that the month or more of river travel had toughened him, made him harder and more powerful. He could feel the difference in his shoulders and in his belly: the muscles were larger, like knots, and tireless. He welcomed every new test of strength, meeting each challenge to his endurance with a new confidence and with a cheerful sense of mastery.

Nevertheless, he had to stop. He hid the canoe in a thick stand of lodgepole pines, out of sight from the river, and made up a pack which he strapped across his shoulders – blankets, a knife, an axe, a tinderbox. His breeches were worn through at the knees, and thin in the seat; his shirt was in tatters. He seriously considered leaving his boots, for each had a small hole in the sole, and they wouldn't last until he could get moccasins. But he wore them anyway.

Away from the river, the land rose sharply in broken, rocky sweeps; the earth and sky seemed vertical, and unending. His vision traveled far, over patches of dark green that shaded the lower slopes of the mountains, over lighter green far in the distance, and earth-brown, and the reddish yellow of hard, bare rock. To the southeast was the mountain he was looking for. Tall, peaked, pointing to the sky; at the foot of this mountain was the painted cave. An eagle soared in the distance; a grasshopper whirred before his feet. He started to walk among the oaks, firs, madrones and willows of the river bed, straining his ears for the sound of the falls he knew to be ahead.

At midday he was hungry, but decided to wait until reaching the falls before allowing himself to think of food. It was too early in the season for fruit or berries; perhaps he could catch a fish, he thought, and regretted not having brought more food. But he quickly forgot about it, not caring in the slightest for his stomach.

He saw the falls before he heard them – saw them perhaps a half-hour's distance away. The river bank sloped sharply upward, even here, and he started to climb, clinging at times to roots and saplings, trying to keep the falls in view. At the top, finally, he lay down to rest under a Douglas fir, and the feeling grew inside him that Eagle Camp must be close by. Perhaps an unexpected noise, or the faint trace of a trail, or perhaps a thin odor of smoke –

He stood up to study the land more carefully, and saw the Indian before the Indian saw him, and leaned against the fir to watch him.

The man was tall, slender, graceful; his hair hung in two braids down his bare shoulders. His breechclout was narrow and beaded, and hung halfway down his thighs, following the movements of his legs as he stepped. His face was angular, with jutting cheekbones and chin, deep-set eyes, wide mouth with thin, sensitive lips. He was picking flowers, and had loaded one arm with the same lavender daisies Ephraim had picked for Cyrus. Ephraim judged him to be somewhat older than Cyrus – perhaps thirty-five, perhaps forty. The muscles of his buttocks flexed softly as he walked; in back, the breech cloth covered only the cleft and a bit more. Narrow waist, slender hips –

Ephraim moved, and the Indian looked up. They gazed at each other in silence, and Ephraim smiled slowly in greeting. The Indian raised his hand, and the faint trace of an answering smile crossed his face; an eyebrow wavered upward. He came toward Ephraim, not taking his eyes from Ephraim's face. Ephraim continued to smile in as open a manner as possible, but his glance flicked momentarily down to the Indian's long, wiry body.

The Indian lowered his hand. "Hello," he said softly.

"Hello," said Ephraim, but his throat caught. "Hello," he repeated more clearly.

"I was hoping you would come today," the Indian said pleasantly. Tiny, expressive quivers played about his lips and eyebrows.

"Have you been expecting me?" Ephraim asked.

"Ah, yes. Someone from downriver raised a smoke signal several days ago to tell of your coming, and of the fact that Mr. Calvin and his strange companion had passed without causing difficulties. Either I or one of my companions has been waiting for you here since yesterday." His voice was very soft, with a melodious lilt.

"This is Eagle Camp, then," Ephraim said.

"Close by, yes. Would you like to come with me?"

"Yes, thank you," Ephraim said. "Actually, I was beginning to be afraid of missing the camp; I see now that I had nothing to fear."

"Nothing at all." The Indian smiled and turned, leading Ephraim to a trail through the woods. Ephraim contemplated the

Indian's back, his legs; he was a small-boned man, with slender ankles and knees, yet the muscles of his calves and thighs swelled sharply, and softly, as he walked. And again the gentle flexing of his buttocks – Ephraim's heart began to beat faster.

"May I ask you your name?" Ephraim said. The Indian turned and gazed at Ephraim. "My name is Tlasohkah; I am sorry that I didn't tell you before."

Ephraim smiled. "My name is Ephraim, which you undoubtedly knew already."

"Yes," Tlasohkah said. Then he turned and continued to glide along the trail.

They were joined at length by a younger Indian, possibly eighteen, who greeted Ephraim with a happy yelp and then conversed with Tlasohkah in an Indian tongue that Ephraim couldn't understand. He caught his own name once or twice at the beginning, and then they must have proceeded to another subject, for he didn't hear his name again.

Ephraim felt a bit slighted, but decided not to worry about it for the time being. All the while, the young man punctuated and emphasized his conversation by touching Tlasohkah in one way or another – on the back, on his shoulder, or by taking his hand momentarily – casually, but knowingly. At times he glanced and smiled at Ephraim. There was an adolescent smoothness to his body that Ephraim found uninteresting, but perhaps, all the same, he and Tlasohkah were lovers. Ephraim didn't like this idea at all.

Suddenly, the young man ran off, disappearing down the trail. Tlasohkah turned to Ephraim and explained, "We were discussing the plans for the evening's games and entertainment. Very few of the young men now at Eagle Camp speak English; I hope you didn't feel left out."

"Not at all," Ephraim lied, and the lie showed on his face. "I think it is up to me to learn your language, and not the other way around."

Tlasohkah smiled, almost gravely. "Possibly so. But it is a very difficult language; only one white man has learned to speak it well, and that man is Cyrus Wheelwright."

"I didn't know that Cyrus spoke Indian –" Ephraim mused.

"He does. I taught him. He is a very intelligent man, and was able to learn our tongue in a very short time. But after all, there are other ways of communicating than by means of words –" He touched Ephraim lightly on the shoulder.

"Quite so," Ephraim replied, smiling, and touched the Indian's back in return. Perhaps, he thought, the young man was not Tlasoh-kah's lover.

The path led out of the forest and twisted sharply around the low, rocky hill; on the other side was a flat, open meadow, studded with pines. Among the trees were a scattering of tents, and in the center, a permanent wooden council chamber. The sides and roof were formed of carefully hewn slabs of cedar, carved and painted with designs reminiscent of the Indian blankets Ephraim has seen in Astoria. There was a handful of young men in the camp, many of them the same age as the adolescent Ephraim had seen earlier. They had been playing a type of hoop-and-stick game when Tlasohkah and Ephraim appeared, but they quickly dropped the game and stared eagerly at Ephraim, chattering among themselves and to Tlasohkah in their own tongue. Ephraim smiled in greeting, and the young men smiled shyly in return. Several of them were strikingly handsome; all were graceful, muscular.

Tlasohkah led Ephraim into the council hall, and the young men continued their game; their calls and shouts floated in, contrasting sharply with the peaceful darkness inside. "You may sleep here if you wish," Tlasohkah said. "And I thought that perhaps you would like to exchange your clothing for what the Indians wear."

"Yes, I would," Ephraim said. "I would particularly like some moccasins; my boots are falling apart."

Tlasohkah stooped and opened a wooden chest in one corner of the dark chamber; from this he pulled out a pair of moccasins, In-dian-style leggings, a sleeveless deerskin jacket and a beaded breechclout. He handed them to Ephraim. "Try these on," he said.

Ephraim pulled off his boots and shirt; Tlasohkah was watching him closely. But as he started to unbutton his breeches, the Indian turned and walked out of the hall, leaving him alone. Ephraim was slightly disappointed. Perhaps, he thought, he's not at all curious –

He pulled the breeches off quickly and reached for the breech-clout. But he detected the soft sound of approaching footsteps, and delayed putting it on, pretending to examine the beaded design.

It was Tlasohkah, standing in the doorway, regarding him with interest. Ephraim felt the blood rushing into his cock, and quickly tied on the cloth in confused embarrassment. He is interested, he thought.

Tlasohkah brought a bowl filled with a warm stew, and offered it to Ephraim wordlessly, but Ephraim noted a pulsation in the vein at the Indian's temple. "Thank you," he said. "I haven't eaten." He sat down and began to eat, sipping the liquid and eating the rest with his fingers.

Tlasohkah still carried the flowers he had picked when Ephraim had first seen him; he sat down opposite Ephraim and began braiding them into chaplets, exactly as Ephraim had done for Cyrus. "How odd," Ephraim said. "I made one exactly as you are doing several days ago."

"Sometimes," the Indian said, "people with similar thoughts will do or say similar things. But it is a strange coincidence. Would you like to help?"

"Yes, certainly," Ephraim replied, and they divided the pile of flowers. From time to time Ephraim glanced at the Indian's breech cloth, but could learn nothing. They worked in silence until they had made chaplets from all the flowers.

Rising, Tlasohkah placed one about Ephraim's neck and one about his own, smiling his grave, almost sad half-smile as he did so. Ephraim thanked him with his eyes. "If there is going to be an entertainment tonight," he said softly, "I think I should sleep this afternoon."

"Yes," Tlasohkah answered. "You can sleep in here, where you won't be disturbed."

"Thank you," Ephraim breathed, and touched the Indian lightly on the chin. Tlasohkah's eyelids quivered, then he turned and left.

Ephraim spread his blankets in a dark corner, took off his breech cloth and lay down. He was asleep immediately.

The sound of drums awoke him – gay hoots and laughter coming from the outside. Sitting up suddenly, he discovered a bowl of the same stew by his blankets, and ate it gratefully, knowing that Tlasohkah had placed it there.

He began to think about, to consider this Tlasohkah. The thought was exciting. Tlasohkah was extremely attractive, with his long, slender, pliant body; the pliability of a steel spring, the suggestion of steel, of steely grace – and yet willing, receptive; soft, perhaps – soft to the touch, yet hard. The body of a long-distance runner. Ephraim wondered, fascinated, What does he look like naked? and found himself thinking of the soft flexing buttocks, the cock, the belly hair, then the buttocks again. Nevertheless – had Tlasohkah shown any particular interest in him? No – and yes. He couldn't decide.

He rose, stretched, put on the breech cloth, chaplet and moccasins, drew a blanket around his shoulders and peeked out the door. The moccasins were wonderfully comfortable. He wriggled his toes, and ran his fingers through his hair.

A short distance away was a campfire; a group of Indians sat about it in an open clearing. Noticing a trickling stream nearby, Ephraim first splashed the sleep from his face with icy water, drank, then walked over to the fire, holding the blanket tightly wrapped around his body.

Tlasohkah was off to one side with a drum between his legs, beating the leather head with his long fingers. Ephraim sat beside him; Tlasohkah stopped drumming and smiled at him. Ephraim said, "Good evening."

"Ah, good evening," Tlasohkah replied softly, melodiously. "Did you sleep well?"

"Yes," Ephraim answered, "and thank you for the food."

"You knew it was I who left it there?" He began drumming again, a new rhythm, practicing, limbering up his fingers.

Ephraim didn't feel like answering right away, but Tlasohkah's eyes were upon him, expecting a reply. "I felt it was you," he said finally. "My feelings know."

Tlasohkah smiled broadly for the first time, showing a row of beautifully white, even teeth. The long lines on either side of his lean cheeks deepened with the smile. He was pleased, and turned to watch the group of young men, evidently considering the conversation fulfilled.

Ephraim too turned to watch the young men about the fire, some were watching him, also; others were still eating, but most were simply playing around aimlessly, chattering and laughing. He turned back to Tlasohkah's drumming, watching his fingers, trying to catch the rhythm of his beating, but it changed from one rhythm to another just as he thought he had learned it. Tlasohkah noted his frowning concentration, and called out an order; one of the young men ran off and returned shortly with another drum. He placed it on the ground before Ephraim. Ephraim thanked the young man, and was given a happy smile in return; then, turning his attention back to Tlasohkah's drumming, he began, tentatively and lightly at first, to imitate the rhythm. Tlasohkah nodded as he became surer, then stopped his own drumming, allowing Ephraim to continue alone. It was a simple beat, but strong, and moving. They continued with new beats until Ephraim had learned several easy ones, and one that was a bit more difficult.

A jangle of bells and rattles at his side made Ephraim look up startled. Someone had dropped what looked like deer antlers by his side, and thongs having many small metal bells attached to them. He looked at Tlasohkah in puzzlement, then he saw the others, and began to understand. They were fitting the antlers on their heads, tying the bell cords around their calves and arms. Tlasohkah started the first rhythm, the one Ephraim had learned first. "Watch this dance, and learn how to do it. When you think you know how, you should join them. It is called the Elk Dance, but I think it is as much a game as a dance; or perhaps there is no difference."

The dancers slowly began to organize themselves in a row. Ephraim counted fifteen of them. The drumbeat continued; louder now, and steady; some of the dancers began the step, then all fell in. Ephraim watched their feet. Some were singing, but not all.

The step seemed to be simple; Ephraim was sure he could do it, and was putting on his antlers when one dancer, with a bound, detached himself from the group and turned to face them. Ephraim stopped to watch.

The single dancer pawed the ground with his feet, lowered his antlers, and charged, still in step with the others, around in a circle. A jeering went up from the row of dancers; the soloist bellowed challenges. He leaped, pawed and charged until another dancer leaped out to meet him.

They faced each other pawing and snorting, circling, charging past each other. Then, with precision, they locked antlers and circled, still in step, first one way, then the other. Ephraim saw that it wasn't a game of strength, but of skill; the first dancer was leading, changing direction rapidly; the challenger was trying to follow. Then the challenger was thrown out of step by a swift right-left maneuver. They straightened up, laughing, and the line of dancers hooted. The loser retired to his place in line, and another took his place to try his skill.

Ephraim finished fastening his antlers and bells and fell in line, still wrapped in his blanket, holding a pair of gourd rattles. He caught the step rapidly, and concentrated both on his own feet and on the maneuvers of the mock-fighters. As new challengers won or were defeated, he noted that losing was merely a question sometimes of being forced to dance one step or even a half-step too many on the same foot; the dancers' timing had to be perfect in order to follow the fast, surprising changes of direction.

After half an hour of continuously dancing the jogging, hopping step, Ephraim felt warmed up and limber enough to issue a challenge. A brief spell came when nobody wanted to solo, so Ephraim leaped out with a cry, throwing his blanket aside.

A delighted roar filled his ears. He pawed the ground and snorted, enjoying himself, laughing at the jeers. Almost immediately an Indian leaped out before him to take up the challenge. It was a man Ephraim had noticed before – somewhat older than the rest, broadly muscular, with black, shining eyes. He laughed at Ephraim, pawed, charged, leaped and snorted. When Ephraim was ready, he lowered his head and they locked horns, circling in place to the right. It was more difficult than Ephraim had expected, for the circle was very tight, and the dancing was performed in a bent-over position, but he managed it well enough. Then he switched to a leftward circling, and his challenger followed him easily; Ephraim began to admire the other man's skill. Thereafter Ephraim tried every trick he dared in order to throw his challenger off balance, but none of them worked; the Indian followed him effortlessly.

After many minutes of fruitless circling back and forth, a murmuring grew in the line of dancers, some laughing calls, and Ephraim knew he should give up; his dancing had been equaled. He backed off and straightened up, smiling broadly, and threw his arms about the Indian's shoulders. The Indian smiled back in surprise.

"You are a good dancer," Ephraim said, and retired back to the line. The Indian didn't understand, and looked to Tlasohkah in puzzlement. Tlasohkah called out a translation, and all the dancers cheered, laughing and shaking their rattles.

The drumming stopped, and the dancers dispersed. Ephraim picked up his blanket, walked over to Tlasohkah and sat down. Someone had brought a kettle filled with liquid; a young man served Tlasohkah and Ephraim in a hollow gourd. Ephraim tasted; it was mildly fermented, somewhat like beer, but white in color, and with a greenish taste.

"Newketle," Tlasohkah said, and took a sip. "For festival occasions."

"It's strange," Ephraim said.

Tlasohkah shifted his position on the ground. "What you said to Ya-nah was unexpected, and was very pleasing to everybody," he said. "It is not necessarily the custom to compliment one's challenger, especially one who has defeated you –"

"But it was true – he was very good. Perhaps after I've had some practice, I will be able to defeat him, but certainly not now."

"And something else that perhaps you didn't realize," Tlasohkah added. "If he accepts your challenge, that means usually that he is interested in you. In this case, I am sure that he is."

"Really? I didn't know that."

"And now you do know." Tlasohkah tapped on the drum, staring into the fire. "Ya-nah is eagerly sought after by many young men. Are you interested in him?"

Ephraim considered his reply very carefully. Finally he said, "I don't think so."

Tlasohkah, expressionless, glanced at him levelly, then turned to his drum, beginning the first measures of a new dance. Ephraim went off to get more newketle.

When he came back to sit beside Tlasohkah, the dancers had seated themselves in a large, loose circle around the fire, leaving a broad space about the center.

Ephraim had many questions to ask of Tlasohkah, but decided to keep still. A dancer had come into the circle, and he settled back on one elbow to watch. The young man, stripped to the loin cloth, was carrying a hoop of the same type that Ephraim had seen that afternoon. He danced exuberantly, joyfully, with an occasional suggestion of thrusting in his loins. He played with the hoop, spinning it rapidly and skillfully about his arms and legs, sometimes about his hips. The step was wild and energetic, but simple enough to allow many leaps and turns. The man's body gleamed with sweat in the firelight. He seemed to be dancing more for the benefit of one young man in the circle than for any other, and Ephraim recognized the pair as having done the Elk Dance together.

Tlasohkah leaned over and whispered, "Watch, and you will learn many things."

Then the young man who was the dancer's favorite picked up a lance decorated with feathers, and leaped, dancing, into the circle. They were on the far side of the fire from Ephraim, but their maneuvers brought them around the fire several times, so that Ephraim saw much of the fierce joy of the contest.

The young man with the hoop continued his dazzling spins, backing slowly away from his adversary; the lance-man, meanwhile, twirled the pole, throwing it up and catching it, thrusting, twisting, seemingly with no reference to the hoop-man. But suddenly, with a lunge, he tried to jab the lance through the hoop. He missed; the hoop was carried spinning behind the dancer's back, and reappeared on the dancer's wrist, still spinning. The spectators roared, the hoop-man laughed, and the lance-man turned his back and continued dancing as if nothing had happened.

They continued around the fire in this fashion for several minutes, lunging, parrying, spinning. Finally the lance-man succeeded, and wrenched the hoop from the other's grasp with his lance; he held up his arm in victory, and the hoop slid down to his shoulders. The spectators cheered, whooped, and shook their rattles.

Tlasohkah looked at Ephraim, eyebrows raised, a quizzical smile playing about his eyes. Ephraim smiled back and shrugged his shoulders, then turned to the new couple in the ring. This one was a lancer, to everybody's amusement; another young man was soon trying to trap his lance with a hoop. Ephraim noted that the two previous dancers had spread out a blanket and were lying together, half reclining, barely within the circle of the firelight. With an inner smile, he recognized at least one purpose of the dance. But the hoops? The lances?

Altogether, five couples competed in the hoop dance, and each then withdrew to a blanket at the edge of the firelight. One young man then challenged the group with both lance and hoop, and was met by another carrying the same; the contest was fiercely fought,

underneath the smiles and laughter, and the victor was wildly ap-
plauded. This, Ephraim surmised, was the only "real" contest of the
evening.

During a lull, he turned to Tlasohkah. "Do you do this dance
often?"

Tlasohkah laughed quietly. "Yes, often. Every time they have an
entertainment. It is very popular."

The significance of the "they" was not lost on Ephraim. "Do the
same –?" He paused, then began again. "Do the same couples do this
dance with each other every time?"

"Not usually," Tlasohkah answered. "Otherwise there would be
no point to the dance."

Ephraim nodded his head and smiled faintly in understanding.

A new lance-man came out – the man with whom Ephraim had
done the Elk Dance. He paused directly in front of Ephraim, giving
him to understand with his eyes that he wanted him to take up his
challenge. Ephraim smiled and shook his head, excusing himself,
indicating with gestures that he didn't know how to compete with
such a skillful dancer. The other smiled back, with a glint in his eyes
meaning that he could wait; that perhaps next time – And he danced
away. When he and his eventual challenger were finished, Tlasohkah rose and got more newketle. Ephraim was beginning to like the
strange, almost herbaceous taste.

When Tlasohkah came back, he asked, "Are you interested in
anybody here?" There were still a handful of uncommitted young
men.

Ephraim sipped the newketle. "Oh, yes," he replied.

Tlasohkah's eyebrows quivered, but his face was otherwise calm.
"Does he know you are interested?" he asked.

"I don't know, really," Ephraim said. "But he should."

"And what is he like?" Tlasohkah's voice was calm, melodious,
showing only a hint of concern.

Ephraim glanced at him, smiling. "Oh, he is handsome, very
handsome, like a hawk diving through the summer air. His body is

graceful and lovely, an alder tree in the wind, and his voice is a mountain stream playing in the meadow. I think I love him."

"Ah," Tlasohkah replied. "And perhaps this person loves you too."

"Perhaps. If so, he can teach me many things. And I am quite sure that I love him."

They were interrupted by a young man in a blanket who whispered to Tlasohkah. The two conferred – smiling and laughing at times, at times very serious. Finally Tlasohkah turned to Ephraim, raised his eyebrows wordlessly, and began a strong, slow beat on the drum.

All the dancers sat up with new interest; their faces were serious, intense. Those on the far side of the fire moved around to Ephraim's side, forming a half-circle. Ephraim too sat up.

The man who had conferred with Tlasohkah – tall and lithe, already out of adolescence – walked slowly into the clearing, in time to the music. He spread a blanket on the ground and stood on it, facing his audience. His mouth spread in a near-mirthless grin, almost a mocking challenge, and he untied his breech cloth and let it fall to the ground. Ephraim's heart jumped. The man stood motionless, hands on hips, looking down at his cock, waiting, waiting, until it rose, engorged, glistening; then he looked up at the audience suddenly. His cock stretched out, an almost violent distortion of his body.

Another man strode into the clearing, stood on the blanket within arm's reach of the first, and dropped his breech cloth also. The two naked men faced each other; the one with cock outstretched, the other with his cock rising strongly, rising until it met the first one – touching it momentarily, glancingly.

They clasped right hands quickly and began wrestling Indian fashion, straining against each other. The drum beat slowly, deeply. Their muscles stood out; sweat trickled down their bellies as each tried to throw the other off balance; their cocks met, crossed, glanced apart and met again. Finally, the second man lost his footing. They dropped hands and stood panting.

Ephraim knew what was going to happen, somehow, and yet he didn't know. He knew intuitively, without putting his knowledge into words.

The second man dropped to his knees on the blanket, then lay flat on his belly, legs wide-spread, cradling his head in his arms. The first man knelt behind him, between his legs. His cock stood tall, a mysterious, bulbous thing rising out of his loins. He called out in Indian, and someone threw him a pouch of some sort. He caught it in one hand, opened it and spread its contents on his cock – slowly, lovingly, until it shone in the firelight. Then he inserted a glistening finger up the other man's ass.

Ephraim's eyes opened wide as the couple united – step by step, precisely as he knew they would. He had known somehow, that this was what they would do, that this was how it was done, and yet he didn't really know. It's true, he thought. He gets on all fours, like so; the other spreads his legs; he touches his asshole with his cock, like so; he pushes, the head goes in, like so, then another inch, slowly; then all the rest – a strong push, hard, and he's all the way in, but he pulls out, an inch, then back in, hard; then out, then in, hard – he's ready to come; his legs are quivering with the excitement – in, out, hard, fast, he's coming – he's come and he falls on his lover.

Ephraim pulled the blanket tighter around himself, not wanting his erection to show. He trembled, and stared into the fire, not wanting to speak.

As if from a distance, he heard Tlasohkah's voice, and forced himself to listen. "This is not often done," he was saying, "unless two people wish to make a more public declaration of their love. Perhaps you should not have seen it. Did you find it shocking?"

Ephraim looked away from the fire, toward Tlasohkah. All the dancers, all the young men had left silently in the darkness. "Yes, and no," he answered. "It was shocking, and it was beautiful." He swallowed. "Yes – very beautiful."

"I am glad you said that," Tlasohkah murmured. "There are so many other things you could have said that would have been so wrong –" He paused to sip the last of the newketle. "And," he continued, with the barest flicker of a smile on his lips, "are you still interested in any of the persons present?"

Ephraim smiled, relieved. "Ah, yes. Very much so."

Tlasohkah looked around him, making sure that all the others had gone. "Would that person be close by, by any chance."

Ephraim felt a surge of excitement. "Most certainly," he breathed. "And do you know, by any chance, if that person is interested in me?"

"I am quite sure that he loves you – loves you desperately, almost – and that he is longing for you to possess him, strongly, powerfully, as you saw a man possessed tonight."

Ephraim let the blanket fall to the ground and stood up. He smiled down at Tlasohkah and untied his loin cloth. His cock sprang free; he felt proud of its size and thickness, its rushing fullness, and of the coppery glint of his belly hair in the firelight.

He held out his hand to Tlasohkah. "Show me the way, my love, and I will possess you with all the force that is in me."

Tlasohkah's gaze lingered on Ephraim's cock; he untied his own loin cloth and stood up. His cock was like the rest of his body – long, slender and graceful. His testicles hung down fully a hand's length between his thighs – hung freely, independently, swinging as he moved. Ephraim swallowed again, and felt the hair prickle on the back of his neck. He slid his arm around Tlasohkah's waist, and walked with him toward the wooden council hall. As they walked, Ephraim let his hand slip below the Indian's waist, down to his buttocks, and felt the soft movement of flesh; he reached further, feeling the long hair around Tlasohkah's asshole. He began to pant.

They chose a patch of moonlit meadow by the streamlet, and Tlasohkah brought a blanket from the council hall. He spread it on the ground. They embraced, and slowly lay down on the blanket together. Tlasohkah spread an oil on Ephraim's cock, then handed the container to Ephraim and rolled onto his stomach.

The moonlight silvered his long body. Ephraim touched and

kissed the soft buttocks, then inserted his oiled finger – gently, lovingly, with a growing sense of wonder, of quickening eagerness. He poised on hands and knees behind the Indian. Tlasohkah whispered; he bent to listen. "Enter me slowly, my love – you are large, quite large –" Then he reached around and directed Ephraim's cock, and with an upward thrust of his buttocks, indicated that Ephraim should proceed.

Ephraim pushed. The head slid in; it was tight, and warm. He waited, trembling, for another upward thrust, then pushed again, another inch, and waited. "Go ahead," Tlasohkah whispered, and Ephraim eased forward. Slowly, it slid all the way in until his belly hair met the black hair of the Indian's ass; met, and tangled as he writhed. Then he fell onto Tlasohkah's back, panting, almost ready to come. "Rest now," Tlasohkah said.

His cock felt like a pine tree – more enormous than life. He was acutely aware of the Indian's buttock, pressing against his belly; his fingers found the thickly hairy armpits; his lips touched the Indian's ear, his jaw.

"Go now, my love," Tlasohkah murmured finally, "as hard as you wish."

Ephraim thrust savagely, once, and again, in a mounting frenzy; he ground his belly hair against the softness, and it gave under him, softly. The base of his cock was tightly circled, maddeningly, sweetly; it was a pine tree reaching into darkness – It burst in a cloud of love into the darkness. Ephraim cried out in the agony of joy, panting, trembling on the Indian's back.

Tlasohkah drew a breath and let it out in a sigh. His eyes were closed.

৵

They bathed their sweat-soaked bodies in the stream and returned wordlessly to the council hall to spread their blankets. Ephraim pulled the Indian down to his side and held him tightly. Finally he spoke. "You are indescribably beautiful," he whispered, "and I love you, wildly; I want more of you, often, all of you –" He slid his free hand down the Indian's back, down to his buttocks, then around, and grasped. It was half-limp, half-erect; he squeezed and pulled gently, then let it fall, and explored further, felt the loose, free testicles lower down on his thigh. "Oh, my love," he whispered, "I want to make love to you my way –"

"Anything you do gives me pleasure," came the answering sigh.

Ephraim freed himself and buried his face in the Indian's belly hair, then took him, still half-limp, in his mouth. Tlasohkah groaned with pleasure, and a feeling of intense beauty rose in Ephraim as the Indian slowly hardened, lengthened, expanded. He savored Tlasohkah's growing excitement, enjoyed the insistent upward thrusts of the Indian's loins, and was deeply, beautifully happy when he felt the hot, sharp spurts.

As Tlasohkah's body relaxed, Ephraim kissed his lips, his eyes, his cheek, murmuring, "My love, my love –" Then he lay on the blanket, pulled Tlasohkah tightly to his side again, and went to sleep.

The night passed for Ephraim in a wakeful slumberous awareness of the body next to him. Listening to Tlasohkah's deep breathing, he was flooded with a profound tenderness, and pulled him closer; recalling their love-making, a flash of desire passed like a shock through his veins.

He twisted and turned during the night. At one point he awoke to find himself between Tlasohkah's legs, his head resting on the Indian's belly hair. He kissed the man's belly and curled up closer. Tlasohkah slept on peacefully.

In the morning he awoke to a sound in the council hall. It was Tlasohkah, beginning to dress. He had just put on a sleeveless leather jacket, and wore nothing else. Watching the Indian's flat, lean backside, the hairy cleft parting his buttocks, Ephraim sighed and held out his arm. Tlasohkah turned and saw that Ephraim was awake. He smiled radiantly and strode to his side, squatted on his heels. They kissed, lightly.

"Good morning, my love," Ephraim whispered.

"My handsome one," Tlasohkah breathed. He smiled again. "I do love you, Ephraim – much more than I thought I would or could." His voice was barely audible.

Ephraim sighed and rose to his feet. He was pleased that Tlasohkah watched him as he walked, swingingly. He almost decided to make love again, but instead looped his breech cloth under his crotch and fastened the cord, and Tlasohkah did the same.

He put his arm around the Indian's waist and, pushing aside the door flap, walked outside.

They were met with a shower of pink and lavender flower petals, thrown by a laughing crowd of young Indians. Ephraim dropped his hand from Tlasohkah's waist in confusion, but Tlasohkah pretended to duck the shower, laughing and shouting. He spoke to the group of young men; many jokes and pointed remarks passed back and forth, much teasing. The exchange was rapid, and judging from the facial expressions and sharp laughter, some of the comments must have been very pointed.

Finally Tlasohkah turned to Ephraim. "This is a custom sometimes, but they have caught me by surprise. They want to know if I am going to keep you to myself or not, and if so, I must make a public declaration of my intention. And also, since I am older than this group of young rabbits, and more a chief than a comrade, they find it amusing that I should fall. I also think they are a little jealous."

"Tell them," Ephraim said after a hushed pause, "to forget their disappointment at not having either of us, for we love each other."

Tlasohkah translated, and was met with a chorus of whoops and laughter. He turned again to Ephraim. "They want a declaration," he said.

"What does that involve?" Ephraim asked, feeling a certain anxiety.

Tlasohkah shrugged his shoulder. "Oh – it could be anything," he said, and called out an order to the group. A young man ran off, and returned immediately with two brilliant columbines. He gave the flowers to Tlasohkah, who said to Ephraim, "I will place this here, in your hair, to show that I love you."

Ephraim took the other columbine and asked, "May I place this anywhere I wish?"

"Yes, of course." Tlasohkah started to grin.

Ephraim inserted the stem of the flower in Tlasohkah's loin cloth; the vermillion blossom rested low on his belly, next to his hip. "I place this here because I love you," he said, smiling up at Tlasoh-kah.

The young men were pleased, and murmured their approval.

Tlasohkah rested his hands on Ephraim's shoulders and looked into his eyes. The Indian's face showed deep tenderness and a calm, intense joy.

They kissed, broke apart, joined hands and walked to the fire, surrounded by the laughing group of young men, who continued to pelt them with pink and lavender petals.

They took breakfast from a common pot, which was already beginning to cool, and with surprise Ephraim noted that it was mid-morning, for the sun was several hand-breadths above the jagged horizon. He hadn't slept so late in months and enjoyed the deep lassitude in his muscles.

Tlasohkah finished, and asked, "Would you like to go with me to work in our cornfield this morning? There is little to do, since I pulled the weeds the day before yesterday, and we can spend the afternoon at the river."

Ephraim was surprised; he had never heard of cornfields among the Indians of this area. "Of course," he answered. "I think I will enjoy it."

Tlasohkah picked up a shoulder basket and asked for food at various tents; from the council hall he brought a blanket, which he gave to Ephraim to carry, and a long, stringed musical instrument similar to a guitar. Ephraim examined this curiously. "I made it myself," the Indian explained, "patterned after a guitar I once saw in Vancouver."

"Did you teach yourself to play it?"

Tlasohkah smiled. "Yes, my love. There isn't another one like it."

They followed the streamlet to a narrow, open meadow, where Ephraim found himself in an irregularly shaped cornfield. The shoots were perhaps six inches high, and planted not in rows but at random. He found it impossible to estimate the size of the field because of its odd shape, but judged that there must have been about twenty acres in all, stretched along the stream bank.

Tlasohkah picked up a long, fire-hardened stick and proceeded to dig out certain weeds, while Ephraim pulled the others by hand.

"This is," Tlasohkah explained, "one of three fields that the Society has under cultivation. The yield isn't high, but we don't want to plant more, for that would attract attention. Actually, we don't need any more; most of our needs, which are quite simple, are supplied by hunting, trapping and trading. Until a few years ago, we obtained all of our corn by trading with Indians to the south of us; but now we are taking our furs to Astoria, and sometimes to Fort Boise. But I think it is a good idea to plant corn, don't you?"

"Oh, yes," Ephraim answered. "It is enjoyable work."

"And it is a good excuse to bring some of our young men together for part of the summer. They come at cultivation and planting time; some will go back down to the coast, or east to the mountains until harvest season, and then they will all return. Others, of course, will stay here all summer."

"Do some of them –?" Ephraim hesitated. "Won't some of them pair off eventually, in more or less permanent arrangements?"

Tlasohkah straightened up. The sun was hot, and sweat was beginning to trickle down his forehead and chest. "Oh, yes," he answered. "By harvest time, all will have made some kind of arrangement for the winter. Some of their preferences are becoming apparent now; amidst all of the playing around, you will notice that certain young men tend to pair off with each other more often than not, and by the time the leaves have begun to fall, they will be firmly attached to each other. Until next spring, of course, when it is customary to search for new lovers, to renew ties with old ones; but, as often as not they will remain with the same lover for several years. Especially as they grow older."

"And yourself?" Ephraim asked.

"I do not know, this year." Then he laughed. "Ask me the question after you have talked to Bear-who-dreams – after you have finished your spirit quest." He paused, gazing off at the horizon. "I had thought of going down the river in August, and coming back before the harvest; but we shall see."

They worked in silence to the end of the long, narrow field. Ephraim enjoyed the work immensely. The sun prickled on his bare skin, sweat dripped from his eyebrows and chest and down his legs, and his back ached slightly from the constant stooping. Tlasohkah broke the silence occasionally with low humming, sometimes breaking into an Indian song, but neither felt a need to speak. Ephraim glanced at the stooping form from time to time – at the long lines of his thighs, the lithe, sharply muscled belly – and knew, with a flush of excitement, that soon he would possess that body again; soon they would be locked together in mysterious, joyful passion.

They came to the end of the field and turned back. Tlasohkah put an arm around Ephraim's shoulder as they walked, and asked with a flickering smile, "Do you understand now the meaning of the hoop dance from last night?"

Ephraim grinned slyly. "No. Tell me about it."

Tlasohkah laughed. "Oh, innocent one!" Regaining his composure, he continued. "The dance is, however, a mere formality – a way of beginning. During a long night of love-making, it makes very little difference which man held the lance and which one the hoop during the dance. Very likely the roles will be reversed several times."

"And so it must be with us," Ephraim said quickly. Then he stared at the ground, almost frightened at what he had said.

Tlasohkah looked at him. "Have you ever –?" he asked softly.

"No."

"And you want to?"

"Yes."

"Then we shall, my love," Tlasohkah replied slowly. "Tonight, perhaps, if you wish." He shivered. "Do you desire this?" he asked delicately.

"I must know," Ephraim said.

"Know then, that it will be done with love – with all the tenderness and love in my soul."

"I know, and I am thankful," Ephraim replied quietly. "I am glad it is you."

Tlasohkah sighed; his expression was grave.

They picked up the blanket, guitar and shoulder basket, and followed the streamlet without speaking, through the camp, down a sudden ravine, and finally arrived at the base of the falls. Here the river formed a broad, deep pool, overhung by firs and spruces.

Tlasohkah spread the blanket on the sand at the water's edge and they ate slowly. Sunlight pierced the dark trees, forming bright, lacy patterns on the water and on the sand. Falling water flashed in dizzy sparkles, and a hollow tinkle echoed through the ravine. Ephraim listened: a rustling chatter of squirrels, the hoarse cry of a jay. A hawk wheeled across a brilliant, diminished sky. The rest was silence.

Leaning closer to Tlasohkah, Ephraim whispered into his ear, almost touching the bronze cheek with his lips:

> Softly in the moonlight your form
> Silvered softly in the dark night
> Leading me downward in the pale light
>   Onto your flesh your hair your lips
> Downward drifting into desire
> Passion's penis rising higher
> Seeking your chest your loins your hips
>   My hardened penis downward dips
> Into your asshole darkly tight

Warmly endlessly lost from sight.

Tlasohkah smiled. Then he rose and strode to the water. He threw off his breech cloth and stood facing the stream for an instant, then dived. His muscles snapped like steel, and he landed far out, with a sharp crack that sent the squirrels scurrying through the treetops. He swam in long, easy strokes across the pool, climbed out the other side and disappeared in the thick underbrush. A minute later, Ephraim saw him standing on a high rock overhanging the pool – straight as an arrow, arms at his sides. Sunlight caught the black gleam of his hair. Then, like an arrow he sprang, then curled, somersaulted in the air, straightened out and pierced the water cleanly, with scarcely a splash.

Ephraim stood up and called "Bravo!" when the Indian's head reappeared; then he untied his breech cloth and dived in.

Tlasohkah was waiting for him on the other side, smiling; to-gether they clambered up the steep path, Tlasohkah leading. He pulled himself up with feline agility, holding onto roots and branches; Ephraim was struck again by the supple grace of the man's body. The muscles of his back rippled like wavelets as he climbed. He watched the black-haired cleft as the Indian climbed, legs stretching apart, and longed to touch, to caress, to probe –

They reached the top, and Ephraim looked down. The rock rose perhaps fifteen feet above the water; Ephraim had never dived from this height, but he was suddenly possessed with a desire to equal Tlasohkah's feat, to show that he too could perform with grace and bravery.

The water was clear as crystal; he could count the pebbles on the bottom. He poised at the edge of the rock in the sunlight, feeling Tlasohkah's admiring gaze, and again felt proud of his tanned, mus-cular body, of his heavy penis.

He sprang up and outward; the air whistled past his ears, the world turned, spinning crazily; blue sky, green water; then he straightened, arched his back and pierced the water, touched bottom.

He shot to the surface and looked up, pleased with himself.

Tlasohkah was delighted. His shell-white teeth shone in a broad, admiring smile. Then the Indian stood on the ledge with his back toward the water, arms straight before him; he leaped out and back, slender body stretched high, feet pointed, penis downward-hanging, and struck the water a short distance from Ephraim.

Ephraim was overcome with admiration. When Tlasohkah surfaced, he called, "You are beautiful, my love!"

Tlasohkah flashed an answering smile. "And you, my love. Had you ever done that before?"

"No," Ephraim answered. "Never."

"You are quite good," Tlasohkah said.

They swam lazily to the side of the pool and stood up; Tlasohkah wrung the water from his long hair, and Ephraim lay down on the blanket, hands locked behind his head, watching. Suddenly he knew that he needn't wait longer to make love; he wanted to possess Tlasohkah now, immediately –

Tlasohkah sat close to Ephraim and picked up his guitar. Ephraim decided to wait, but amused himself by running his fingers up and down the Indian's thigh.

Tlasohkah tuned the instrument, then started to pick a soft, delicate melody. He sang:

> Strong as the Douglas fir, bright in the sun
>   Lovely, handsome one
> Bright in the sunlight and proudly alive
> With a questioning look as I quietly arrive
>   Ah, my handsome one
> As I quietly come through the woods to your side
> Burning with amorous passions inside
>   Ah, my handsome son
> Amorous passions inside my soul
> Through my veins like a flood in the springtime they
>   roll

Handsome as the sun
Like a flood warmly rolls through my veins as I see
You in the sunlight and smiling at me
    Handsome in the sun
Smiling at me with a start of surprise
And perhaps a vague promise of love in your eyes
    Brother of the sun.

"How strange," Ephraim mused, "that you should echo what another has said of me. Brother of the sun!"

"It is not at all strange," said Tlasohkah, "that you should inspire similar feelings in different people – that many should love you and express their love in the same words." He looked away, at the water-fall, and continued calmly. "I am quite certain that I am not alone in my love for you, Ephraim, and that other hearts are troubled by the thought and memory of your face, your voice, your manner of being. If this disturbs me, I will not tell of my disturbance, for such is not my way.

"Know, however, that I am happy to make love to you now, to-day, and would be happy to make love to you when the leaves have fallen and the ground is covered with snow. If you should wish to prolong my happiness for a winter, my life would be deepened beyond anything I can imagine. But for the present, I am content with the beauty you have brought into my life, and consider my moments with you now as self-fulfilling. I ask nothing more; you have given me already more than I am in the habit of wanting."

Ephraim was deeply troubled, and pondered a long while before answering. Finally he began, hesitantly. "It is true that I love others, but I hadn't thought of them until this moment. While I am with you, I love you only, and think only of you." He paused, then began again. "I can't say what I will decide until after my spirit-quest; every-thing has changed for me, too rapidly, and sometimes I feel like a leaf on the wind – I fall in love with everyone I see." He laughed. "But I am not a seventeen-year-old; I am perhaps deeper than I seem." He shook his head, confused. "I don't know, this summer is beautiful, and I have learned to live in the present. That present, right now, is filled with you."

"That is our way," Tlasohkah replied softly.

"And I want to possess you now – here," Ephraim said. He pressed his face against the Indian's hips.

Tlasohkah passed a hand gently over Ephraim's back, then Ephraim let himself be pushed, gently rolled, face up; Tlasohkah was over him, on all fours, his genitals hanging down, down, testicles almost touching the golden belly hair. Ephraim relaxed, sensing that the Indian wanted to take charge, to proceed in his own fashion; his mind drifted into passive acquiescence.

He felt the Indian's fingers on his belly, stroking, caressing; his lips and teeth on a nipple, biting, kissing until it stood up hard, and then the sweet warmth of the mouth on his cock.

An insistent hand was on his buttocks, urging, and he rolled over; Tlasohkah's lips touched his backside, then the cleft; Ephraim spread his thighs and felt the warmth of Tlasohkah's touch. He flexed with mounting pleasure as Tlasohkah probed sweetly – spread his thighs still more widely apart, arched backward as the Indian explored.

Suddenly Tlasohkah stood up, and Ephraim rolled over; the Indian was half twisted around, lubricating himself with one hand. Then he stood over Ephraim, straddling his hips. Ephraim propped himself on his elbows to watch, and the Indian knelt so that his buttocks touched Ephraim. Slowly he lowered himself, and Ephraim entered Tlasohkah; the Indian's body came down, surrounding darkly the thick penis, until he was sitting on Ephraim's belly hair.

Then he rose an inch or two and held himself steady; his stomach muscles stood out, taut and rigid. Ephraim thrust upward. Tlasohkah's body swayed with the thrust. Ephraim thrust again, and then again. The tightness around him gathered meaning and sweetness into his loins, and he felt himself possessed with a frenzied urge to prove out the meaning by grinding his belly hair against the Indian, to establish this sweetness as the law of the world by uniting himself inseparably with this being. He thrust powerfully, again and again, until they were inseparable, until sweetness was the law of the world, and he burst into the Indian's darkness with frenzied splendor.

Later, chest still heaving, he followed Tlasohkah into the pool. Lazily, half sleeping, he bathed; Tlasohkah smiled at his languor, and they played in the water – casually, affectionately exploring each other's bodies until afternoon shadows covered the pool.

That evening before the campfire, Ephraim sat next to Tlasohkah, leaning on one hand, rubbing his chest hair against the Indian's shoulder. The others had gathered, but Ephraim paid little attention to them; his world was this man whom he longed to hold tightly, closely.

"I love you," he whispered into Tlasohkah's ear, and the Indian smiled. They rubbed cheeks, and Tlasohkah murmured, "My love –"

Ephraim pressed his face against the Indian's shoulder, vividly aware of the silken skin, the vibrant muscles; Tlasohkah was drumming intermittently, but finally called to another in the circle, gave him the drum and turned to Ephraim. His back was toward the fire, his face in shadow. Ephraim also turned from the fire, still leaning on one hand; with the other he stroked Tlasohkah's hard, muscle-knotted belly, traced the outline of his loin cloth with one finger, sought the penis underneath. "Tell me," he asked, "do you love others, Tlasohkah?"

"Yes," Tlasohkah answered. In the dark it was impossible to see his face. He added softly, "Of course."

Ephraim's mind was a tumult of questioning feelings, of tenuous connections and pangs of unnamed emotion. Finally he organized a feeling into words. "You are wise in the Way of the Loon, my love, and I am not; and although I love several, I do not understand how I can do so. Not without –" He paused. The words eluded him.

"Without causing unhappiness?" Tlasohkah asked.

"Yes. Without hurting anyone."

Tlasohkah sighed. "Ah, yes, my love, you have a decision to

138 | *Song of the Loon*

make, and so have I. But why do you think that such a decision should cause unhappiness?"

"Suppose," Ephraim said, "I were to choose another partner for this winter. Wouldn't you be unhappy?"

"It would simplify my own decision. And I would wait for your coming in the spring."

"But would you be unhappy?"

Tlasohkah waved a hand vaguely in the air. "If you were the only man I loved, I would probably make sad poems, I suppose, and weep poetic tears in the autumn moonlight and search for another lover."

"Poetic tears?" Ephraim asked uncomprehendingly. "But would you really be hurt? Would anybody?"

Tlasohkah shook his head in bewilderment. "Now it is my turn not to understand *you*. Since we love each other, there are only two things that can happen: either we make love this winter, or we wait until spring. If we are together through the winter, then the spring winds will scatter us onto different paths. If we are not together this winter, then certainly we will see each other in the spring. Our love will remain warm however, on any path where we happen to be. You love me, and will not hurt me, Ephraim."

"How do you know I'm not pretending?"

"*Pretend* to *love*?" Tlasohkah's tone revealed true bewilderment. "No one does that. You use words in impossible ways, Ephraim!"

Ephraim sighed and remained silent, deciding it was better not to disagree. Finally he said, "You are wise, Tlasohkah, and I am not. You must forgive my ignorance and my possible cynicism, since my whole life has been led in another Way."

Tlasohkah leaned closer, touching Ephraim's cheek with his lips. "That is true, my love – sometimes I forget that you are a white man, new to our ways."

"But I have one last question, and then we will speak of other things. Suppose we were living together in happiness, and another man came, and I fell in love with him, and left you. Would you not be deeply hurt?"

"Ah –" Tlasohkah breathed slowly. "Now I am beginning to understand. In the back of your mind is a word that we never use, and that word is jealousy. In fact, that word does not even exist in our language. It is as Bear-who-dreams has said: you must learn to speak our language before you can think in our paths. My only answer to jealousy is to say that it doesn't exist if two people love each other as we do." He began to caress the inside of Ephraim's thigh with long, graceful fingers. "If I am 'jealous' as you say, then many things are happening in my mind that have nothing to do with love. Perhaps I am afraid that you will not come back, which is foolish. That would mean that I do not love myself, and a man who does not love himself cannot begin to love another. Or perhaps I do not want you to enjoy your life, which is cruelty, not love. That is how Mr. Calvin thinks, they tell me. Or perhaps I want to own you as I would a dog, which is a desire for power over others – the same desire that poisons the lives of witches, not of happy men. Furthermore, anyone who wants to be owned is not worth loving anyway, I think. But I have never met such a person in the Loon Society. Have I answered your question?"

"But how do you know that I really love you?"

Tlasohkah answered simply, "I know. That is all."

Ephraim noted that the Indian's penis was hardening inside of his loin cloth; he kissed him on the shoulder and rose, and went to bring newktle.

There were several young men standing around the deep clay bowl holding the newktle; Ephraim stood among them and drank a gourdful, then filled it again, and another for Tlasohkah. He could see his lover on the other side of the fire, watching him, and wondered what he was thinking. The newktle made him light-headed, and instead of returning to Tlasohkah, he drank some more. Several of the young men were watching him surreptitiously, and it was pleasant to know that his near-naked body was exciting to others but Tlasohkah was the handsomest man present, he thought, and probably the most sensual, and the gentlest. Ephraim frowned fleetingly. In spite of all the Indian had said, he knew that for himself there would always be preferences, perhaps jealousies, and sad nights. He walked back, conscious of his hairy thighs gleaming in the firelight as if sprinkled with gold dust. Tlasohkah smiled in welcome as he sat down.

"You are the handsomest man here," Ephraim said flatly.

"You should not say that," Tlasohkah replied.

Ephraim noted, however, that the Indian was flattered."Perhaps not, but you will excuse me, since I am new to the Way. Nevertheless, it is true, and I would be very unhappy without you."

"You are very charming, my love." He smiled and drank newktle.

Ephraim finished his drink quickly, leaned his head against Tlasohkah's chest and placed his hand on his loin cloth. The penis underneath was large, but not yet hard. He felt the Indian's lips on the back of his neck. "I want you to take me," Ephraim whispered, "as I said this morning." Tlasohkah's cock began to stir; Ephraim felt the outline of its head pressing forward beneath his fingers. He stroked it softly, and traced the whole length of it, stopping at the base.

"Yes, my love," Tlasohkah murmured.

"Do you want to be inside of me, to fill me?" He felt dizzy; there was a humming in his ears.

"Oh, yes," Tlasohkah breathed.

"Then, now –" Ephraim said, and rose to his feet.

Tlasohkah's expression was anxious; he rose and enfolded Ephraim's waist with an arm. His hand trembled. Ephraim picked up the blanket and led the Indian out of the firelight.

In a moonlit glade beneath an enormous pine, he spread the blanket and untied his breech cloth. Tlasohkah stood before him, breathing deeply; Ephraim reached out and pulled off his breech cloth also. The long penis jutted outward; Ephraim took it in both hands and knelt to kiss it. It swelled beneath his lips. Then he lay on his stomach and spread his legs, waiting –

Tlasohkah knelt behind him and spoke. "You have given me permission, Ephraim, to perform an act of love such as you have never experienced. Know, my love, that my desire to do this rises like a maddened river within me; it strikes my loins like spring thunder. I shall enter you, plunge into you, with fierceness – but a gentle fierceness that is one with my love for you. And I shall leave a part of my soul within you." He swallowed, and then continued. "You are in the moonlight, so soft, so white, covered with fine golden hair –"

Ephraim felt the Indian's lips on his buttocks, then his warm, moist tongue. He thrust backward. Then a long finger probing gently, inward, inward, and then Tlasohkah was on his hands and knees, his lips touching Ephraim's ear. "I am going to enter you, my love," he whispered. "Relax –"

Ephraim felt the penis. Tlasohkah pushed; the head went in, and Ephraim gasped. He writhed but Tlasohkah pushed harder. Ephraim felt the enormous-seeming organ entering him gradually, pushing strongly inward; finally Tlasohkah lay trembling on his back.

Slowly, Ephraim grew accustomed to the enormity of this strange thing filling his body. He felt the Indian's belly hair on his backside, and thrust, and was answered by a grinding push. Tlasohkah began to push inward and withdraw, slowly, rhythmically; he was panting and moaning. Ephraim began to answer the thrusts; the hard belly hit his backside fiercely, and with a furious explosion of savage thrusts the Indian came, and fell shuddering onto Ephraim's back.

He withdrew slowly and fell on the blanket, exhausted. Ephraim sat up; their eyes met, but they didn't speak.

Ephraim looked at the long, naked body before him, and suddenly wanted to possess it again, and he rolled the Indian onto his belly. Tlasohkah spread his legs, and without preliminaries Ephraim plunged inward. The Indian's answer was an ecstatic writhing; unbelievably, he met Ephraim's every lunge. The soft flesh of his backside quivered. Ephraim watched, looking down as he pushed, at the thick base. He marveled at its thickness, at the black hairiness of the Indian, at his own gold belly hair, and came suddenly, sharply, piercingly.

Later, when he lay beside Tlasohkah on the blanket, the Indian began to laugh softly. Ephraim raised his head questioningly. "I came again," Tlasohkah explained. "I can hardly believe it."

Ephraim laughed, and pulled the Indian tightly to his side.

ҩ

Some time in the middle of the night he was awakened by the chill, and woke Tlasohkah. Together they returned to the council chamber, shivering from the dew on their bare feet.

The following day they set out for the cave of Bear-who-dreams. Tlasohkah led; their paths twisted upward, steadily rising over rocky and sometimes barren mountains.

During the daytime, they wore only moccasins. The constant sight of the Indian's naked loins filled Ephraim with lust, and they made love on the hillsides and along creek bottoms, at night and in the mornings, with the sun streaming down on their naked, sweat-streaked bodies. Sometimes they united standing up, or with Tlasohkah leaning against a tree. Ephraim grew accustomed to the Indian's penis in his asshole, and learned to take pleasure in the Indian's passion. He asked everything and denied nothing.

On the fourth day, Tlasohkah pointed out a cave in the distance, and they parted, sadly and tenderly, but exhausted.

Ephraim went on alone.

Book Four

Ephraim saw the old Indian from a great distance; his scarlet blanket and graying hair were clearly visible against the background of black lava. He was waiting calmly, seated on the ground, watching Ephraim's approach.

Coming closer, Ephraim was astonished to find that it was Ixtlil Cuauhtli. The Indian's grave, lined face flickered briefly in recognition as he stood to greet the white man.

"May your soul walk in peace," he said. His voice had the same kind, patient tone that Ephraim remembered; it was the same voice he had learned to love and trust during the black days in Astoria.

"It is a joy to see you again, grandfather," Ephraim said. He embraced the old man warmly. "And a delightful surprise. I hadn't expected to find you here."

The old man took Ephraim's face in his gnarled hands. "I thought it best to follow you, my son. Something warned me that you would meet trouble. For three nights in a row I dreamed that you were being pursued by mixtli – the mountain cat – and so I came, down the coast, and up the river. From Singing Heron I learned that you had passed safely, but then I was warned by the danger sticks of the white men's coming. After that I traveled only at night. I must have passed you at Eagle Camp; I did not wish to awaken the men there to ask for you. My dreams had told me by then that you were safe, and I was anxious to reach the painted cave. Has it gone well with you, my son?"

"Ah, yes, grandfather," Ephraim laughed. "Very well. Almost too well."

The old man permitted himself a sly smile. "I thought perhaps it would. And I have a message for you from downriver."

He pulled a deerskin scroll from his blanket and handed it to Ephraim.

Ephraim's eyes widened with surprise as he began to read. It was from Singing Heron.

> Sun brother, the sky has been empty and the nights
> very dark since your departure. I spend the long hours
> lamenting the need for sending you onward.
>
> It was best that way, I know, and by now I am sure
> that you know it too. How cruel of me to send you
> away as I did! But it was right, for otherwise you would
> not have known the love of many others.
>
> Now that your knowledge of love is deeper, now that
> you have learned many things, I can offer myself to you
> wholly, knowing that your choice will be a free one,
> and a wise one.
>
> From Singing Heron, who sings of you often when
> the poor-wills cry in the twilight.

Ephraim rolled up the deerskin with trembling fingers and turned to the cave. Ixtlil Cuauhtli took his arm silently, and they climbed up to the entrance.

Once inside the cave the old man spoke. "Do not be disturbed, my son, if the decisions facing you seem to be difficult. Your heart will know what is best before the moon has waned, for your spirit quest will tell you many things." His voice trailed off into hollow echoes as they descended the twisting tunnel of the cave.

The old man lit an oil lamp and gave it to Ephraim. The walls of the cave were cool; the two men's breathing echoed in resonant sighs from a great distance beneath. Ephraim felt Ixtlil Cuauhtli's reassuring hand on his arm, and he was led on into the darkness.

From far ahead he could see a light, not of the day, but yellow, from another lamp. Ixtlil Cuauhtli snuffed their own lamp and they continued on toward the light. The walls widened, and Ephraim found himself in a high-vaulted chamber. Another man was painting figures on the walls; he ignored them utterly.

Ixtlil Cuauhtli indicated a place for Ephraim to sit, and then sat beside him.

Ephraim looked around at the walls, at the other man. There were vague outlines on the walls – of figures in violent motion, of men, of animals – but the light was too dim to make them out clearly.

The man turned to them. His eyes were pools of indigo darkness, and his cheekbones jutted sharply from a calm, fragile face; his long, black hair gleamed in the flickering light. He was perhaps fifty.

"It is Bear-who-dreams," murmured Ixtlil Cuauhtli.

Bear-who-dreams sat on the floor in front of Ephraim and placed the lamp by his side.

"How are you, Ephraim MacIver?" he asked in a soft, lilting voice.

"I am very well, my father, and I hope that you are the same," Ephraim whispered.

"Thank you, my son." He paused, staring piercingly into Ephraim's face. Ephraim lowered his eyes. "Since my brother Ixtlil Cuauhtli is here, I shall speak in my own tongue, for the thoughts form themselves more truly in the Indian way. My brother will translate into your language. I find your language cruel and untrue."

"Very well, my father," Ephraim answered.

Bear-who-dreams uttered a soft, slow, singing statement in the Indian tongue, and Ixtlil Cuauhtli translated at intervals.

"He says that he knows of you from several sources: from myself, from Singing Heron, who wrote another letter which I also brought, and from the fact that the unhappy missionary has been seeking you.

"From these reports he senses that you have in your soul already the gentleness out of which love is born – both the love of other men and the love of all creatures. Do you feel that you have this gentleness in your soul?"

Ephraim thought for many heartbeats, eyes downcast. Finally he glanced briefly at Bear-who-dreams, and spoke haltingly. "I do not know," he said, "I hate no man, for such is not my nature. But I fear many, and I sometimes think that hate and fear are the same. It is also true that love cannot exist in a fearful heart."

Pinpricks of light flashed in the pools of blackness, then disappeared. "Why do you fear others?" Bear-who-dreams asked. "Is it the companion of Mr. Calvin that you fear?"

"Yes," said Ephraim. "I fear him. He can harm me in many ways."

"You must learn to guard yourself, my son, in many ways, wherever you think he can harm you. Fear walks with the weak man, and the stupid."

"Yes, my father."

"Perhaps he has broken something in you that you wish restored. Perhaps," he said slowly, "he carries within himself, still, a part of your soul."

"No," Ephraim said vehemently. "That cannot be."

Bear-who-dreams sighed. "Are you certain that you don't hate him?"

Ephraim faltered. "No. I'm not –"

Bear-who-dreams interrupted. "It is as you have wisely said: fear and hatred are perhaps the same thing." He stared at Ephraim while Ixtlil Cuauhtli translated, then continued. "Let him keep the part of your soul that he still possesses. You gave it freely, and generously, and it would be small and mean of you to demand it back. Give, my son, and forget the past. Hatred and vengeance are poisonous."

Ephraim sighed and remained silent, but his thoughts were a turmoil. Suddenly he burst out, glaring at Bear-who-dreams, "But how can I forget the past? How can I help but remember the way I was nearly broken? How can I think of it without bitterness?"

Bear-who-dreams met his glare calmly, and his answer was soft: "You need not forget the past, my son, but be guided by it in the future – without anger, without hatred and bitterness. If you allow hatred and anger and bitterness to remain in your heart, he will have succeeded in breaking your soul just as surely as if he were still by your side."

He paused to let these words stir through Ephraim's mind, and lit a long Indian pipe from a straw held over the lamp's flame. Ephraim had no reply.

Bear-who-dreams drew on the pipe and passed it to Ixtlil Cuauhtli, who passed it in turn to Ephraim.

Ephraim felt the old man's eyes upon him, appraising him, noting his every reaction. When the pipe had come back again, Bear-who-dreams spoke. "You are handsome and strong, my son, and many eyes will turn in your direction." He stopped, waiting for a reply.

"I have never thought of myself as either," Ephraim said, "until this summer, perhaps."

"You will begin to think of yourself thus more and more often as your experience with the Loon Society grows, because it is true, and many will tell you so."

Ephraim thought for a long time; at length he answered, "I have known many who love only themselves, and they have made me suffer. I do not wish to be that sort of person. Nor do I wish to be the sort of person who takes no pride in himself, or who hates himself."

A trace of a smile passed over Bear-who-dreams' lean face. "You are quite correct, my son, but often a childish self-love can grow in a man without his knowing it. How would you know if such were happening to you?"

"I do not know –" Ephraim paused, troubled. "But I can recognize it in others by these signs: a desire to satisfy only oneself when making love, and a way of being friendly only to those people who can be useful in one manner or another. If this ever happens to me, and I do not recognize it, I would hope that my friends would tell me, for such a person is very distasteful."

Bear-who-dreams passed the pipe again. "It seems that you have already attracted many people."

Ephraim sighed, and said nothing.

"What do you intend to do about this?"

"I don't know," Ephraim whispered unhappily. "I wish I did know."

"Do you love them all?"

"Yes."

"And they all love you?"

"Yes. That is my understanding."

"Do you think," Bear-who-dreams mused, "that if a choice could be made clear to you, you could love that person, and the others also?"

"I think so," Ephraim answered slowly, "yet I don't know how that can be possible. Isn't it wrong to love more than one man at a time?"

Bear-who-dreams stared at the smoke drifting in the lamplight. "No," he said finally, "but I will not tell you why. You must find that out for yourself."

After a long silence he added, almost as an afterthought, "Your choice will become clear in your medicine dream." Then he rose and returned to his painting.

Ixtlil Cuauhtli touched Ephraim on the elbow, and they got up to leave. Once in the sunlight, he said, "My brother is pleased with you. You gave very wise answers for one so inexperienced. And he will think of you this afternoon, and make prayers for you."

Ephraim smiled, greatly relieved.

In spite of his fatigue, he spent the afternoon chopping wood and bringing water for the two Indians. In the evening he shared their meal in the chamber of the paintings, and curled up in his blankets that night in the same chamber, next to Ixtlil Cuauhtli, vaguely aware of the flickering lamplight dancing on the spinning painted figures.

In the morning he was awakened by a frail, monotonous chant

coming from nearby. Drawing the blankets from his face, he saw Bear-who-dreams sitting next to his head. The Indian reached out and covered his face again, and continued to chant.

The singing stopped, and he heard the voice of Bear-who-dreams as from a great distance. "Lie still, my son," he said. "I am preparing you for your spirit quest; I am telling the Earth to send you forth again, into the world of men –"

He started to chant again, and continued monotonously for what seemed hours. Ephraim dozed, but his limbs ached, and he longed to stand up, to stretch and run.

Suddenly the blanket was pulled away, and Ephraim sat up. Bear-who-dreams was still sitting in the same place, filling his pipe, smiling into space. "You are almost ready to go forth," he said. "To make your journey easier, you must not wear any clothing that is fastened with knots; nor must I."

Ephraim saw that Bear-who-dreams was covered only with a blanket. Looking down at himself, he realized that he would have to take off his breech cloth. He untied it and let it drop to the floor.

"Take the blanket," the Indian said, pointing. "But you must leave your moccasins."

Ephraim threw the blanket over his shoulders and kicked off his moccasins.

Then Bear-who-dreams lit his pipe, and a sweet, acrid smell filled the chamber. He handed the pipe to Ephraim.

It was not tobacco, Ephraim decided. He inhaled deeply, and Bear-who-dreams indicated that he was to finish the pipe by himself. Ephraim sat down.

"When you are finished, go, my son. Eat nothing on your journey, but at sunrise, eat this, and you will know when to come back."

Ephraim heard the Indian clearly, but he was far, far away. He held out his hand and was given a little button – amazingly, impossibly, from such a distance he couldn't see the button. The walls of the cave were bright in the darkness.

Ephraim stood up, and the world receded. A sweet, tiny old man with white hair and a red blanket took him by the hand. He was so sweet, so godlike, that Ephraim kissed him on the forehead.

He allowed himself to be led through miles of tunnel toward a brilliant pinprick of light, far, far in the distance; but the journey was swift, for soon he was in a newly cleansed world, bright, and incredibly beautiful.

The sweet old man was Ixtlil Cuauhtli; Ephraim suddenly remembered the face and the name. Ixtlil Cuauhtli was doing something. A feather – he blew it in the air and watched it float – a puff of nothing curling off – and then Ixtlil Cuauhtli spoke. "Go south, my son. That way is your world, your spirit."

Ephraim smiled in gratitude and kissed him again. He turned southward and began to walk across the bright earth. His bare feet touched the ground rarely; he could smell the newness of the sun.

Slowly, slowly, his feet began to touch ground more often; slowly the world began to age and the colors to fade.

He walked, ever away from his shadow. When the sun was high, he found a southward flowing stream, and lay down to rest. His feet hurt, and he shut his eyes against the glaring sun.

He awoke to a gray and ancient world. He leaped up anxiously and ran along the stream bank, following the water, being careful not to fall in, fully aware of the dangerous fish that lurked in the dark pools. But could they see him? He didn't know, and shuddered. Anyway, they couldn't get out of the water.

He ran on and on, and then stopped suddenly. What was the point of running? He thought uneasily that the birds could fly faster than he could run. They could catch him if they really wanted to. Perhaps it would be better to act calm and not attract attention. He walked carefully, trying to control his breathing.

When the sun was near the horizon, he found a tree that would hide him from the birds, and climbed up, finding a broad limb he could hang onto in case one tried to carry him off during the night. He pulled his blanket tightly around himself and began to watch for the birds – slyly, without moving a muscle.

One came, of course, and it was just pretending to be little. When it flew away to tell the others, Ephraim scrambled down and ran some more.

Night fell, and he crept into a hollow log. He didn't dare shut his eyes; the sounds outside were too suspicious. He wasn't positive, but somewhere he thought he heard a weasel, waiting for him to doze off.

He awoke with a start, and wriggled out of the log. The sun was rising – *again* – and he trotted off, away from the evil place.

He stopped. Before him was a lake, deep blue, almost purple. It looked friendly, and he sat down, trying to remember what he was doing.

In his hand was a little green button, and he remembered vaguely that – something. He didn't know what, but he ate it anyway.

Suddenly, before his eyes, the lake drained away, leaving a huge blue hole. The earth was flat, then, and this was a hole in the earth, and he was looking through to the sky on the other side. He scuttled backward, terrified lest he fall through. He watched this other sky suspiciously through narrowed eyelids.

Then he saw it, coming at him, and he screamed – a bird, a huge bird, not pretending now. It had Montgomery's eyes.

He leaped up and ran stumbling, falling, running again. He found a gopher hole and dived in, just in time – and the bird screamed down at him. He turned around in the hole and waited, panting, then peeked out. The bird was sitting not far off, changing itself into a snake. Ephraim knew what they meant, and decided to run for it.

He ran, leaping over blue cracks in the earth, but the snake was behind him.

When he saw that the snake had changed into a huge cat, he knew he would have to make a stand and fight it out. He backed up against a friendly Ponderosa pine, and waited.

The cat slowed to a walk, then sat down before him. In a twinkling it changed back into Montgomery.

Montgomery smiled viciously, entirely pleased with himself.

"What do you want?" Ephraim muttered hoarsely.

Montgomery laughed; he held his sides and laughed until the tears came.

"You –" he said, gasping for breath, "you don't know what I want?" He roared with laughter and fell to the ground. Finally he stopped, and looked up with a sneer. "I am going to kill you, you little fairy." He stood up and pulled a pistol from his belt.

"No!" Ephraim shouted. "You can't kill me!" Desperately, he searched for words. "You can't do it, because you're not real! You're not real, do you understand?"

"You think not?" Montgomery replied coolly. "What makes you think so?"

Ephraim took an aching breath. "I can get rid of you. I know you're not real because of *your language* – that word – it proves that you don't exist in *this world*. All I have to do is *think you out of existence*."

"Ha!" Montgomery laughed. "It'll take more than you to think me away. I'll bet you can't do it." He raised the pistol and pointed it at Ephraim's chest. "Go ahead and try."

Ephraim beat his mind into concentration; he forced his thoughts into a single convergence, and his muscles ached from the tension. Montgomery began to fade.

Ephraim smiled triumphantly, and Montgomery came back, clearly, face grim, pistol still pointing.

He concentrated again, but Montgomery held his own; slowly, the finger strained to pull the trigger. Ephraim watched the pistol, horrified.

Suddenly Montgomery fell backward, the shaft of an arrow vibrating in his chest. He was dead.

Ephraim spun around – and saw. The Ponderosa behind him had no face, no arms, no legs, yet it had killed Montgomery. And he knew who the tree was.

He kissed the tree, and wept. Tears stained the rough, brown bark, and the tree was happy. Ephraim fell sobbing, still clinging to the tree; he kissed it again, fervently. "My love," he choked, "I know you now."

The tree sighed as it waved its stately branches protectively in the breeze. "Come to me, my love," it whispered.

Ephraim curled up at its feet and looked back. All that was left of Montgomery's body was a patch of blood-red flowers, nodding sadly in the soft wind. The lake was filled with water again, smiling happily at Ephraim, and the birds in his tree were friends now. The sun was high, and Ephraim dozed.

When he awoke, the sun was midway down the sky toward the horizon, and he sensed that his lover's spirit was preparing to leave the pine tree. Quickly he pressed his lips against the bark and whispered, "I want to stay here this winter, by this lake. This is a good place."

The tree sighed in loving assent.

Ephraim muttered, "I will wait for you here, my love."

Softly, faintly in the distance, he heard the reply. "Send me a mess – ssage –" and the spirit was gone, leaving only a tall majesty.

A striped ground squirrel played where the red flowers had been; it watched Ephraim curiously, then frisked away.

For the first time, Ephraim felt the weakness in his body. His knees trembled, and his feet were sore. He walked down to the lake and drank, and bathed himself in the cool water. Then he turned northward and began the wearisome trek back to the cave of Bear-who-dreams.

There were no spirits now in the forest. The birds no longer threatened his soul, and the fish in the streams were unconcerned. Signs of game were plentiful; in a distant valley, at sunset, he spied a beaver pond. The deer were sleek and almost tame.

Slowly, his heart filled with hope and a new calmness, and he began to make plans for the remainder of the summer, for the coming autumn and winter.

At nightfall he rested until moonrise, then continued, always toward the north star. His head was light, but his thoughts were clear.

He went on painfully during the night, fighting off weariness and the night's chill. At dawn he saw the mountain of Bear-who-dreams much further away than he had expected. His feet were numb, and his thoughts strayed.

He looked for his lover in the pines as he passed them, and felt a presence, an encouragement, and pressed on.

He stumbled, and a pine murmured, "Be careful, my love; you will soon be there."

The sun was high as he climbed the last slope toward the cave. A red shape careened dizzily downward, he felt rock on his face, against his teeth. He tried to get up and only felt rock under his feet. Then soft, warm blackness.

It was the same voice, leading him back to the world. "Ephraim, Ephraim," it sang. He opened his eyes in panic and saw the face of Ixtlil Cuauhtli hovering over him. "Ephraim," he chanted. "You are here."

He saw the cave then, and knew he was not back in Astoria. He sat up and smiled weakly. "I have seen many strange things," he whispered.

Bear-who-dreams left his paintings and came close. "Tell me what you saw, my son, before you forget," he said, and sat down next to Ixtlil Cuauhtli.

Ephraim lay back and tried to gather his thoughts. Slowly, haltingly, he told the whole story, ashamed at times to admit his fear, but omitting nothing.

When he was finished, Bear-who-dreams sat silently for a long while. Then he spoke in Indian, and Ixtlil Cuauhtli translated. "You have had a true vision, and an Indian vision: it is strange that a white man should do so.

"I also know that the lake you came upon is the center of the world; only I and Ixtlil Cuauhtli and perhaps two others know of it. Our vision was different from yours, but they mean the same thing.

"Many things you saw were what a white man would see, but you saw them in the Indian way. We do not put flowers on the body of a dead man, but red is the color of death.

"Montgomery is dead for you. He means nothing. His old self is also dead, shot and killed by the spirit of the pine tree. He is born anew. You will see him again, and know.

"You are now one with the world."

Bear-who-dreams went to a dark cranny of the cave and brought something in his hand. "I think that in your soul you are already an Indian. And I will give you this to wear, to show that you belong to the Society of the Loon." He placed a thong around Ephraim's neck; hanging from it was a small stone bird.

"You will eat now," the Indian said, "and I will make a prayer for you."

Ixtlil Cuauhtli brought a bowl of hot corn meal, which Ephraim ate carefully. Surprisingly, he wasn't very hungry.

When he had finished, he said to Ixtlil Cuauhtli, "I want to send a message downriver." He hoped Ixtlil Cuauhtli would find a solution to the problem of getting the message delivered, and didn't care how it would be done.

The old man gazed silently at Ephraim, then said, "You write the message, and I will think of a way to deliver it." He brought a piece of deer hide, a quill pen, and some paint.

Ephraim spread the hide on the floor and began to write.

My love:
I saw you in my spirit quest; you were a pine tree, and my heart was filled with your power and majesty. The thought of your presence, your embrace and your love bring longing and a sweet sadness to my soul; come, and we shall be fulfilled.
I am leaving soon to build a cabin by the lake where I saw you. You know the way, I am sure, for it was there that you saved my soul from destruction.

Ixtlil Cuauhtli took the deerskin, rolled it up, and tied it with an orange-painted strip of hide. "Tomorrow," he said, "I shall take this as far as Eagle Camp, and there I can find a young man who will deliver it downriver."

Ephraim thought for a minute. The letter would have to go downriver; yes, that would be fine. "I'll go with you, my father; the journey is long, and you have only recently arrived."

Ixtlil Cuauhtli sighed, then smiled. "For you, my son, I came here from Astoria, and the journey to Eagle Camp will be very short. It will take us two days, perhaps." He rose and left the cave; Ephraim dressed and followed him, limping on tender feet.

~

The next morning, Ephraim was awakened by Ixtlil Cuauhtli; they left the cave and found Bear-who-dreams in prayer, standing in a patch of dew-heavy flowers. He was wearing only a breech cloth, and his slender, erect body, vigorously sinewed, glowed in the early sunlight. He turned to Ephraim and touched him on the cheek, lightly, with a lingering trace of tenderness. "You are good, and I love you," he whispered. "May the spirit of love and brotherhood walk with you always." Then he disappeared into the cave.

The image of the Indian's graceful, upright body hovered in Ephraim's mind, and he wondered to himself.

Ixtlil Cuauhtli's eyes were on him, appraisingly. "Perhaps," the old Indian said, "what you are wondering in your mind is possible, and perhaps, under other circumstances –" but he cut himself short, smiling softly, and Ephraim looked at the ground in confusion.

They busied themselves with preparations, and left within the hour.

The journey seemed endless to Ephraim, but to his surprise it took less time than it had before. Ixtlil Cuauhtli was tireless, and they stopped only to sleep.

Within two days they arrived at the river above the falls. Ixtlil Cuauhtli stopped, and motioned Ephraim to sit down.

"I think I shall stay here, my son, for a week or more, but I want you to return. Know, however, that I have changed many plans since spring; I think it is unsafe for me now in Astoria, and I wish to stay with Bear-who-dreams this winter, as I have done many winters in the past. I also want to be near you, Ephraim, to enjoy your happiness, for such things are of great importance to me. Go, my son, but we shall see each other often; the winds of early spring will tell you of my coming."

Ephraim watched the old man's eyes, and realized the depth of their friendship. "I will go, my father, because you wish it, and because I love you." They embraced, and Ephraim turned back toward the cave.

He did not hurry on his return journey, but paused often to watch the chipmunks at play, and the wheeling flight of hawks; he picked flowers and fished; the first berries were ripening on sunny southern slopes, and the wild plums were turning purple.

A strange dreaminess filled his heart, and he almost wished, like Amatus Sum, to be out of time. As he approached the cave, the dreamy timelessness increased.

On the evening of the third day he stepped again into the dark chamber, and Bear-who-dreams was there, painting by the yellow light of an oil lamp. He turned his deep lavender eyes to Ephraim in greeting.

Ephraim brought wood and water, and built a fire at the cave entrance. There were two snared rabbits ready to broil, and corn meal. He turned the rabbits on a spit, and when the smell of their cooking penetrated the cave, Bear-who-dreams came out and sat down, facing the sunset. Ephraim served him, and they ate in silence.

Finally Bear-who-dreams asked, "Ixtlil Cuauhtli did not come with you?"

"No," Ephraim answered. "He wished to stay at Eagle Camp for several days. But he will come back."

Ephraim sensed the Indian's brooding gaze as he put more wood on the fire. He looked briefly into the black-purple eyes, and then away.

The dark mountain shapes were silhouetted in old rose as Bear-who-dreams spoke again. "Do you wish to make love to me, Ephraim MacIver?" His words were spoken toward the thin line of dark pink on the horizon.

Ephraim's heart jumped in an unnameable emotion. His tongue was dry. "Yes," he whispered, "if you wish."

The Indian asked, still facing away, "What does your heart tell you, Ephraim?"

Ephraim hesitated, trembling.

Bear-who-dreams continued, "I know your desire, and I am pleased, and I know your fear. But remember, my son –" He caught himself suddenly, then cried out angrily, "Your language forces me to use words that are not true! I am not what you call me, nor are you what I –" He stopped speaking.

Ephraim leaped to his feet, still trembling. "Must we have names for everything?" he cried in a strangled whisper.

"Names often lead us astray," Bear-who-dreams mused. "You are wise, Ephraim. Some things should not be named."

Ephraim went to stand before Bear-who-dreams and gazed down at him. The Indian stared into the darkness. His eyes were in shadow, his face immobile. Ephraim finally held out his hand, palm upward, toward the Indian.

"Is this what your heart wishes?" the Indian asked.

"Yes," Ephraim whispered.

Bear-who-dreams stood up, leaving his blanket on the ground. His face and eyes showed only a fierce pride, and haughtiness, but his voice was soft. "We shall be lovers then," he said. There was pride in his gesture as he untied his breech cloth.

Ephraim stared helplessly at the Indian's cock; it was broad and thick, twined with veins. The fist-like head hung down heavily.

He loosened his own breech cloth and let it fall. Bear-who-dreams lit a lamp from the fire, and turned into the cave.

Ephraim continued staring – at the Indian's gently out-curving belly, marked by a thick line of black hair down from the navel, and at the suggestion of softness on his back, just above the hip. Suddenly he was struck by a rush of desire as Bear-who-dreams walked ahead of him down the passageway. He reached out and touched the Indian's soft, flat buttocks, then let his hand fall. Bear-who-dreams looked at Ephraim's erect, forward-pointing cock and sighed with a quick out-rush of breath.

When they reached the inner chamber, Bear-who-dreams set the lamp down beside his blankets and turned to Ephraim, arms limp at his sides, palms turned outward. His cock was beginning to lengthen. In a maddened rush of desire, Ephraim embraced him, enclosing his body tightly in his arms, kissing his face, his eyes, forcing his tongue past the Indian's lips. He pulled Bear-who-dreams down onto the blanket and fell on him, panting, moaning, pushed by an urge to somehow enfold this man's body in his own – to devour him. Bear-who-dreams sighed in rapture as Ephraim ran his hands roughly up and down his body, frenziedly excited at its graceful pliancy. Then, sensing that he was about to come, he rolled off, panting heavily, still clutching the Indian's hand.

Bear-who-dreams sat up. Their eyes met, and then he gazed at Ephraim's body for a long while – at his erect, swollen penis, at his coppery hair. He reached out and ran his fingers through the hair, tracing the hairiness up to his chest. He touched Ephraim's nipples, his chin, his eyes, then bent down, straddling Ephraim's head with his thighs, and took his cock in his mouth, down to the base.

Ephraim buried his face in the Indian's belly, and thrust his loins upward, gently, then forced himself to relax. He took the heavy, half-erect cock in his mouth and felt it harden against his tongue.

Bear-who-dreams stopped and stood up, motioning for Ephraim to do likewise. His cock was swollen and hard; he touched Ephraim's cock with his, and they gazed at the heads pressing against each other.

Ephraim stepped back, hands on hips, legs planted firmly apart, watching. When Bear-who-dreams began to thrust his hips rhythmically, knees half bent, Ephraim forced him to the floor, pinned his thighs wide apart and took him in his mouth. The Indian writhed slowly and groaned, and came suddenly, in a hot flash of urgency.

Ephraim rose to his knees, determined to come onto the black belly-hair, but Bear-who-dreams rolled onto his stomach and spread his legs, lifting his hips off the ground; Ephraim thrust blindly downward, grinding the Indian's hips against the floor, pounding, rocking from side to side, pushing crazily upward, inward, to the Indian's heart, and then he floated, toes twitching, legs thrashing, on and into the Indian's soft buttocks inward, inward…

He lay on Bear-who-dreams for many minutes, enjoying the pressure of the Indian's buttocks against his belly and the tightness around him. He thrust gently from time to time, and was met with answering thrusts. Finally, reluctantly, he pulled away.

Before he went to sleep, with Bear-who-dreams wrapped tightly in his arms, Ephraim heard a whisper next to his ear. "One such as you, my lover! You must come to see me this spring, and we will make love again, and you will push your youth and strength into me and I will hold you there for many hours. And I will enjoy again the sight of you. Some day I want to see you come – to spurt out onto me, hotly and strongly. But now I must sleep, for I am not as young as you. Hold me tight, my lover, and share your strength with me."

Ephraim kissed the shadowed eyes and drew him closer.

In the morning, after a silent, thoughtful breakfast, Ephraim made ready to leave, but lingered in the entranceway. Bear-who-dreams sensed his hesitation, and stood deep in thought. Finally he looked up at Ephraim and said quietly, "Last night I said that some day I would want to see you come."

Ephraim's blood began to race at the strange thought. "Now," he said. "But you must undress, for the sight of your nakedness excites me."

They undressed, and stood facing each other, naked. Ephraim began the stroke, watching the Indian's heavy genitals, staring at his hairiness. Bear-who-dreams watched him intently.

Ephraim paused, dropped his hands and stared at himself for a minute, then started again. When he felt he was ready to come, he moved closer to the Indian, asking with his eyes what he should do. Bear-who-dreams tensed, thrust his loins forward, and stood waiting, watching intently as the spasms began. He sighed, and they watched Ephraim's cock until it was limp.

The Indian fastened his breech cloth without removing the semen. "When I do the same to myself, what you have just done," he mused, "I shall think of you, and of your body, and of your coming." He paused, looking into Ephraim's eyes, and added, "It is strange that you should be attracted to a man of my age."

"Strange, perhaps," Ephraim whispered, "but I love you."

"That is good. It makes me happy. It is a path in our Way that few have cared to explore."

Then, oddly, Bear-who-dreams turned back to the fire and caught a handful of smoke. He held his cupped hands for Ephraim to see. "Do you remember our talk yesterday," he said, "– about words, and about naming things?" Ephraim nodded, Bear-who-dreams continued: "What I have just captured is now confined and molded by the shape of my hands. It does not float lazily in the air; it does not curl off into the woods. My hands are enclosing it."

Then he opened his hands before Ephraim's face, and spoke softly, slowly, his black-purple eyes intent on Ephraim's eyes: "But it is still smoke."

Ephraim gazed at the faint wisps and comprehended. "Goodbye, my father," he whispered.

"Walk in beauty and happiness, my son," Bear-who-dreams murmured softly.

They touched lips and Ephraim turned to go, thoughtfully, and pensively.

Book Five

He chose a site for the cabin in a meadow overlooking the lake, sheltered from the wind by a grove of hemlocks and firs; a tiny stream was close by, gleaming in the summer sunlight.

He began by chopping down trees – lodgepole pines and Ponderosas – with an axe borrowed from Bear-who-dreams. From sunup to sunset he labored – felling, trimming and notching, calculating the number of logs he would need – how many split logs for the floor, how many for the roof. He left the more distant logs where they had fallen, but managed to roll the closer ones to the cabin site.

Then he began to gather rocks for the chimney, sweating naked in the sun, muscles straining as he carried boulders up from the lakeshore. There was clay-mud on the lake bottom that would do for mortar.

He snared deer and rabbit, and caught an occasional fish; there were bitter wild cherries, and plums, and currants. He dug roots and trapped birds.

Not having bothered to put up a temporary shelter of any kind, he slept in the open and awoke with dew on his face, shivering in the pale, cold dawn.

For three weeks he toiled, and then decided to quit until his partner came. He rested, and passed the days exploring the lakeshore, or simply lying in the grass, staring at the sky.

He tried to remember what he had learned about the tanning of hides, and even tried to chip a stone scraper from one of the lakeshore rocks, but gave it up in disgust and boredom, and threw the stone away.

Then Ixtlil Cuauhtli came unexpectedly, and with expert hands chipped out two stone scrapers. Together they soaked, scraped and tanned the deer and rabbit hides that Ephraim had saved. The old Indian made an awl out of bone, and they stitched the hides together into a small tent. Then Ixtlil Cuauhtli left, without having said a word about Ephraim's partner.

Again the days of idleness, of watching the ground squirrels in the afternoon sunlight, of lazy swimming in the lake, of singing at the moon. At times desire rose in him like a hot flood, and dawn would find him cavorting in the lake, pale and trembling.

Ephraim watched the mountains to the north, thinking that some sign might reveal his partner's approach, but he saw nothing but an occasional soaring eagle far in the distance, close to the mountain of Bear-who-dreams. Once he saw a tiny speck of red, and imagined it to be Ixtlil Cuauhtli.

The days were warm in the sunlight. In the open spaces of black rock and white pumice, grasshoppers whirred in the afternoon, and sparse clumps of grass waved in the wind. But in the deep shadows of the woods, cool ferns grew, and columbines and sorrel. Ancient logs rotted on the forest floor, crumbling to the touch.

He found a small yew tree in a ravine leading into the lake, and decided to make a bow. With unthinking patience he shaped a yew branch, using only his hunting knife, and for days the time passed quickly. In the end, however, he was at a loss as to how to fashion a suitable arrowhead; he put the bow away unstrung in his tent, and returned to snaring.

One hot afternoon he sought out the Ponderosa pine, the former dwelling place of his lover, and sat down in its filtered shade, leaning back against the rough trunk. The air was still, and except for the humming of the midsummer cicadas, there was scarcely a sound. He gazed drowsily across the lake, eyes half-closed against its brilliant reflections, half-listening to this own heartbeat and to the cicada's monotonous song. He dozed, aware of the peaceful shadows and brilliant green before him. His thoughts wandered sleepily – pale and green like the new ferns, and in time with his heartbeat.

A strange sound awakened him – a heavy stamping in the grass, the creak of leather. He leaped to his feet, suddenly terrified, and was enfolded in the strong arms of his lover. Tobacco smell, prickling beard, bare chest deeply muscled, covered with thick, silken hair. Ephraim pulled back and looked at the smiling blue eyes.

"Cyrus," he whispered.

"I have come, my love," Cyrus murmured. He was dressed Indian-fashion – moccasins, leggings and breech cloth.

Ephraim was suddenly shy, and couldn't speak; he looked at the ground. Cyrus put an arm around his shoulders and pointed out two pack mules. "I went again to Fort Vancouver, and brought many things we will need," he said. They walked aimlessly toward the lake, with Cyrus leading the mules.

Ephraim showed him the cabin site and the logs he had cut. Cyrus scratched his beard pensively. "Have you ever built a cabin before?" he asked.

Ephraim nodded. "Twice," he said. "Or at least I've helped with two cabins."

"We'll have to build some kind of corral or stable for the mules, if we decide to keep them, and do some haying this fall." He sat down on a log and filled his pipe. "But there's plenty of time. We can finish the cabin in three weeks, and even go back to Fort Vancouver in September for more supplies if we have to."

Ephraim looked at him sharply. "We?" he asked.

Cyrus smiled slowly. "If you'd like," he said.

Ephraim sat down beside him on the log, frowning. "And Montgomery?" he asked.

Cyrus drew deeply on his pipe. "Ah, yes; Montgomery," he said. "Do you want to hear a very interesting story?"

Ephraim nodded, relieved for the distraction. He was also curious. Surely, he thought, his medicine dream had had some correspondence in reality, as Bear-who-dreams had said. The thought crossed his mind, fleetingly, that perhaps Cyrus really had killed Montgomery.

As Cyrus prepared to speak, Ephraim allowed his eyes to wander over the powerful body next to him down to the taut loin cloth –

"I went down the Willamette," Cyrus began, "and soon figured out that I was right on the heels of Montgomery and Mr. Calvin; they were perhaps a day ahead of me. Finally I had to pass them, since they were traveling very slowly. I slipped by at night, thinking that I'd seen the last of them, that certainly they or at least Mr. Calvin would stop at the Mission. At any rate, imagine my surprise when I saw them in Fort Vancouver two days after my arrival, and just before I had figured on leaving.

"Now, something struck me as odd about those two almost immediately. I remember what you had said about Montgomery, and after giving the matter a good deal of thought, I decided to stay around for a while to see what was happening.

"Montgomery, it turned out, spent his evenings in a certain tavern, sometimes playing cards and sometimes drinking by himself. Mr. Calvin, you understand, doesn't drink. Anyway, I struck up a conversation with Montgomery one evening at the bar. We talked about this and that for several hours; he was very pleasant, almost ingratiating, and I have to admit that he can make a very good impression when he wants to. Then in comes Mr. Calvin, looking for Montgomery, wanting him to leave. Montgomery has no intention of leaving, and laughed at the suggestion. It was a cruel laugh, or rather just thoughtless, brushing Calvin off as if he were a very minor annoyance. But Calvin simply sat down without a word and began to wait. I watched him out of the corner of my eye, and I'll be a ring-tailed polecat if that poor man wasn't suffering the tortures of the damned – and do you know why? I couldn't believe my eyes, but there it was: obviously, Mr. Calvin had fallen desperately in love with Montgomery."

Cyrus laughed thunderously, slapped his thigh and stood up, facing Ephraim. "Would you believe it? Calvin, who has spent his whole adult life trying to destroy people like you and me – passionately, unmistakably in love with Montgomery, of all people!"

"Are you *sure?*" Ephraim asked unbelievingly.

"Oh, yes," Cyrus said with finality. "Montgomery after a while got annoyed at Calvin's presence, and to amuse himself, I suppose, he gave him the choice of either sharing our bottle or of being thrown out bodily. You probably can't imagine what a difficult choice that was for a man like Mr. Calvin, but finally he decided to drink. For all I know, it was the first liquor he ever tasted in his life; but at any rate, it went to his head in a hurry, and within an hour he was wildly, pathetically drunk. Poor man, he managed to preserve a certain amount of dignity, but that didn't save him at all from Montgomery.

"Past midnight, when there was nobody left except maybe a handful of trappers and so on in the bar, word began passing up and down the street that the austere, erect, pure, Mister Missionary Calvin was getting drunk in such-and-such a saloon, and some two dozen or more came running. Poor Calvin – he took it all in silence: the jokes, the questions; he just sat there without a word, until Montgomery said to him, 'Go on and tell them; tell them why you're getting drunk for the first time in your life. I dare you.'

"Well, Calvin stared at him for a full minute, and then he said, 'All right, I'll tell them.' And he climbed up on the bar and stood there, waiting for the noise to quiet down, as if he were going to give a Sermon. Then he started in: 'Gentlemen,' he said, 'I have been asked to tell you why I am getting drunk for the first time in my life, why I am drunk for the first time in my life. Are you listening? Because I want you to get it straight,' and here he smiled a little, 'I don't want you to go around telling lies about me. It's because for the first time in my life I've fallen in love. Perhaps not the first time, but anyway the first time I've ever admitted it to myself.'

"You could have heard a mouse breathe in that saloon. 'Yes, gentlemen,' he said, 'it's a wonderful thing to be in love, and sometimes a terrible thing, but either way, I'm too tired, too weary, to deny it. And do you want to know who it is that I love? Do you?' He was pacing up and down the bar then, like an enraged grizzly. I looked at Montgomery, and he was the color of old, wet ashes – open-mouthed, aghast. 'Gentlemen,' Calvin thundered, 'I am in love with this son-of-a-bitch right here,' and he pointed straight at Montgomery.

"Poor Montgomery was petrified; he couldn't move. 'And he's afraid,' Calvin went on, 'ashamed, maybe, to admit that he loves me.' Then he went on to tell all the details of their affair, which must have begun when they reached the coast, after we saw them. He stopped talking only to take another drink, but finally he came to the end. Tears were streaming down his cheeks, and he turned to Montgomery. 'Now that I have destroyed myself,' he said, 'I can still say that I love you, and I can still thank you for making me realize the truth. With or without you, my life will be a happier one. But you, you cowardly wretch, will never have the honesty or the guts to face the meaning of love.'

"Then he climbed down and sat at the other end of the bar, as still as death, staring straight ahead.

"Montgomery came to his senses then, so to speak, and jumped up, yelling. 'He's lying!' he screamed, and pulled a pistol on Calvin; but Calvin just looked at him without moving, without even blinking. I had to hit Montgomery pretty hard, I guess, because I knocked him out. Calvin passed out about then, and when Montgomery came to, all he could say was, 'You don't believe him, do you?' But everybody around sure believed Calvin, because they just walked out without saying a word, staring – contemptuously – at Montgomery. Finally, he passed out too.

"I carried him up to my room and threw him on my bed, and had another bed made up for myself. I woke up at dawn – I shouldn't have slept at all, because Montgomery wasn't to be trusted – and there was Calvin in my room, slumped on the floor in the corner, waiting to take Montgomery home. He looked like the Hangover God in person, but he was awake. I got up and got dressed, and we didn't say a word. Finally I asked him, 'Do you think he'll try to shoot you again?' I'm not sure what he expected me to say, but this was a relief to him.

'I don't know,' he said; 'I don't think so. Anyway, I don't care.' So I said, 'He's very likely to try it again. Better let me talk to him.'

"Calvin was suspicious at this. 'Who are you?' he asked. 'And what are you going to say?' I skipped the first question, and said, "I'm going to tell him exactly what you told him last night – that if he has an inch of backbone, he'll begin to face things. I know his type, and I happen to know a little bit about his particular background.' Then Calvin asked, 'Do you know a man by the name of Ephraim MacIver?' I said yes, I'd heard of you, and that Montgomery had played the same game with you that he was apparently playing with him – with Calvin, that is. Calvin said, 'I thought as much.'

"Just then I noticed Montgomery with his eyes open, listening, and I said, 'I don't know anything about it, but my guess is, he isn't going to live very long around here if he keeps going the way he is. By now, everybody in town knows what a yellow-bellied skunk he is.'

"Now, I'll tell you, Mr. Calvin surely wasn't expecting *that*, and neither was Montgomery, because he sat up in bed and yelled, 'What do you mean, a yellow-bellied skunk?' and I said, 'Calm down. I meant just what I said. And furthermore,' I said, 'it's true.'

"Montgomery said, 'How do you figure I'm a yellow-bellied skunk?' and I said, 'How do you figure you're not?' and he floundered around with some long story about how Calvin this and Calvin that, and how he himself was as pure and innocent as a choirboy, and I said, 'I've changed my mind. You're not a yellow-bellied skunk at all. You're a *lying* yellow-bellied skunk.'

"All he could do after that was sputter, so I said, 'Look, it's none of my business what you do with whom in bed, but I'll tell you this: All those men downstairs last night have been around; they know North from South, so to speak, and all of it from personal experience. They saw right through you last night, just as if you'd been made of glass. If you were to go out tonight and admit the truth like a man, they'd respect you. Otherwise you're a coward in their eyes, and they'll probably run you out of town. Think it over.'

"'Bring me some booze,' Montgomery said, and Calvin ran down and brought back a bucket of beer instead of booze, but Montgomery was too busy thinking to notice the difference. Finally he eyed me and said, 'What about you? You're a funny-looking one to be telling me these things.' And I said, 'That's where you're wrong.' and he said, 'You mean –?' and I said 'Yes.' Then he had to think a while, and finally a brilliant idea struck him. 'Okay,' he said, 'prove it. Do such-and-such – right now, right here.' I stood up ready to brain him, but I managed to say, 'No. I won't; because I don't even like you; I can barely stand to look at you. You're a *feeble-minded* lying yellow-bellied skunk.' He was frightened then, and we finished the beer without another word.

"Finally, Calvin suggested that they go home, and Montgomery got up to leave. But just as he was going out, he turned to me and said, 'All right, I'll think about it. But first I'm going to find out if you're telling the truth or not.' 'The truth about what?' I said. 'About the other men in this town,' he answered. 'You'll find out,' I said, and he left.

"I followed him around all the bars that night, from a distance, and it was just as I thought it would be. People talked to him a little, of course, but they were all very cool, and sometimes obviously contemptuous. But I guess you know how thick-skinned Montgomery can be, especially when he's drunk, and he was pretty drunk that night. Finally he brought the subject of himself and Calvin up with a good-looking young trapper who'd seen the whole affair the previous night. This trapper said to him, 'Look. You remind me of a man I used to know around here. This fellow loved to drink, but he thought there was something wrong with drinking, so as a consequence he thought drinking was all right as long as somebody else invited him, or if somebody else paid. This meant that whenever he felt like drinking, he'd hang around the bars begging for liquor, which he was honor-bound not to pay for himself. Then, after he'd gotten drunk and had his fun, he'd blame everything on the men who'd paid for his drunk; it was all their fault, not his, and we could never get him to admit that he really liked the stuff, that he really liked to get drunk. No, he didn't like it; it was us who had forced him into it.'

"Montgomery asked, 'Whatever happened to him?' and the trapper answered, 'We had to help him out of town.' Well, this set Montgomery to thinking, and he may be a lot of things, but he's not stupid. Finally he asked the trapper, 'What do you think about drinking?' 'For myself, or for somebody else?' the trapper answered, and Montgomery said, 'Me, for instance.' Then the trapper said, 'It's really none of my business if or what or how much you drink, just so long as you do it like a man, and don't cause any trouble. And if,' he went on, 'you're lucky to have a good drinking partner, don't poke fun at him just because he likes the same things you do.'

"Well, I couldn't have put it better myself. Montgomery loaded himself up with enough booze to last a week, and left; he went to Calvin's hotel and stayed drunk for four straight days, with Calvin and sometimes me taking care of him. When he came out of it, he was more or less ready to face reality, and to accept Calvin's love for what it was, although he made no promise to love Calvin equally in return. They are now living together honestly, I believe you'd call it."

Cyrus stood up and faced away, toward the lake, arms crossed over his chest; the white skin of his powerful buttocks showed in the space between his loin cloth and leggings. "This is a strange way, Ephraim, to begin our reunion – with a long story about your former lover. But I must know what you think about all this."

"What do you wish to know?" Ephraim asked softly.

"How do you feel about Montgomery now?"

"As far as I am concerned, he is dead," Ephraim answered; and he told Cyrus his medicine dream.

Cyrus must have been smiling when he said, "That is the old Montgomery who died. And if you were to meet him again?"

Ephraim stood up. "Even assuming that Montgomery has changed, which I find hard to believe, I couldn't love him now under any circumstances. Too much has happened, my love."

"He spoke of you, Ephraim."

"That's interesting," Ephraim said coldly.

"He feels guilty about the way he treated you."

"He should."

"You sound bitter, my love."

Ephraim sat down without answering.

"He is very handsome," Cyrus continued. "I didn't realize how handsome he is when I first saw him on the river. Handsome, and graceful."

Ephraim sat in frightened silence, watching the broad, strongly curved shoulders, the resolutely turned head. Suddenly he cried out, "Why are you saying these things, my love? Do you want me to go back to him – to leave you, to go raking around in some sickly, painful garbage heap?" He stood up again and continued. "Leave it alone, Cyrus. It's dead." His voice choked.

Cyrus' head lowered. "I'm sorry, Ephraim. It is because I love you so much, and I'm afraid – Somehow it is different this time, and I'm so afraid. This is no longer a game with me. And will you do me a favor? Please don't say you love me until I ask you. No – I'll ask you now, and then later, perhaps, I'll ask you again. Do you love me, Ephraim?"

Ephraim's voice caught as he answered. "Yes, Cyrus, I love you; more, I think, than I have ever loved in my life."

"Thank you," Cyrus answered softly. Still facing the lake, he pulled off his leggings; Ephraim's heart beat wildly at the sight of the thick, muscular thighs, and he undressed quickly, watching Cyrus slowly, deliberately untie his loin cloth and let it fall. The sun caught the fine, soft hair against the glowing white skin of his buttocks, flexing rhythmically as he turned to face Ephraim. Their eyes met; Cyrus' face was stern, and frightened. "Actually, Ephraim," he said, "I want you and love you so much that I will be happy to have you under almost any circumstances."

"Don't say that," Ephraim whispered. Still looking into Cyrus' eyes, he was aware of the huge projection that sprang forth from the darkness of his loins, but didn't look down, and continued to gaze at the agony and desire in Cyrus' face. "Don't say that," Ephraim repeated.

Cyrus looked down, then, at Ephraim's body – the whole of it, but lingering on his full, out-stretching cock. "No," he said, "I shouldn't say that, but it's true; and this time I have so much at stake that I can't bear to be taken lightly. You must know that."

"I understand you," Ephraim breathed. "I feel the same way."

Finally he let his eyes fall to Cyrus' body – the mass of dark hair covering his chest, his lower belly, the jutting penis rising outward from hairy denseness. He took a step forward, and was met by the hard, tense body in a sudden shock of arms and chest and belly, of stinging whiskers on his lips. Cyrus groaned in pleasure as he thrust his tongue into Ephraim's mouth; his body writhed, and Ephraim felt rough, callused hands up and down his spine, on his backside.

They fell to the grass, and Ephraim pressed the huge shoulders against the ground insistently, and rubbed his cheek, his lips against the deep curve of Cyrus' chest, down to his belly. Cyrus struggled up onto his elbows, and Ephraim took his cock in both hands and kissed it on the tip. He felt a hand on his shoulder, pulling tentatively, suggesting that he wait, but Ephraim shook his head and took him in his mouth, and Cyrus leaned back again, giving himself over voluptuously to Ephraim. He came in a choking flash, twisting on the grass, groaning deeply.

Ephraim sat up, watching the great, heaving chest before him, the slowly falling penis. Cyrus was watching him, and his cock began to rise again; Ephraim bent to kiss it, but he was pulled forward, and sat on the broad chest. Cyrus stroked him gently, then urged him farther forward; Ephraim fell to his hands and knees, and was seized wholly, entirely, in Cyrus' mouth. Ephraim shuddered at the unbearable warmth, the miraculous rapture, and weeks of pent-up desire shot from him.

He rolled onto the grass, thinking of the love-making to come that night.

๛

They began building the cabin on the following day. Cyrus had brought tools – an adze, saws and hammers – and they worked together silently, each knowing almost instinctively when the other needed help, and what needed to be done next. Ephraim was calmly happy as he hitched the mules to a log or split and smoothed planks to the floor. Cyrus' muscles flexed like a stallion's as he helped lift the logs into place; sweat streaked his face and beard and chest hair, and he would smile suddenly when he saw Ephraim watching him.

Ephraim let his beard grow, and it came out the color of polished bronze, like his body hair. Cyrus smiled, and did not disapprove.

They slept locked together in the open, and made love as before, and not as Tlasohkah had taught him. Ephraim often passed his hands over the powerful muscles of Cyrus' backside, enjoying the feel of the silken hair, but held back. He knew Cyrus wanted to be loved in that way, and he himself wanted to; yet he waited, not quite knowing why.

They labored for days on the chimney and on chinking the walls; the clay from the lake bottom was a long distance away, and had to be hauled up in iron kettles.

Finally they decided to keep the mules over the winter, and spent another two weeks building a stable and corral connected to the house. This meant also that they would have to cut hay for the winter, and they didn't have a scythe.

Ephraim never spoke of Tlasohkah or Bear-who-dreams, but one day while working on the stable roof, Cyrus said casually, "I met a young man who said his name had been Amatus Sum; he said to tell you that his name is now Amabam-et-amo." Ephraim looked at Cyrus sharply, and saw a sly smile in his eyes. In the same tone, he replied, "That young man has quite an ability with foreign languages. I wonder who could have taught him all these new verb tenses?"

"Ah, yes, who?" Cyrus said, and they both laughed quietly.

That afternoon as they were hanging the stable door, Cyrus mentioned Amabam-et-amo again. "It was that same young man I was telling you about who told me of Singing Heron's letter to you."

Ephraim glanced up, but said nothing. Cyrus was intent on setting a hinge.

"When I learned of the letter," he continued, "I was saddened, and resigned myself to spending the next year or two alone."

Ephraim continued to work silently, not knowing immediately what to say.

"Did you receive the letter before your spirit quest?" Cyrus asked.

"Yes," Ephraim replied.

"Could I ask you what you thought when you read it?"

Ephraim waited until the door was properly hung, and then stood up and began pacing the floor; finally he leaned against a post and asked calmly, "Why do you ask me these things? What do you wish to know?"

Cyrus sighed and shrugged his shoulders, but said nothing.

"We have both loved many people, have we not?"

"Oh, yes," Cyrus whispered. "But possibly this time it is different."

Ephraim went out, pretending to examine the chinking in the walls, and came back to find Cyrus leaning against the wall, waiting. "I think you are right," Ephraim said in a low voice; "I think I knew, somehow, that I could learn what I need to know from you, and from no other."

"In time, we will know," Cyrus said. His eyes were kindly, and serious, and he turned back to his work.

Ephraim watched him working, watched the space of naked skin between his leggings and loin cloth as he stooped, and knew that this was the time. Deliberately, he bent over the half-crouched body and seized it from behind, wrapping his arms around Cyrus' waist and chest, pressing his loins hard against Cyrus' backside. He rubbed his cheek against the swelling back muscles, pushed his fingers down inside the loin cloth and tangled them in the thick hair. Cyrus held still, sighing.

Ephraim found the knot of Cyrus' loin cloth, untied it and pulled it off; trembling, he kissed the dark, silken hair of the cleft, explored inward with his tongue, and then with a finger, two fingers.

He stood up and pulled off his clothes, surprised at his own size, at the pulsations of desire that made him unsteady on his feet. He went out to get a blanket, and returned to find Cyrus naked. He was only half erect; he caught Ephraim by the shoulders and pulled his face to his lips.

"Now, my love," he whispered, and lay face down on the blanket on the stable floor, legs spread, buttocks rising, insanely beautiful –

Ephraim dropped to his knees between Cyrus' legs, filled with an urge to throw himself savagely into the dark and mysterious recess –

Instead he lowered himself gently onto Cyrus' back, hips between the man's thighs, rubbing his belly against the swelling muscular softness of Cyrus' buttocks. He whispered into Cyrus' ear, "Tell me, my love – is it different this time because this time it is to be forever?

Cyrus moaned, "Yes, my love; take me forever."

Ephraim worked his hands under Cyrus' chest, twining his fingers in the thick, sweat-dampened hair. He pressed his belly hard against Cyrus' backside. "This is to be reality?" he whispered.

"Take me in reality," Cyrus murmured, "and take me hard." He spread his thighs wider, lifted his hips off the ground. "Hard; with all your strength and passion, forever –"

Ephraim drew back and placed himself against Cyrus, widening him slightly with his fingers. Then he steadied himself, and drove furiously inward; with the first thrust, his belly met Cyrus' backside. "Like that?" he whispered.

Cyrus moaned again. "Yes, ah, yes – hard, my love. Drive, fill me, oh, my love –"

But Ephraim rested, wanting to prolong the act. He worked his hands under the hairy body again, and down. "I want you forever, my love – your body, your face, your hairy thighs – I need you – you are a place to live. You are not a game, a poem –"

Cyrus flexed his buttocks and groaned, "take me hard, hard –"

Ephraim drew back until all but the head was out, then slowly pressed inward. "You are beautiful, Cyrus," he whispered. Then he moved savagely, drawing almost completely out, and in again, hard – once, twice; then he rested.

Cyrus groaned again with pleasure, sensing the gathering warmth.

"Ask me, Cyrus," Ephraim whispered. "Ask me if I love you."

Cyrus whispered, half moaning, eyes tightly shut, "Do you love me, Ephraim?"

"Yes!" Ephraim cried, and thrust hard from the hips, "Yes!" Another thrust. "Yes! My God, yes!" and he came in a violent explosion of lust and love; at the same time, he felt a warm burst into his hand from Cyrus.

He collapsed on Cyrus' back, panting, writhing still. "I love you for that, and for other reasons equally strong –" Then he added, "I want you to take me in the same way as soon as you wish. But soon, my love."

☙

They completed the cabin and stable three days later, and decided to go to Fort Vancouver on the following day for more supplies.

Cyrus was strangely thoughtful, almost nervous, that afternoon. He checked and rechecked their gear, apparently worried about the pack saddles, their rifles and other equipment; then he suddenly pulled out his cock and showed it to Ephraim. It was soft, yet was the length of his hand and more. "Do you think," Cyrus muttered, almost angrily, "that you can take all of this?"

Ephraim touched its head lightly with his fingers. "Yes," he said calmly. But he wondered, and was afraid.

"Do you want to now?" he asked.

Cyrus backed away. "I've wanted to since I first saw you," he whispered.

"Then now," Ephraim said. He undressed, brought a blanket, and sat down, watching Cyrus, who stood as if frozen. "Take me, Cyrus," he said.

Slowly, Cyrus pulled off his breech cloth and leggins. His cock was hard; they stared at its length, its thickness. Ephraim lay on his stomach and waited, apprehensively.

He felt Cyrus' finger in his anus; he took a deep breath and waited. The head came in suddenly, and he stifled a gasp.

Cyrus paused, trembling.

"Don't stop," Ephraim groaned. "All the way!"

Cyrus pushed, slowly, and Ephraim gritted his teeth. "All the way," he moaned, and felt the huge, unbelievable organ forcing its way endlessly, agonizingly. "All the way –" he gasped. "Hard –"

Finally it was in, and Cyrus lay heavily on his back. Ephraim panted in relief. "Rest now," he choked.

Gradually he grew accustomed to the strange hugeness; the idea of possessing Cyrus, inside himself, grew on him. His spine tingled; the muscles of his backside felt warm, almost sweet.

Cyrus whispered, "I am lost to you, lost to you, Ephraim –"

"Go –" Ephraim breathed, and flexed his back.

Cyrus thrust tremendously, like a bull, a stallion, and Ephraim felt his hips crushed against the floor. Cyrus thrust again, and again, in a grinding frenzy, instinctively, like a huge animal. With a rumbling, agonized groan he fell, finally – shuddering, trembling. "Lost to you –" he panted. "Never before."

That night before going to sleep, Cyrus pulled Ephraim to him and muttered fiercely, "Now I am yours, and you are mine – I'll never let you go. Never –"

❧

They set off light-heartedly the next morning for Fort Vancouver, riding the mules, laughing and singing. Cyrus seemed beside himself with joy, sometimes smiling at Ephraim for no reason, and his rumbling laughter boomed across the mountains.

To Ephraim's surprise, the trail led gently downward, through dense, deep green forests of pine, cedar, and Douglas fir. The sunlight was filtered through the trees, and the air was cool.

While watering their mules in a mountain stream, Cyrus caught Ephraim around the waist and pulled him close, whispering a poem, half laughing, kissing Ephraim's eyes and lips as he spoke:

> What caused these deeply heart-felt sighs?
>   Your eyes.
> My mouth at what sweet fountain sips?
>   Your lips.
> What strikes my tongue with lightning's shock?
>   Your cock.
> And thus my love my senses flock
> To be by yours so sweetly stung –
> My eyes, my lips, my thirsting tongue,
> Your eyes, your lips, your lovely cock.

Within several days they came to the Willamette, flowing broadly and peacefully through a gentle, smiling plain. They left the mules with an old trapper, a friend of Cyrus', and borrowed a long, deep canoe to carry them downriver.

They saw an occasional Indian, a few trappers, and several wiry, sun-browned settlers hoeing their fields. Cyrus bartered with one of these for the pants he was wearing, figuring that Ephraim would attract too much attention in Fort Vancouver dressed as an Indian. He offered the farmer a beaver skin hat, and the farmer accepted readily.

❧

Soon the Columbia's powerful current swept them downstream, irresistibly, toward Fort Vancouver. Ephraim had to squint his eyes against the reflected sunlight, and he found himself wishing, suddenly, that they could turn back. He stroked the water without enthusiasm, almost fearfully; the deep, lunging river carried the canoe along like a leaf, like a dry twig, mindlessly, uncontrollably, rushing in its incomprehensible channel. With all our skill and craft and strength, Ephraim thought, we are only going along with the river, swerving a little bit here, steering a little there, but it's the river that carries us, and carries us only where it was already headed. He shipped his paddle and closed his eyes, letting Cyrus steer, and thought back to the long struggle upstream in the late spring. He had hardened then, and grown, and now he was drifting, almost lazily, back toward the ocean, almost a full circle.

'Ah, no,' he thought, 'not full circle.' Not back to Montgomery. It isn't even the same Montgomery, he thought suddenly, and laughed to himself.

He gazed across the broad, clear, sparkling water, at the high cliffs along its bank, at the white eddies over rocks that jutted treacherously. He laughed again, silently. 'This river,' he thought, 'will carry me to the sea, if I wish.'

Cyrus, from behind him, was calling softly. "My Ephraim," he called, "above the murmur of the waters, what are you thinking?"

Smiling distantly and peacefully, Ephraim turned to face him. "Of the river," he answered, "and of currents, and full circles –"

Cyrus gazed at him for a long time, thoughtfully. "Were you thinking of me?" he asked finally.

"Not directly," Ephraim said, "but you were there, in the back of my mind."

"Did you love me, in the back of your mind?"

Ephraim smiled. "You have asked me," he said.

"Yes, I have asked you. Do you love me?"

"Ah, yes, I love you," Ephraim answered simply, and turned around, and took up his paddle again.

They found a hidden inlet above the town and drew up their canoe. It was late afternoon. The trading post was perhaps an hour's walk. They washed and dressed carefully, and divided Cyrus' money between them, concealing it in their shirts.

"I'm not sure how I'm going to like this," Ephraim said.

"How do you mean?"

"Oh, several things," Ephraim mused. "I've been away from towns for many months, and without really thinking about it, I've just assumed that I'd never go back. I don't think I'll like it."

"I know. The confusion, strange faces and stranger ambitions –"

"And there's Montgomery. Even in spite of what you've said, I can't bring myself to believe that he's changed. I don't trust him."

"Perhaps we should stay together at all times?"

"Well, now, it's not that so much," Ephraim answered uneasily. "I'm not afraid of him. But he's liable to do anything. I simply don't know–"

"Something embarrassing?"

"Perhaps."

"Dangerous?"

"Equally possible."

"We'll keep any eye on him." Cyrus said, and caressed Ephraim's shoulder. "Just remember that I have many friends around the fort, who will stand beside us in any difficulties –"

"Well, in any event," Ephraim sighed, "it will be a relief to have the whole matter settled once and for all."

Cyrus laughed. "It is rather untidy, isn't it?"

"The whole background, all the threads leading into and out of a relationship such as ours – it's always untidy," Ephraim agreed.

In spite of himself and greatly to his surprise, Ephraim found the fort exciting. They found a hotel with a restaurant and a saloon, evidently the headquarters of all the trappers and river men; Ephraim rested on the unfamiliar-feeling bed while Cyrus went out to look for supplies. He couldn't sleep because of the noise from downstairs, so he sat up and stared out the window.

The wooden sidewalks in front of the hotel window clattered and thumped with the heavy steps of woodsmen and men from the town – tall, strong-thighed trappers, lithe and wiry farmers, broad-chested, graceful Indians. He studied their faces, and the ways they walked. There was a cautious alertness in all their eyes – a probing, a searching. If men shook hands or slapped each other on the back or touched one another's shoulders casually, their eyes probed intently at the same time, looking for a flickering, concealed response. Their eyes met, surmising, appraising, asking, sometimes refusing, sometimes tentatively answering. And always a wary, urgent sureness in the hips, in the taut buttocks, in the lazy thrust of a muscular thigh. 'Odd that I didn't see this in Astoria,' Ephraim thought.

He went downstairs burning with strange eagerness, and walked into the bar after checking to make sure that Montgomery wasn't there. He stood where he could watch the passageway into the hotel, in case Cyrus should pass, and ordered a shot of rye.

The bartender appraised him with wary eyes while pretending to polish the glassware. There was a desultory card game in one corner of the room, and one solitary drinker at the bar. Ephraim took them in at a glance, and then stared at his reflection in the long mirror behind the bar.

He studied his face intently, surprised at the change. His beard was much longer now, silken and wavy; in the shadows of the saloon it was buckeye-colored. His face was leaner, stronger, more mature, with sharp cheekbones and a clean, hollow sweep leading into a strong, gently angular jaw. Heavy, wild eyebrows, wide, sensitive eyes. He smiled to himself in self-satire. Very handsome, he thought wryly; and yet, very handsome, just the same.

The bartender moved closer, polishing the bar at Ephraim's elbow. "You new in town?" he asked.

Ephraim gazed at him coolly. "Yes," he answered.

The bartender was a big man, and dark, with black, curly hair. "You a trapper?"

"Yes."

"This is a fine post," the bartender continued. "Lots to do."

Ephraim didn't answer, and gazed out the opened street door, squinting into the autumn sunlight. Tiny particles of dust floated in the still air like flecks of gold. The other man at the bar was watching them covertly in the mirror.

Ephraim swung his gaze back to the mirror and ran his fingers through his hair. He noted in passing that the bartender had been studying him intently.

The bartender lowered his eyes quickly and turned back to his glassware. But soon he moved back again, still polishing. "You come alone?" he asked.

"No," Ephraim said.

"Who you come with?" the bartender asked softly.

Ephraim looked briefly at the black eyes and allowed himself a faint smile. "A friend," he answered. "Give me another shot, would you please?"

The bartender sighed and reached for the bottle. Ephraim strode out to the latrine.

On his way back, he bumped into the card dealer hurrying along the path. "Oh!" the dealer said, wide-eyed, surprised. "I'm sorry." He smiled hopefully and lingered, but Ephraim only nodded with a vague half-smile and returned to the bar.

He smiled again at his drink, thinking, and considered a course of action. Some town, he thought.

A shadow loomed in the doorway, and Ephraim looked up; it was Cyrus. "Hello!" Cyrus called. "Couldn't sleep?"

"Too much noise," Ephraim said.

Cyrus leaned one elbow on the bar and faced Ephraim, almost protectively close.

"Give me a shot of rye, Matt," he called, and the bartender served him.

"You two come to town together?" the bartender muttered.

"Yep," Cyrus said. "We're old friends." Ephraim looked up impassively at the bartender.

"I should have known it," Matt said.

"What's the matter, Matt?" Cyrus laughed. "You look unhappy."

"Oh, nothing's the matter; nothing at all. I just should have known, that's all I said."

"Known what?" Cyrus said. He was trying to control his laughter.

Matt gave him a disgusted look and moved away.

"Matt and I are old friends," Cyrus explained, and laid a hand on Ephraim's shoulder, massaging gently. "Aren't we, Matt?"

Matt grumbled, "Sure. Old friends."

Cyrus laughed, and then spoke only to Ephraim, voice lowered. "I've bought a few things – scythes, of course, several hones, some baling wire, needles, an awl and some chisels. I left it all at the stable. What else, do you think?"

Ephraim arched his back, enjoying the strong fingers on his shoulder. "Nails?" he said.

"Maybe a few. And a bigger hammer."

"We could use a good two-man crosscut, but we can do without one, too. More soap. Tobacco. Potatoes and carrots, but we can trade for them downriver. Paper. Ink. Some twine. Whiskey." He stopped to think. "We could really do without all that, but we might as well get it, as long as we're here."

"Right." Cyrus dropped his hand, but moved his foot so that it touched Ephraim's. Then he dipped his finger into the whiskey and wrote on the bar, "I love you." Ephraim smiled and rubbed it out.

"Shall we get something to eat?" Cyrus said. "I feel like eating something green, and something made out of flour, and some tame meat."

"Let's go," Ephraim said.

Cyrus paused at the door and called to the bartender. "Good-bye for now, Matt. We'll see you later."

"Together, I suppose."

"Of course," Cyrus laughed. "In spirit, if not physically."

Matt snorted, but he had to laugh.

They sat down in the adjoining restaurant and ordered a huge meal. Ephraim wondered at the unfamiliarity of plates and glasses, napkins, forks and spoons. He ate all the bread before touching anything else.

"Matt really is an old friend of mine," Cyrus said while eating, "even though our styles are totally different. He is something of a satyr, and since I'm not, he thinks I live in a perpetual state of timid frustration – which isn't too far from the truth at that, but still it's far from being exact. What surprised him was the fact that I'm connected now with such a startlingly handsome person as you. And being the kind of person he is, he interprets our relationship as an extremely shallow one. So he will make certain suggestions to you. Which you may accept, if you so wish."

"I don't so wish," Ephraim said emphatically.

Cyrus was frowning thoughtfully, but remained silent.

"Wouldn't it put you in a rather – awkward – position if I did so? In his eyes, I mean."

"Not ultimately," Cyrus answered slowly.

"Some people don't perceive ultimates and final ironies," Ephraim said. "And besides, I'm not sure that I'm even attracted to the man."

Cyrus continued eating slowly.

When they finished the meal, Ephraim stretched and yawned. "Now I am sleepy," he said, and stood up. "I think I'll go upstairs for a short nap."

"I'll go with you," Cyrus said. He picked his teeth carefully while going up the stairs. "But I won't stay. I'll be down in the bar."

Ephraim lay down on the bed without undressing, and Cyrus sat beside him. "I think you'd better lock the door after I leave," he said; he gazed down at Ephraim, and one hand was on his thigh.

Ephraim stretched voluptuously and touched Cyrus' cheek. "Go, my love," he whispered.

Cyrus brought his head down; their tongues met. "My love, my Omega," he sighed.

He rose, and left; Ephraim locked the door and lay down again. He dozed peacefully.

Feeling strangely alone, he awoke several hours later. There was water in the pitcher at his bedside, and he splashed his face quickly to wake up, combed his hair, and felt his way down the dark corridor and stairs.

At the door of the bar, he looked inside, then drew back quickly, heart pounding.

Montgomery was there – with Cyrus, and another man who must have been Mr. Calvin. Ephraim turned and slipped out the back door, breathing deeply, found a pump, and splashed more water on his face. He dried carefully, and combed his hair again.

"Well, I can't avoid it," he whispered, and walked into the bar, poker-faced, erect.

Cyrus saw him first. He raised a hand in greeting, and pulled a chair over to the table beside himself.

Ephraim sat down quietly and signaled for a beer. His face, he knew, was flushed, and he held his hands clenched together in his lap.

Cyrus tapped Montgomery on the shoulder, saying, "I'd like you to meet a friend of mine."

Montgomery's head swung around, eyes out of focus, and he looked at Ephraim uncomprehendingly.

"Hello, Clarence," Ephraim said calmly.

Montgomery brought his eyes back into focus, and he stared at Ephraim's face without recognition. Then suddenly he knew. "You are Ephraim MacIver – with a beard," he breathed.

"Yes," Ephraim said.

Montgomery stood up, laughing and whooping, and pounded Ephraim on the back. "Well I'll be! If it isn't old Ephraim! Where've you been all this time, pal? You sure went and got yourself lost, didn't you? Have a beer. It's sure good to see you! You already have a beer. Well, have another one. Hey, Cal, here's my old friend Ephraim. Where've you been all this time, pardner? And how'd you get hooked up with this old carcajou over here?"

Ephraim laughed and went along with the back-slapping, but he studied Montgomery closely, looking for the old familiar clues, the signs of duplicity. And they were there, but Ephraim couldn't be sure of their meaning.

"You sly old dog!" Montgomery was saying to Cyrus. "You knew all along."

Cyrus laughed, freely and openly, but part of him was on the alert also, observing intently.

Mr. Calvin sat quietly, and Ephraim shivered.

'Montgomery is clearly embarrassed,' Ephraim thought. 'The joviality doesn't mean a thing – he just hasn't decided what to do about me yet.'

Cyrus filled his pipe, smiling almost paternally. 'You are sly,' Ephraim thought.

"Many changes," Cyrus observed to Montgomery, "have taken place without your having been aware of them."

Mr. Calvin replied, "Could you be more explicit, perhaps?"

"Oh –" Cyrus shrugged his shoulders elaborately, then lit his pipe, shrewd blue eyes fixed on Mr. Calvin. "I could mention several things, but the most important for now is my relationship with Ephraim, and his with me."

Mr. Calvin's mouth widened in a slow, satisfied smile. "You two are lovers, then."

Cyrus answered, "That is our relationship; yes." He smiled beatifically.

Montgomery's face, Ephraim noted in an instant glance, was uncomfortable, with a trace of chagrin. But he recovered quickly. "How very nice!" he said. "I'm truly delighted." He sounded utterly charming, and Ephraim shivered again.

An hour passed in hurried, convivial chatter, and with no further mention of the past. Montgomery switched to rye and drank quickly, nervously. Mr. Calvin drank beer very slowly, as did Ephraim. Only Cyrus seemed calm.

Finally Montgomery invited them all to his cabin. Cyrus accepted, after a surreptitious, reassuring glance at Ephraim.

∾

Montgomery and Calvin lived in a secluded two-room cabin at the edge of town. It was furnished with unusual care, containing an upholstered divan and chairs, a braided rug, and a wide fireplace. Calvin poured rye for everybody, and the conversation continued.

They spoke of nothing. Ephraim remained silent, almost aloofly distant. Calvin was politely reserved but intensely interested; his steely-cold, oddly handsome face followed every word, every gesture, every glance. Montgomery and Cyrus did most of the talking; Montgomery had a gift of witty incisiveness, and his stock of humorous tales was inexhaustible. Cyrus skillfully kept the conversation limited to generalities, away from the past, and Ephraim began to relax. After several drinks, he went to the latrine.

It was the opportunity that Montgomery needed. He followed Ephraim quickly, carrying a lantern. "You'll lose your way in the dark," he explained.

"No fear of that," Ephraim said.

Inside the latrine, Ephraim unbuttoned his pants and began to urinate, staring straight ahead. Montgomery placed the lantern on the ledge between them, and did the same. Unwillingly, from the corner of his eye, Ephraim was aware of the other man's penis – a vague shape hanging outward. Staring down, he tried to hurry.

"What's the matter?" Montgomery said softly. "You didn't use to act this way to me."

"That's very true," Ephraim said. He finished and buttoned his pants. Montgomery was shaking his penis – a nodding blur. Ephraim turned for the door.

"Don't go," Montgomery commanded.

Ephraim opened the door.

"Wait, I want to talk to you." He spoke softly now, still pretending to urinate.

Ephraim stepped back in, but stayed close to the door, ready to spring out.

Montgomery spoke over his shoulder. "Have you forgotten so soon?" His voice was bland, and half-drunk; he turned slightly, so that Ephraim could see his penis. It was hard.

"Certainly not," Ephraim said. He looked first at Montgomery's penis, then at his eyes. "But it's all over, Clarence."

Montgomery stood as he was and stared at Ephraim. "No, look," he said. "I know I gave you some rough times, but couldn't we get together again some time, like now, for instance?" He turned to face Ephraim squarely.

Ephraim felt dizzy. Montgomery was there, before him; he knew every line of his body. His heart began to pound faster. But he remembered, and hated himself. All the other times – the stupid, drunken, demcaning times.

"Forget it, Clarence. I said it's all over." He pushed out the door and tramped down the dark path toward the cabin.

Montgomery followed, trotting, and caught up. Ephraim turned. "Clarence," he snapped angrily, "you really don't understand, do you? It's not that I'm angry with you or want revenge; it's simply that I don't love you. I love someone else."

Montgomery set down the lantern. "Listen, Clarence," Ephraim continued. "I want you to be happy, so go to Mr. Calvin. Go to him; try to give yourself to him. Take what he has to give to you, of course, but give yourself to him. And try giving yourself to yourself –"

Montgomery's right fist clenched. "Very wise, aren't you?"

Ephraim looked at the fist, and laughed suddenly. "You wouldn't dare. I'd pound you into the ground up to your eyeballs."

A twig snapped in the woods. Ephraim wondered who it was.

"I suppose I wouldn't," Montgomery sighed, and his fist unclenched. He picked up the lantern, and they started toward the cabin. In a very small voice he added, "Actually, Calvin is a very good man."

"I'm glad to hear that."

Montgomery passed a hand over his forehead. "I guess I'm drunk; I don't know how to explain it." He stopped. "Ephraim, what I was trying to tell you back there was that I've changed, a little. Do you understand me? Regardless of what you may think, I have learned to give – learned to try to make others happy. But I can't do it all the time, and I forget, sometimes."

"Your words, back there, were the same as always."

"I know. My words come out wrong, always. That's what's so good about Calvin – he knows when I mean one thing and say something else. Like, I'll say one thing," he started walking again, hands in his pockets, "and he knows regardless of what I say – maybe I'll say I hate his guts – still he knows that what I mean is that I want to –" He paused, struggling for words. "Want to kiss his cock. He knows that."

"He's been through the same thing, Clarence."

They came to the door. "Right. And anyway, what I'm trying to do is say more what I mean, instead of just the opposite." He groaned, and leaned his head against the door.

"Let's go in," Ephraim whispered. "You'll be all right."

"No, wait –" Montgomery's voice was hushed and urgent. "I had a dream about you –"

Ephraim's eyes widened, and he sat down on the step. "Tell me," he whispered.

"I dreamed that I was going to kill you; I was going to shoot you and get rid of you. I had found you out in the woods, wandering around alone. I took aim, and was just about to pull the trigger when something knocked me down, and there was Cyrus standing over me –"

"It was really Cyrus? You recognized him?"

"What do you mean? Of course I recognized him. Anyway, he was laughing fit to kill. You were gone, somehow. And he said something silly. He said, 'You don't know what two and two are, do you?'

And I said, 'Of course I don't. There's no such thing as two and two.' So he laughed, but he was angry, and he shouted, 'Two and two are four, stupid!' and I woke up in a cold sweat, shaking. I told Calvin about it, and all he said was, 'Of course, that's just what I'm trying to teach you."

Ephraim stood up. "He's right, too; and maybe you'll learn from him."

"You understand it too?"

"Yes. Of course I do."

"Tell me what it means," Montgomery pleaded. "For the love of God –"

"I already have," Ephraim said softly, and pushed open the door. Montgomery followed him helplessly.

Cyrus was strumming a guitar when they entered. He looked up expectantly, tensely, then smiled when he saw the distress on Montgomery's face, and Ephraim's significantly arched eyebrows. He continued strumming, and Montgomery poured himself another drink.

Mr. Calvin came in through the front door. He looked first, briefly, at Montgomery, and then at Ephraim; there was a deep thankfulness in his eyes, and the hint of a tear. Obviously, he had witnessed the whole scene outside. Ephraim sat next to Cyrus, happy to have lost a potential enemy. Mr. Calvin sat on the floor in front of the fireplace.

"I would like to sing a song for you, and for me," Ephraim said, taking the guitar, "if you would care to hear it."

"By all means," Calvin murmured. "I am sure it will be most il-luminating."

Strumming the guitar, Ephraim began singing in a soft voice:

I found my pleasure traveling many ways
    and sought a labial, lingual joy at first –
    your lips and tongue set swollen nerves ablaze
    a supine sweetness, warmly rising burst –

And then a darker path and deeper lust,
  a mystic hidden vortex underneath
with urgent lunges entered, spinal thrust,
  a violent writhing in the velvet sheath –

But, lo! Our bodies curl, entwine, unmesh,
  you take your pleasure, mad and wild and free.
At times your wondrous penis fills my flesh,
  for as I enter, so you enter me;
And as our bodies meet and intertwine
  this darkest pleasure seals your love to mine.

Montgomery, who had been listening with closed eyes, stood up suddenly. All eyes turned to him; his hands were thrust in his pockets still, and he was struggling for words. Finally he said, looking intently at Mr. Calvin, "Do you remember the speech you made a month or so ago at the bar when you were drunk?"

"How could I forget?" Mr. Calvin sighed.

"Well," Montgomery continued, "I'm going to make a continuation of that speech, and tell these people what I think of *you*." He paused, and drew a deep breath.

Mr. Calvin looked at him apprehensively. "Later, please, Clarence," he pleaded.

"No, it has to be now," Montgomery insisted. His face was drawn, his eyes wide and nervous. "First, I find you extremely handsome. I've never said that before to you, have I? But it's true, and I've always thought so. Now stand up."

Calvin stood up warily, not knowing what to expect.

"Your face is hard and cold, and handsome, and it excites me; and your body is like your face, and it excites me too. Take off your shirt."

Mr. Calvin looked at Ephraim and Cyrus, hesitating.

"Go ahead, take it off," Montgomery said. "You will be very surprised at what I have to say."

Mr. Calvin unbuttoned his shirt and pulled it off, letting it drop to the floor. His skin was a nacreous white; black, curling hair spread across his chest and down his belly. He stood nervously, watching his lover.

Montgomery reached out and touched Calvin's chest. "I want you to know," he said, "that I think you are beautiful – broad-shoul-dered and lean, and your hairy chest makes me want to touch you, to play with your body, to kiss you. I want you to know this, and I want these people to hear my confession." He paused, stroking Mr. Calvin's chest, his beard, as if in a trance. "Do I love you?" he continued. "I don't know. Perhaps. Probably."

Mr. Calvin was trembling.

"Now," Montgomery said, "I am going to take off my clothes and lie down on my belly or any way you want me, and you will take me. And I'm going to love it, because I want to have you inside me." He started taking off his shoes. "These people can stay or leave; I don't care. That's up to you and them." He tore off his shirt, then reached for Calvin's belt buckle, unfastened it, and began to unbut-ton his pants.

Suddenly, Calvin remembered Cyrus and Ephraim, and looked at them with wide, startled eyes. "I'm sorry –" he said. Montgomery pulled down his pants, and Mr. Calvin was naked; his thick penis was lengthening and rising outward. "Please go for now – another time –"

Montgomery had ripped off his own pants, and was caressing Calvin hungrily, rapturously.

Cyrus stood up. "We understand," he murmured. "And – we are happy for you." Calvin didn't answer. Cyrus took Ephraim by the elbow as Montgomery was pulling his lover to the floor in a straining, panting embrace. Cyrus and Ephraim left quietly.

"That," Cyrus remarked as they walked home in the moonlight, "was remarkable."

"I find it hard to believe, yet I saw it with my own eyes," Ephraim said.

"Do you think they should be in the Loon Society?"

Ephraim pondered the question. Finally he answered, "Perhaps next year, but I'm not sure."

"We should think about it," Cyrus mused, "and consult with Bear-who-dreams."

"Ah, yes," Ephraim answered. "I should like to see Bear-who-dreams again."

☙

Ephraim awoke the next morning with a slight headache and a feeling of uncertainty in his stomach. Cyrus, on the other hand, was the same as always, and he led Ephraim through the supply stores with inexhaustible energy, shrewdly bargaining for the equipment they needed, calmly good-natured as always. He perceived after a while that Ephraim, in spite of his efforts to conceal his discomfort, was losing interest in their transactions, and they returned to the hotel for lunch.

"You should take a nap," he said to Ephraim after eating. "Then you'll feel better."

"I think I drank too much last night," Ephraim commented.

"Ah, well!" Cyrus laughed. "Then we know the illness isn't fatal. Go lie down, and I'll come after you in several hours."

Ephraim undressed and fell into bed, to sleep deeply for perhaps an hour, until he was awakened by a movement, a sound in the room. He opened his eyes and saw Mr. Calvin sitting on the floor in the corner.

"Good afternoon," he whispered sleepily.

Calvin stood up. "You're awake," he said. "I wanted to talk to you. Cyrus gave me the key."

Ephraim moved over in the bed. "Sit down," he yawned. "I'm sorry I can't offer you a chair."

Calvin smiled and sat down carefully, almost gingerly, on the very edge of the bed. "I had to tell you," he began, "that I followed Clarence out last night, and I heard all that went on between you."

Ephraim decided not to mention that he had already guessed. "That's good, I suppose," he said. "Now you know how I feel."

"And I want to thank you for what you said to him," Calvin continued softly. "I think it has made all the difference."

Ephraim smiled. "You can thank Cyrus also for a few things, from what I understand."

"Yes, I've done that."

Ephraim thought for a while, gazing absently at the neatly clipped beard. "However," he observed, "I don't think, in the long run, that we are responsible really for anything. We have helped, of course, but the person who is really responsible is you."

Calvin's eyes were troubled, questioning. "I don't think so. I couldn't have done it alone."

"Ah, no, perhaps not," Ephraim answered. "But I myself couldn't have done it under any circumstances. Do you know what Clarence wants? What he wants really is precisely what you have, and which I have perhaps now, but certainly didn't at the time I knew him, and that is strength and determination. Underneath, Clarence is almost childlike; he needs and wants someone to lead him – someone to help him grow up."

Calvin laughed. His teeth were small, even, and brilliantly white. "Growing up!" he said. "It's difficult, isn't it?"

"You have seen this?" Ephraim asked.

"I think of it all the time. And he is growing."

"Last night, particularly. I was stunned."

Calvin sighed, smiling distantly. "Ah, yes, last night. Perhaps you have had the same experience –" He paused, groping for words.

"Not with Clarence. I am sure you were the first –"

"That's not what I mean," Calvin interrupted hastily. He blushed a deep pink, and looked nervously at the floor. "What I meant was –" he gestured vaguely in the air. "What I meant was – the indescribable beauty of the act – with someone you love – after – well, after everything that's happened."

"I understand you," Ephraim said softly. "It has happened to me."

Calvin lifted his head. "You understand me, and I had to talk to someone who did." He sat in silence for several seconds, gazing out the window. "I hope you weren't embarrassed by – by Clarence's haste."

"Oh, no," Ephraim said carefully. "Embarrassed, no –"

Calvin looked at him questioningly.

Ephraim spoke nervously, wondering if he too were going to blush. "I mean, I found out that what Clarence said was true –"

Calvin continued to look at him; one eyebrow went up slightly, and there was the trace of a smile on his lips. He said nothing, waiting for Ephraim to continue.

"That is," Ephraim went on, "that you are, really, a handsome person –"

Mr. Calvin stood up and walked to the window, staring out. "And so are you," he said. "And I want to kiss you before I leave."

Ephraim lay still, saying nothing. Calvin turned around and came to the bed, sitting closer this time. "And nothing more than a kiss," he whispered. He leaned down and pressed his lips against Ephraim's cheek, and then their lips met, gently. Mr. Calvin's lips were soft and sensitive; he was breathing deeply.

He sat up, smiling faintly. With a forefinger he traced the outline of Ephraim's loon medallion under the sheet. "Some day," he whispered, "when I am one of you, you and I will see each other again."

Ephraim was startled. Calvin shouldn't know this yet.

"And then," Calvin continued, "I would like to see you naked, as you have seen me, and we shall make love."

"Ah, yes," Ephraim breathed.

Calvin stood up, and gazed down at Ephraim with thoughtful eyes. "Good-bye, Ephraim; I am very grateful to you."

"Good-bye," Ephraim answered. Mr. Calvin turned and left, closing the door carefully.

Fitfully and uneasily, Ephraim continued his nap, until he was awakened again by Cyrus' naked body moving in beside him. While running his hands down the hairy, rippled abdomen, Ephraim was seized with a longing to return to the wilderness. "We should go home soon," he sighed, touching his lips to Cyrus bearded jaw. "There are too many people here."

Cyrus' soft breath brushed his ear. "Tomorrow, my love," he breathed.

☙

The snows began in late October, and by mid-November the cabin was covered with drifts; it was a soft, wet snow that packed down hard, and crusted, and squeaked under snowshoes. On sunny days the air was balmy, and the nights were seldom piercingly bitter.

The snow stayed, regardless of the brilliant sunlight, and more snow fell, covering the trees again, blocking the doorway once more.

They set traps for mink and fox and beaver, and the game was plentiful. Most days were spent in hunting or following the trap lines. When the weather was stormy, they stayed in the cabin and cared for the mules, sometimes sewing more winter clothing, sometimes carving furniture.

Ephraim had feared the winter, but he came to love it. Life went on, he noted, in the forest – many birds were gone, but the jays remained, and the chickadees, and the hawks. The tracks of many animals unknown to Ephraim darted across the snow, and he learned to recognize the prints of rabbit, lynx, and mountain lion. Life was muted, and silently white.

Ixtlil Cuauhtli came in November, trading corn meal for venison, dried fruits and berries for beads and sea shells, salt and tobacco.

He brought news from Bear-who-dreams and from Eagle Camp,

and reminded Ephraim that he must begin learning the Indian language. They spent days before the fireplace, endlessly practicing words and phrases. Ixtlil Cuauhtli was patient and intelligent. Within a week, Ephraim could utter some simple phrases – it was very difficult, but Ixtlil Cuauhtli laughed and told him he was doing well.

Cyrus told him of Mr. Calvin and Montgomery, and Ixtlil Cuauhtli looked noncommittal. "We shall see," he said. "Perhaps next summer I shall go to Fort Vancouver."

Before he left, he promised Ephraim to return in the spring with a message from Bear-who-dreams, and whispered that Bear-who-dreams sang of him often. He also mentioned to Cyrus that the tracks of a carcajou – a wolverine – had been seen south of the cave.

"If he bothers you, and you want me to come and help hunt him down, Ixtlil Cuauhtli, just send up a signal," Cyrus said.

Ixtlil Cuauhtli nodded, and left.

In mid-December, Cyrus pointed to a faint puff of gray-black smoke on the northern horizon. His eyes were grim. "The carcajou," he said. "I shall have to go." He began to build an answering fire.

He was ready to leave by nightfall, but decided to stay until morning. "It may take some time," he said softly, "because carcajous are mean, vicious, and extremely cunning animals." Ephraim's heart skipped uneasily. "If one of them decided to stay around for a while, he can destroy a trapper's whole season, just for meanness. And if he decided to leave, he can be halfway to Astoria in one night, I haven't seen or heard of one around here for several years, and believe me I'm not happy about this one. The last time, it took me over a month to catch him, and I was extremely lucky to do so. The Indians and other trappers didn't believe I'd really caught him until I showed them the pelt." He paused, staring into the fire. "I hate to go, Ephraim, but this is serious."

"Can't I go with you?" Ephraim asked.

Cyrus turned to him with bemused, kindly eyes. "No, my love. Who would take care of our cabin and the mules? I will be back from time to time, when I'm able, but you must stay here." His eyes narrowed. "If the creature discovers our territory and our traps, leave them; don't set any more. And if you chance to see him, which is unlikely, shoot to kill. Don't take any risks."

He left in the morning, and Ephraim's days were empty, dragging monotonously into cold, lonely nights. He followed the trap lines anxiously now, watching for signs of the fearful beast. He too had heard tales of the carcajou, from trappers, in Astoria, told in low tones – tales of appalling ferocity, of uncanny shrewdness.

Ephraim slept fitfully at night, alert for strange sounds; he awoke with relief when nothing had happened, only to realize that another bleak, lonely day lay before him. It was the same in the evening, on returning home – joyful on seeing the cabin undisturbed, and quickly depressed by the bitter loneliness.

White, gleaming days followed one another. Ephraim found it more difficult, more pointless, to follow the trap lines, and soon gave them up entirely, leaving the house only for wood, and occasionally to hunt. There was food to last more than a month, and he sensed danger in the air.

On the twelfth day, while hunting, he saw unfamiliar tracks only a mile from the cabin, and he hurried back, deciding not to go out again unless absolutely necessary. He slept in the stable, with a rifle at his side.

The fifteenth day was cloudy, and by mid-afternoon the sun was a pale yellow disk in a metallic sky. The wind rose, bending the hemlocks southward, tearing the snow from their branches, shrieking ill omens.

Ephraim forced himself into frenzied activity. There was wood to be brought in, and hay to be thrown down to the mules. He brought the largest log he could carry and blocked the stable door from inside, and brought more logs for the drop-windows. He propped open the door that connected the cabin and stable, and threw more wood on the fire. The wind howled and shrieked.

Soon it was a gray world. Peering outside, Ephraim saw nothing but flying grayness, and he shivered. It was strange snow – sadly, bitterly cold – and the cabin was covered by nightfall.

In the morning, the storm continued. Ephraim could hear its muffled fierceness coming down the chimney. He struggled to dig a pathway from the door, fearful that Cyrus might try to come, but soon saw that his efforts were futile.

There was a lull at nightfall, but by midnight the sad howling had begun again, and it was the same in the morning.

The afternoon was quiet, and Ephraim tried to dig himself out again, only to find the same stinging fierceness when he broke through to daylight. Nevertheless, he widened the path, trying to slope and pack the sides so that his task would be easier the next day, and to indicate the location of the door. He made sure there was smoke coming from the chimney at all times.

He went to bed early, cold and anxious.

At midnight there was a strangeness in the air, and he leaped out of bed, half asleep, rifle ready. Listening intently, he realized that the wind had stopped. The storm was passing. He peeked out the door, and saw that little snow had fallen in the pathway during the night; the stars were shining, and the eerie night was silvered by an icy moon. He went back to bed, after propping a log against the door – again remembering the wolverine.

Just before sunrise, he was awakened by a muffled thumping at the door. He lay still, listening, then cautiously went to the door, rifle in hand. The thumping had ceased. 'If it's the carcajou,' he thought, 'I'd better have a try at him.' He unlatched and unpropped the door and pulled; a huge, hairy bulk fell inward, sprawling on the floor. Ephraim gasped with fear, and raised the rifle to his shoulder, aiming –

Then he saw clearly – it was Cyrus, muffled in furs, coated with ice. He pulled him inside and shut the door.

The blue eyes opened, the snow-covered beard moved, and the

pale face broke into a smile. "You had the door blocked. I was just trying to figure out what to do; must have dozed off."

"Are you all right?" Ephraim asked.

"Kiss me first, and then I'll think about it."

Ephraim knelt and kissed the big man's cold lips, brushing snow from his beard. "God, how I missed you!" he said.

"Did you really?" Cyrus smiled.

"Don't go away again. I missed you terribly. I was frightened."

"I won't have to now," Cyrus murmured. He stood up. "We got our carcajou." He sat on the bed and began pulling off his boots.

Ephraim remained seated on the floor. "Tell me about it," he said.

"Yes, sir, we got him." His deep voice filled the cabin; it was like a warm blanket around Ephraim's shoulders. "We just plain outsmarted him. Or maybe it was luck, or Ixtlil Cuauhtli's magic. Anyway, we got him." He threw his boots in the corner and began to massage his bare feet. "We hunted that creature for eight straight days, the three of us, off and on, and never laid eyes on him. All we saw were his tracks, and the way he tore up every trap in their line. He'd ruined a month's trapping for them – snares, steel traps, everything – and it looked like he'd about decided to settle down for the winter. You didn't see him, did you?" He began pulling off his parka.

"I saw his tracks. Just once."

"That's interesting," Cyrus mused. "That must have been the day we thought we'd scared him off. But he came back. Anyway, we discovered that he was watching us, actually following us, every morning. There is a ledge above the cave, and sometimes he'd watch us from there, and sometimes from farther off. So we talked the matter over one night, and decided that there was a bare chance that he didn't know there were three of us, because it happened that after I came, Ixtlil Cuauhtli stayed at the cave while Bear-who-dreams and I went out."

He took off his shirt and threw it with the parka. His chest hair gleamed in the firelight, and he rubbed his shoulders vigorously. "So we switched. Ixtlil Cuauhtli and I went out the next morning, and Bear-who-dreams stayed behind. There's a small second exit from the cave; it comes out above the ledge where our creature usually sat and watched us, and Bear-who-dreams squeezed up and out – I never would have made it – hoping to catch the carcajou from behind." Cyrus stood with his back to the fire, rubbing himself luxuriously, and began to unlace his leggings. Ephraim peeled off his shirt and tugged at his moccasin-boots.

"And there he was, just starting down off that ledge after Ixtlil Cuauhtli and me when Bear-who-dreams peeked down. The carcajou sensed him immediately, but Bear-who-dreams got one arrow into his left hind leg, and the animal ran right into the cave. Bear-who-dreams hollered for us, and we came running, just in time to see that Indian go into the cave after the carcajou."

He inched his leggings down his hips and left them there, gesticulating with both arms. The thick mat of hair at the base of his belly stood out from the fly. Ephraim's temples began to pound; he stood up and loosened his leggings.

"Now, a cornered wolverine is probably one of the most dangerous animals you'll ever run into, but Bear-who-dreams didn't hesitate one second. It was the bravest thing I've ever seen. He put two more arrows into the animal, and he was still fighting – still strong enough to crush your leg with one snap of his jaws – when Bear-who-dreams finally smashed his head in with a boulder. He was skinning him when we got there."

Cyrus smiled broadly at Ephraim, and finished pulling off his leggings. He sighed deeply, hands on hips, still with his back to the fire. Ephraim took off his own leggings and stood naked. Cyrus' eyes swept his body, and his broad chest rose and fell. Half turning toward the fire, he beckoned to Ephraim, and they stood facing the flames; Ephraim slid his arms around Cyrus' waist, and felt a massive arm wrap his shoulders. The hair of Cyrus' thigh prickled against his own, and he watched the glowing-pink head of Cyrus' cock burst forth as the cock thickened and grew long.

"This happened before the storm blew up; I left that afternoon, so anxious to talk to you again, to hold you, to see you like this! The storm caught me that night." His powerful fingers kneaded Ephraim's shoulder, and he turned slightly so that their cocks were touching. "I came without stopping; I was worried, and I wanted to see you."

Ephraim's hand lowered, and his fingers tangled in the hairiness of Cyrus' backside. "That was dangerous, my lover; you shouldn't have come, but I'm glad you did."

Cyrus released his grip on Ephraim's shoulder, and brought a rabbit-fur blanket, which he spread on the floor. Standing in the middle of the blanket, he caught Ephraim in his arms and pulled his body against his own. Their beards mingled with a bristling sound as they kissed. Cyrus moaned against Ephraim's lips, "I love you so much, Ephraim, so much –"

Ephraim felt both arms clenched around his back, Cyrus' silken mass of chest hair against his own, the massive penis pressing against his belly. "Love me, Ephraim," Cyrus whispered. "Love me. Your love is the lodgepole of my being, from which all beauty spreads and protects me. You love me, you need me –" His hips swayed slowly, grinding his belly hair against Ephraim. "Do you love me, Ephraim? Don't say anything. Give me your love –" His breath came in hoarse sobs.

Ephraim let himself down, slowly, kissing Cyrus' belly as he went to his knees, then pulled Cyrus down to the blanket in a sitting position, half-reclining. He stretched the length of his body against Cyrus, clutching the hard, jutting shoulders, grinding his lips onto Cyrus' mouth, and then he kissed his way down again, touching Cyrus' nipples with his tongue, pressing his cheek against the thick, rounded muscles of his lower belly.

Cyrus was watching him with agonized eyes, and Ephraim lay face down on the blanket, legs spread, waiting for the fierce lunge inward.

It came.

Cyrus tried to speak, but his voice was a choking gasp.

Ephraim thrust his hips upward, against the prickle of hair, and he was ground back down. He felt the mighty thickness in his body slide partly out, then pound in again thunderously.

Ephraim's life was in the mystic hugeness that reached up for his heart, knowing his axis, spreading his thighs, achingly, breaking – and then Cyrus came, in an endless, plunging burst.

He lay on Ephraim's back, moaning and shivering, quaking from the release of tension. His penis contracted slowly, and finally he pulled out, still quivering, and fell over on the blanket in a heavy stupor.

Ephraim stood up slowly, wonderingly, and looked down at the Herculean nakedness at his feet. Cyrus was covered with two weeks of grime and sweat, his feet were blistered, his hands raw and almost bleeding.

There was hot water in the kettle by the fire, so Ephraim moistened a cloth and began at Cyrus' feet, bathing gently, filled with pity at the blisters. Cyrus sighed with pleasure, half awake, as Ephraim bathed his toes, his calves, the backs of his knees; he spread his legs languidly as Ephraim moved up his thighs, and winced when he touched a bruise near his hip.

He threw his arms above his head, and Ephraim washed up his body to the deep, hairy armpits; the hair lay in damp rings on his chest and belly. Softly, Ephraim passed the cloth across the broad, high forehead, over the lowered eyelids. He dampened Cyrus' beard, found a brush and brushed it until it glistened, and the long hair on his head.

Cyrus half opened his eyes; he watched Ephraim in almost helpless pleasure, whispering half-audible words of rapture.

Ephraim brought two more blankets and spread them over the sprawled, stuporous body. Then he washed himself, quickly, and crawled in beside his lover. Cyrus moaned, and searched for Ephraim's lips with his own, one arm enclosing Ephraim's chest.

They slept until the patches of light on the floor disappeared against the wall. Ephraim opened his eyes, feeling alone, and saw that it was midday. Without moving his head, he looked for Cyrus, and saw him standing close to the fire, eating pemmican. He was barefoot, but with a blanket thrown over his shoulders that reached to the floor. His back was turned, and he was less than a yard away.

When Cyrus finished eating, Ephraim reached out, seized one corner of the blanket and pulled. Cyrus spun around, and then he smiled down, hands deliberately placed on his hips.

Ephraim stared up at the naked body and felt his breathing become deeper.

Cyrus watched him for a short space of time; then he spoke, softly. "One of my greatest pleasures, Ephraim, is watching the lust rise in your eyes, in your body, when you see me naked."

"Seeing you naked," Ephraim breathed, "is one of my greatest pleasures, for you are beautiful."

"You make me beautiful when you look at me, my love." He dropped his hands and walked to the door, away from Ephraim, slowly; his hips rolled gently as he moved, and the two powerful muscles of his backside flexed alternately with each measured step. Halfway to the door he bent over, knees straight, examining a long scratch on his ankle. The muscles parted, and his testicles swung back between his thighs.

Ephraim's mouth went dry. "You are beautiful now, Cyrus," he whispered. "Inexpressibly handsome!"

They ate, still naked, and made love, and talked, and drank whiskey, and made love again, and napped some more. At nightfall Ephraim rose to look for food; looking down at Cyrus, dozing and still naked, he noted a tear in his eye, and wondered at it, and knew that Cyrus was happy. Gazing at the sprawled body, his heart filled with fierce love. The big man's cock lay across his thigh. Bending down, Ephraim smiled to see a pearl-like tear at its very tip.

He brought pemmican, and they ate again, and drank more whiskey. They smoked Cyrus' pipe and sang, and Ephraim was tingling with high spirits.

"I have a poem," he said. "Would you care to listen?"

"Always," Cyrus answered, and stretched back on the floor, hands clasped behind his head.

Ephraim recited slowly, caressing Cyrus' thigh.

You came with the morning star
in the pale winter's dawning.
In the cold, calm winter's light
your love flooded warmly –
naked,
your cock outshone, outglowed
The sun that brief December day.

Within, your cock drove fierily into welcoming flesh
into the several vortices of my self
as, without, the wind's howl,
long and thin,
Rose cheerless over hills of gray.

My cock gave love,
gave in opalescent spasms –
redly circled
by your warm lips, your tongue,
gave at dawn;

then, seeking the dark mystery of your ass
drove joyously past the silken hair,
And darkly circled, gave at noon.

At dusk,
I saw two tears of love
(contentment, exhaustion, perhaps)
in your drowsing eye,
at your dormant cock,
glowing with a sweeter, more tender,

and perhaps
A sadder light than waning moon.

Spring came in a faint green haze that floated through the willows;
streams broke loose, roaring down the ravines, and the brilliant green
of new pine needles flashed in the sunlight. Pale fern leaves uncurled
from the black earth; scarlet and brilliant orange darted through the
tree tops. Ephraim watched with a strange, restless longing.

Ixtlil Cuauhtli came, on his way to Fort Vancouver, and secretly
handed Ephraim a message. Ephraim read, painted in violet on white
deerskin:

Hollow
    my earth, and cold.
    Emptiness and winter.
Come, sweet my love, and plant for me
    the seed.

It was from Bear-who-dreams, and Ephraim's heart skipped, thinking
of the black-violet eyes, the thick-veined cock. His mind drifted back
to the others, to Tlasohkah, to Amatus Sum – Singing Heron would
be waiting for his call, longing to run and make love in the moonlit
forest.

His restlessness grew, and Cyrus watched him with quizzical,
knowing eyes.

One April evening they sat on the doorstep, listening to the
poor-wills, silently watching the first fireflies.

Cyrus lit his pipe and leaned back contentedly. "Soon, Ephraim,"
he said, "I shall have to take our pelts to Fort Vancouver or to Fort
Boise, to trade at the rendezvous."

Ephraim listened, and waited, half guessing what Cyrus was going to say.

"You may come with me, if you wish, but –" He paused, and then
smiled. "But I think you probably want to go back downriver, to visit

old friends –"

Ephraim grunted noncommittally, and waited.

"It will take me a month, perhaps more."

Ephraim watched the fireflies, and thought of the silver nights at Eagle Camp, and wondered. He felt torn and divided.

"Ephraim, my love –" Cyrus spoke softly; his voice was deep, kindly. "I want you to go, and you want to go. What is troubling you?"

"I don't know what is troubling me. Yes, I would like to go. But – I love you, and I still want to go. How can that be?"

"Ah, Ephraim!" Cyrus sighed. "It is the most natural thing in the world. We all want to love and to be loved, deeply and meaningfully, as you and I love each other; but we also –" he laughed softly, "– want to explore, to push ourselves outward, to find newness, new experience, *rinascimento*. That doesn't mean," he added, carefully, "that you will not come back to me, for we need this kind of love too, an inward kind of exploration – the kind of love that grows slowly like the pine tree, strong and satisfying."

"Agreed," Ephraim said. Thoughtfully he traced with his fingertips the familiar and exciting contour of Cyrus' thigh. Suddenly he laughed, slyly at first, and then gleefully. "I was just thinking," he said, "of Amatus Sum, or whatever his name may be by now, and of the games we played." He caught his breath and continued. "Montgomery would make love only when he was drunk or when he could invent some reason for it. He pretended to himself that he was using his lover for some ulterior, practical purpose, when in reality all he wanted was love. Amatus Sum, on the other hand, allowed himself to make love only when it had been defined for him as a game or a ritual."

"Of the two," Cyrus mused, "Amatus Sum sounds like a much more respectable person."

"Yes, he was," Ephraim said. "Montgomery was a sick man. They were both playing games, of course, but Montgomery thought it was reality, while Amatus Sum knew it was only a game."

"Montgomery," Cyrus said, "now is living in reality, I think; but can he learn to play games as you and I do?"

"And what will Amatus Sum do about reality, about real loving, the way we have loved? I wonder," Ephraim said.

Cyrus laughed. "I think," he said slyly, "that from what I've heard, Amatus Sum found very soon that he had no more need for games."

Ephraim decided that it was prudent to ignore the slyness in Cyrus' voice, and the 'from what I've heard.' Instead he stretched out his arms and said, yawning, "Yes, I think I shall go down the Umpqua and play a few games."

"They can be very refreshing," Cyrus said.

"Quite so," Ephraim answered, suddenly serious. "But they will still be games, nonetheless."

Cyrus sighed and asked softly, "You will be coming back to me then?"

"You," Ephraim said with his lips close to Cyrus' ear, "are not a game."

Cyrus turned his head, and their lips met – softly, fleetingly.

❧

They spent the last weeks of April preparing for the trips, mending pack saddles, choosing supplies to take, making new moccasins.

An Indian came through on his way to Eagle Camp. Ephraim recognized him from the previous summer, and asked him to tell Tlasohkah of his coming. Then he wrote a message for Bear-who-dreams:

Awake, my lord, for now it's spring,
Oh, come and lie with me, my king!

The shooting-stars are now displayed
Against the sorrel in the shade

Oh, come, I know a mossy glade
Oh, come with me to dance and sing!

Awake, my lord, for now it's spring,
Oh, come and lie with me, my king!

Lie down, my love, beneath the pines
While I among the columbines
Will sing to you my gentle lines
Of how my love's a wondrous thing!

Awake, my lord, for now it's spring,
Oh, come and lie with me, my king!

I'll shed my shirt and leggings too
Stark naked then I'll come to you
Unhidden from your rapturous view
Within the forest's magic ring!

Awake, my lord, for now it's spring,
Oh, come and lie with me, my king!

Throw off your blanket, naked stand
Before my eyes, my lips, my hand
Your handsome body, burnished, tanned!
Your penis lengthens – let it swing!

Awake, my lord, for now it's spring,
Oh, come and lie with me, my king!

The Indian tucked the message into his shirt, and promised to deliver it.

At dawn on the last day of April, Cyrus was ready to leave. Mist
was rising from the lake, and the air was filled with mysterious new-

ness. They stood before the cabin, checking the last details of the pack saddles, silently examining the cinches and halters.

Finally Cyrus laid his hand on Ephraim's shoulder, gazed into his eyes and spoke: "Ephraim, my love, there is still much that we do not know about each other – many things we have not done, new areas of love to be explored. When I come back, we will be new to each other, and we will experience again the familiar, and create again, and explore our creation."

Ephraim looked down at the ground. "You are always new, my love; always a surprise, always beautiful."

Cyrus stared into the distance. "Perhaps," he said, "I shall bring our friend from upriver for a short while, or perhaps Mr. Calvin. That should be extremely interesting."

"Yes," Ephraim said.

Cyrus filled his pipe silently, and went inside to light it. When he came out, he pulled Ephraim close with one strong arm, and whispered hoarsely into his ear. "You will come back, my love?"

Ephraim rubbed his cheek against Cyrus' thick beard. "I need to go, Cyrus, and I need to come back to you. You are both the old and the new – the old earth and the new leaves – and I love you." He paused, and then asked, "And you – are you coming back?"

Cyrus caressed Ephraim's shoulder, his beard. "Ah, yes, Ephraim. I have no choice." They parted, and Cyrus took the lead mule's halter.

"The middle of June, perhaps?" Ephraim called.

"About then," Cyrus answered, smiling. He pulled on the halter, and disappeared into the mists.

Ephraim turned back to the cabin, sadly, and picked up his small pack of supplies. He put out the fire, bolted the windows and door, and started walking northward.

The mists faded away by mid-morning, and the air itself was blue; ahead of him rose the mountain of Bear-who-dreams, still gleaming with snow. Ephraim's head filled with flashing visions – Bear-who-dreams naked in the soft firelight, the sinewy grace of Tlasohkah, and Singing Heron of the white teeth and the strong thighs.

His blood raced and tingled, and he began to run, springing over logs and streams, leaping, twisting, singing. He felt strong, endlessly strong, and radiant with beauty.

"I may be playing games," he sang, "but, oh! How I will play them! How I will dance, and sing, and love!"

He laughed and sprang onward, leaping over the new earth with smoothly flexing thighs, his brilliant loin cloth fluttering in the spring air.

Appendices

Biography of Richard Love
by Cesar Love

My father was born on October 18, 1927 in Halfway, Oregon, near the border of Idaho. Richard Wallace Love was the third of four children in his family. Both his parents were teachers, and both came from families that had lived in Oregon since the frontier days of the 1800s. Later in his life, Richard Love would refer to his native state of Oregon as "Loon Country." Oregon would also become the setting for two of his novels, *Song of the Loon* and *Longhorn Drive*.

In the 1930s, my father's family packed everything and moved to the Midwest. When my grandfather began graduate school at Ohio State University, he moved the family from Oregon to Columbus, Ohio. After completing his studies, Grandfather Love would join the faculty of Ohio State University as a professor of psychology. Richard, meanwhile, would grow up in the North Columbus neighborhood of Clinton Park, attending Clinton Elementary School and University High School. Parts of his 1971 novel *Frost* are set in the city of Columbus. The novel opens with the haunting line, "DeWitt Frost was seventeen, a freshman at Ohio State, when someone first called him 'queer-boy.'"

While a teenager, Richard spent a summer away in Arizona. There in the southwest, he developed a passionate interest in Native American culture. This fascination, which nourished much of his literature, would continue throughout his life. After graduating with the University High School Class of 1945, Richard enlisted in the Coast Guard. He fully expected to face military combat in the South Pacific, but while he was still in basic training, the atomic bombs were dropped on Hiroshima and Nagasaki, ending World War II.

After the war, Richard returned to Columbus and enrolled at Ohio State University, where he graduated with a degree in sociology, but was forced to return to the military life when drafted by the U.S. Army. Afterwards, when finally free of military obligations, he left the United States for Mexico City, where he studied anthropology.

Upon his return to America, Richard settled in California. In 1956, he began work as a schoolteacher in the Salinas Valley town of Soledad, where he taught at the Main Street School. One year later, at the age of thirty, he married and started a family. The first of his three children was born in 1958.

In 1959, Richard and his family moved to the San Francisco Bay Area; they lived in Berkeley for a year before buying a home in the East Bay city of Hayward., where the novel *Frost* is largely set. Although he renamed the city as San Geronimo in the text, he kept the names of Hayward streets and landmarks, including the Aloha Club, a local gay bar. His novel *Naked on Main Street* is also set in the East Bay.

In the early 1960s, Richard taught school in Oakland and began studies towards a Master's degree in Spanish at San Francisco State University. It was as a graduate student at SF State that he secretly wrote his first novel, *Song of the Loon*; he had been given an office on campus, and he took advantage of the privacy his office provided by writing what would become his best-known novel.

Although he was not a native Spanish speaker, the influence of Spanish literature is evident in much of his work. Richard completed his Master's degree in 1965, the year before *Song of the Loon* was published under the pseudonym of Richard Amory. He continued his study of Spanish at the University of California, Berkeley, where he also taught as he pursued a Ph.D. Richard would also continue to write in secret. *Song of Aaron* was published in 1967; *Listen, the Loon Sings* was published the following year. In 1969, three more novels of his were published: *Longhorn Drive*, *A Handsome Young Man with Class* and *Naked on Main Street*.

1970 was an eventful year for Richard. That year, he separated from his wife and family and moved to San Jose, California, the city where he had recently begun teaching. He also joined the Society for Individual Rights (SIR), a San Francisco-based gay rights organization. In addition, he became a staff writer for *Vector* magazine, a publication of SIR, to which he contributed literary criticism, book reviews, and poetry.

It was also 1970 in which perhaps his most significant contribution to gay literature took place, even though it was a year in which he did not add a title to his *oeuvre*. That year, Richard led an effort to bring together gay writers. Many of these authors had, like himself, written their novels in isolation. The group, including Dirk Vanden, Peter Tuesday Hughes, Phil Andros, and others, named themselves "the Renaissance Group." One of their intentions was to launch a gay publishing company that would treat gay writers and their work respectfully; members of the group felt that they had been exploited by Greenleaf Classics, the press that published much of their work. Although the goal of owning a publishing company did not materialize, the Renaissance Group succeeded – in discussions, essays, and a public forum – in defining and advancing the emerging genre of gay literature.

In San Jose, Richard Love, who had always been a talented teacher, taught English as a second language to students of Woodrow Wilson Junior High and Herbert Hoover Junior High. He also joined the San Jose Gay Liberation Front. The dedication in *Frost* reads: "For my brothers and sisters in the San Jose Gay Liberation Front." In 1974, Richard published his last book, *Willow Song*, a novel of magical realism set in San Jose. He died in 1981.

Cesar Love
San Francisco, 2005

Song of the Loon film poster, 1970

Richard Amory's

Song of the Loon

Exclusive Northern California Premiere Engagement

X-RATED

The extremely controversial nature of the subject material presented in the picture was not without problems in filming. Nude scenes and masculine kissing, so much a part of the original script, has been adhered to in the filming. Good taste and an intelligent approach to the material by cast and crew alike helped to circumvent any possible trouble during location shooting. Much thanks is owed to members of the U.S. Forestry Service for their cooperation and understanding during production.

Opening May 13

at the all new,
completely renovated

NOB HILL Theatre

729 Bush - 391-4798

From *Vector* magazine, July 1970
"Song of the Loon becomes a 'Looney Tune'"
by Richard Amory

When the premiere performance of *Loon* was given in Los Angeles a number of weeks ago, I remember being somewhat miffed at not having been invited – it is, I understand, standard procedure for producers to honor everybody in sight at such affairs – but now I think I know why they didn't. They were embarrassed at the twisted, thoroughly pedestrian job they'd done on my book, and didn't want me to find out in their presence.

It was, however, a beginning of sorts, and I sometimes wish them well.

We stood in line at the Nob Hill Theater for over an hour, in the glaring light of Bush Street, before they let us in to stand in the back. We had to start in the middle of the story, of course, at the place where "Acoma" brings Ephraim to Bear-who-dreams. I first realized something was wrong when Bear, the antithesis of conventional Western, "masculine" logic, opens his eyes – they are a very Western baby blue. Minor details of this sort kept cropping up, and before too very long it dawned on me that the movie was never going to get off the ground. Little things – they couldn't pronounce the name "Ixtlil Cuauhtli" (Nahua, by the way), so they changed it to "Acoma." John says "Susilaw" instead of "Siuslaw." Montgomery shoots an African antelope, then pulls a regulation American mule deer from the bushes, and finally loads a Safeway roast into his canoe. Blind alleys and unfulfilled expectations – who the hell is "Running Buffalo," and why bring up Tsi-Nokha's scar if he won't be identified by it later on? And so on and so on. Brainless music. Cyrus uses bad grammar. Artless cutting.

But I'll give them a medal for bravery. They were faced with a book that was virtually plotless in the ordinary sense and which is very easily misunderstood. It *is* a pastoral novel, as I said in the foreword, as close to the *Diana Enamorada* as I could make it, meaning that the organizing principle is a loonish, poetic bubble several times removed from standard reality; it is not a satire, and it is most definitely *not* sentimental. Throughout, I was trying to widen the range of options open to homosexuals, to take our experience out of and away from the bars and the baths, and to give us something else besides Judy Garland and *Finistère*, while taking a hard, close look at such problems as love, promiscuity, self-image, and with at least a sidelong glance at stereotyping (Tsi-Nokha) and the origins of persecution (Mr. Calvin). All this within the strict requirements of the pastoral genre.

Still, the most important element of the book as far as I was concerned was its poetic distance from reality, which per se has little or nothing to do with the homosexual experience, and Sawyer Productions was unable to grasp this basic fact in any meaningful way. There were any number of cinematic possibilities to draw from – Kabuki or folk rock for instance – but they relied solely on the Trinity Alps to get the bird flying, and it didn't work.

Poor loon.

Jon Iverson showed moments of competence, as did Brad Fredericks, Jon Evans, and John Kalfas. Under the circumstances, Morgan Royce did as well as could be expected. Physically, Kalfas, Iverson and Evans were quite beautiful.

However, I didn't really start getting angry about the production until the closing scene. In the book, I have Ephraim leaping through the forest bent on a summer of dalliance, fully intending to return to Cyrus in the fall, but they just couldn't leave it that pretty. Luke, a young white boy, asks the aging Cyrus what has happened to Ephraim, and Cyrus answers, "Oh – he died."

I couldn't understand the statement at first, and it took several seconds for it to sink in. Then, *Ye Gods! They killed him off!*

Now, back in 1966, wasn't that one of the major novelties of the book, that a homosexual could lead a happy existence and not be made to suffer for it?

Still *Tea and Sympathy* or *City and the Pillar* endings?

Is our art so completely at the mercy of third-rate, unimaginative, keyhole Victorians that we can't say what has to be said in an educated, sensitive fashion, *or even say it at all?*

Do we still have to act like clowns in order to claim our place in the sun?

I say that the movie version of *Loon* is NOT a truly gay statement at all, but rather a distorted, exploitative put-down, and I disclaim any responsibility for the whole mess.

I am sickened, and profoundly discouraged.

From *Vector* magazine, June 1970

Richard Amory needs no introduction to the many readers of his famous Loon *trilogy – Vector is pleased to have this opportunity of presenting this well-known gay author to our readers as he speaks out on the gay novel and the gay writer and the exploitative practices of the straight publishing world. First question, Mr. Amory…*

Vector: How did you start your writing?

Amory: I'm not too sure. *Song of the Loon* was the first novel I ever really finished. There were two abortive attempts previously, and *Loon* grew out of a minor passage in the last one. At the time, I was working on a Master's at S.F. State and somehow got turned on to Gaspar Gil Polo's *Diana Enamorada* and took off from there. The *Diana* is one of those highly erotic and extremely artificial 16th Century Spanish pastorals, which are usually laid in a cloud-cuckoo-land that the author is pleased to call Arcadia, and I thought it would be a perfect vehicle for a gay novel. After I changed the setting to the Oregon wilderness and costumed the *zagales* as mountain men and cowboys and Indians, the next two novels practically wrote themselves, except for certain problems of style, which were largely a process of whittling away – no clocks, for example so time has to be measured by the sun and other natural phenomena; no women, because they bring in a whole host of secondary problems that I didn't want to deal with; (at the time, as I recall, everybody was embroiled in questions as to the genesis of homosexuality, and it was fashionable to throw the blame onto Maw, poor Maw; I consider such preoccupations a total waste of time, and besides, they usually end up as a bitchy put-down of women), and so on and so on. In spite of this I wrote *Loon* for myself alone, and didn't really start thinking seriously about publication until I was about halfway through the final typescript. And then, since I'd had such a ball writing it, I thought, 'what the hell, why not?' and sent it off to San Diego.

Vector: What do you think of the gay novel today?

Amory: Right on. I think some very, very exciting things are happening. Take writers like Phil Andros, or Dirk Vanden, or Peter T. Hughes, or Dallas Kovar (of whom I am inordinately fond) – in spite of some incredible editorial ineptness and interference, we're saying some things that weren't even dreamed of ten, or even five years ago, and *Loon* is already beginning to look dated. No one has written the great American gay novel yet, of course, the definitive work, but we're getting there.

Vector: What about the gay novel of the future?

Amory: Well, let's take a look backwards first. I'm no expert on the gay novel (there is room here for serious study), but it seems to me that up until now, we've had two main types of books, neither of them much to my liking. First, there is what I call the "Closet Queen Novel," a dishonest put-on wherein the essentially gay characters are disguised as heterosexuals. These things are much older than *Who's Afraid of Virginia Woolf*, and probably much more common than the straight world would like to believe. The prototype is *La Queste del Saint Graal*, a 13th century Old French tale about an association between Percival and Galahad, and just for the sake of argument I would like to include *Candy* here, too, because of its perverse, clearly disguised misogyny. Then there are at least two popular writers of Westerns, one very good and one very bad, both deceased, whom you have read as closet queens, and of course, Tennessee Williams. The keynote here is a twisted, bitchy view of women, and why the Women's Liberation Front hasn't taken off on *Candy* I'll never know. It's sheer libel.

Then we have what I call the "Gay Grotesque." This is the whole tiresome series of novels from *Finistère* to *Myra Breckinridge*, also written for a straight public, in which the hero is either killed off in the end or straightened out, or else he's so ridiculous and repulsive that he's allowed to live on in a hell of the author's making.

Neither of these two types of novel does us much good, for obvious reasons. I would like to see, and I think it's coming, a genre written by gay authors for a strictly gay audience, no holds barred, telling it like it is, or should be, and *put out by a gay publisher*. This is the crux of the matter. Some of the editors at Greenleaf Classics may be able to fake it for a few minutes, but they aren't gay, and never quite catch on to many of the things that I for one am trying to say. They always end up looking like Arkansas tourists in Finocchio's, laughing their fool heads off, which doesn't bother me an awful lot because that's their problem, not mine, except that they screwed up *my books*, damn it!

Vector: A while back you spoke of "interferences." Would you care to expand?

Amory: *Would I?* How much time do you have? I'll try to keep it short. Start with what they did to *Song of the Loon*. Near the end of the book there is a poem in *vers libre* that is technically what they call a *glosa* in Spanish – very popular in the Renaissance. What you do is take, say, a quatrain as a point of departure and then write four strophes, each one ending in a line of the original quatrain. Some of them are done on the *Ave Maria* or the *Credo* and so on and get to be terribly sacrilegious, so I took the first four lines of Whittier's *Snowbound* – you know, "The sun that brief December day / Rose cheerless over hills of gray, / And darkly circled gave at noon / A sadder light than waning moon," and proceeded to turn it inside out into a fuck poem that would have curled poor old John Greenleaf's hair, by making each line of the quatrain refer back to a previous sex act between Cyrus and Ephraim. This was no mean trick, mind you, but of course the editor had never heard of *glosas* or *Snowbound*, and hardly even of strophes and stanzas, so out of some entirely extraneous considerations which I can't fathom, they excised two of the sex acts leading into the poem, thereby spoiling my elaborate build-up and rendering the poem meaningless. This is sheer Yahoo-ism, and it took a lot of the fun out of the whole thing, and I'm still jangling.

Then what they did to *Song of Aaron* just surpasses belief. *Aaron*, coming right after *Loon*, was an extremely important book for me and even more so, it turns out, for them, and I am still strongly turned on by the blasted thing, but they blew it. In the original typescript, Avispa was called "sheriff" throughout and it made sense, but big, bold Greenleaf Classics ("We take cases clear up to the Supreme Court!") suddenly got cold feet thinking about how some real lawman in, for example, Ashley County, Arkansas, was going to react to a gay sheriff, so the editor in his brilliance rummaged around in his very limited knick-knack box of Pidgin Spanish and came up with the term, "el Jefe." Now, "el Jefe" means THE chief, so you get lines like "Which sheriff?" becoming "Which el Jefe?" meaning "Which the chief?" and my editor, who is Gringo all the way, thought he was being very tolerant and safe and erudite and ritzy-Latin all at the same time. I could have shat, and probably did. (Try, just once, to use the word "shat" in a manuscript for Greenleaf. They'll change it to "shit" immediately, as they did in *Naked on Main Street*, having no knowledge of the English language and no respect for *you*.)

I screamed like a stuck pig on *Aaron*, so they did a fairly decent job on *Listen, the Loon Sings*, but from there on it was one editorial disaster after another, culminating in the absolute mess they made out of *Longhorn Drive*. In *Naked*, for instance, there was a long passage in high school French based on Corneille's *Le Cid*, and they botched it completely. (It's no trick to copy the letters, one by one, of a language that you don't understand except that they couldn't; and their random scatter of accent marks is the sign of a thoroughly second-rate, Yahoo outfit.) In *Handsome* they saw fit to insert the word "brown" in a passage where I most certainly didn't want it, yet my "the editor," the same "the editor" who corrected "shat" to "shit," failed to catch an obvious lie/lay error on my part. *Longhorn Drive* was the most carefully honed thing I ever wrote, but it came out looking like a game of Fifty-two Pickup. (The real name of the game is Grab the Money and Run, and Fuck You, Queer Boy.) I counted a grand total of *fifty* typos in *Longhorn*, some of them quite serious, like skipping all lines on a page between the word, say, "brush" on line two and "brush" on line twenty-two, and I'm not even taking into account their insanely clumsy re-spellings of words in dialect. (The "the editor's" own dialect, by the way, and I think that says a lot.)

Most serious of all is the fact that they really don't know where it's at with gay people – as I said just a minute ago, they're faking it all the way, and even worse, still thinking in terms of the old stereotypes and screwing up our vision of the world. They haven't caught on to the contemporary scene at all – they aren't liberated, they're merely reverse Victorians, like Jacqueline Susann. There was a rim scene in *Handsome*, and they objected; Avispa calls Aaron "Honey" à la Jim and Huck Finn, and they objected; they downgrade, they stultify, they won't advertise, and they never, ever, give you a straight answer on anything unless forced to. (I didn't know that the movie version of *Loon* was finished or even definitely started until I saw the ad in the *Advocate*.)

Vector: Any advice for young gay writers?

Amory: Yes, indeed. If they are published or in the about-to-be stage, write to me or Dirk Vanden, care of S.I.R., Box 41, 83 Sixth Street, San Francisco. We're both of us damned well sick of some things, and may be able to help them. Other than that, some rules of thumb: Demand a contract, and see to it that it's honored. Don't accept a contract that holds you solely liable for actions under local obscenity statutes. Don't accept first refusal options. If you're in a position to be hurt because of your writing activities, see a lawyer and hang tough. Remember that in spite of their put-downs, your publisher needs you more than you need him. And never, *ever*, sell yourself short, as I did.

When you're writing, do your own thing *but* – remember that the gay public is about twice as smart as the publishing houses gives them credit for. Read everything, in translation if necessary, from Horace and Ovid to Miguel Angel Asturias. Read garbage too, like Gene Stratton Porter and Max Brand and Ella Wheeler Wilcox. And for Christ's sake, *don't write down to your editor! Make him smarten up!*

Vector: Do you see the gay novel developing into a new literary genre and moving out of the "underground"?

Amory: It already is an identifiable genre, let's face it, with roots going back into the nineteenth century if not further. (I don't think the *Satyricon* counts.) However, yes – since the early sixties things have changed quite a bit, and I most definitely do *not* think that *Song of the Loon* was responsible for the change. It would have happened anyway – I just had the good luck to hit the right market at the right time with a groovy little curiosity piece.

Anyway, your question hinges on the word "underground" and my guess right now is that it won't, depending. I am thoroughly pessimistic about some things, and mostly I think the crunch is coming if we don't watch out. Back in '67, I used to see the whole *Loon* trilogy on sale in the local supermarket, and I even saw it briefly in the Student Union Bookstore in Berkeley, but now that GC has come out with its new, red-blinding format, you don't see anything on sale except in the standard erotic bookstores, thus ghettoizing my works in a way that I don't particularly like.

What I'm saying is that publishers themselves are perfectly content to operate in and through the underground, and while it may be safer than having to do battle in every court from Muskogee to Sioux Falls, it tends to stamp our work in a very subtle fashion with some peculiar and undesirable characteristics. That is, once you define yourself as an underground writer, you start conforming willy-nilly and unconsciously to the requirements of the genre – hot sex on every page, sloppy writing, (who's going to complain about the writing?), stereotypes, lots of Fannyhillisms (the "nether lips" school); you forget about trying to say something important, and it becomes like a self-fulfilling prophecy – you're down in the gopher hole because that's precisely where you deserve to be. A vicious circle. This is what I mean by being ghettoized, and it does the gay movement no good at all.

The underground situation may be advantageous to the publishers, but in the long run I think they're playing a very dangerous game. For instance, I don't see a particle of legal difference between *Longhorn Drive* and *Valley of the Dolls*, but by operating exclusively through the underground, Greenleaf might be saying that there is, and that's what sank Ralph Ginsberg. He went out of his way to declare that "Eros" was obscene, and thus convicted himself.

This is a roundabout way of saying that I don't have a crystal ball. It will all depend on the publishers and their own self image, and on the writers, and on how much more bullshit we are willing to take. I for one have published my last novel through Greenleaf Classics, Inc., believe me. It keeps coming back to the same problem, doesn't it? The only real solution is going to have to be gay all the way – authors, publishers, and audience; no more outside bullshit and exploitation, forcing us to perform like trained monkeys …

Vector: What are you working on now?

Amory: Oh, something contemporary and very East Bay – I really, sincerely *dig* the East Bay, from Berkeley and Oakland out to Pleasanton and down to Milpitas – and I ought to be finished by the end of July, I hope. We'll see.

From *Vector* magazine, July 1970
"Now is the time, the Walrus said, to speak of many things…"
by Dirk Vanden

I would like to add my two cents' worth to the comments made by Richard Amory in last month's *Vector*. My response to his interview was that, as far as he went, he was "Right On!" But he didn't go far enough.

To my way of thinking – knowing what both Richard and I have gone through with those people – Greenleaf Classics and all the rest of their ilk, got off extremely lightly. (For example, Richard neglected to mention that, in order to get *Song of the Loon* published, he had to sign over all rights to the book, including motion picture rights, and for this received the staggering payment of $750! No matter how many printings the book goes through, and no matter how much money the movie makes [at $5 per seat in S.F.] Richard Amory will not receive one penny more than that original $750.)

I think it is high time we let gay readers know just who gets the benefit of all that money they're spending on gay novels – and now on movies made from those novels (it sure as hell ain't the writers!) – and to let gay writers know at least some of the pitfalls that lie ahead of them if they intend going "underground" for publication.

Also, I think it is past time for us to put some very serious thinking into exploring the current and future status of the gay novel. I'm very disturbed by the crap being foisted off on us, both by the publishers and by supposedly good gay writers themselves.

I'm also disturbed by the welcome reception granted to this crap by readers who seem to feel, "Well, at least it's something," – or even worse: "If it's gay, it's good." This body of trash has become *our literature*, friends. Think about that for a minute.

I call myself a "Pornographer." I do this not because I enjoy the distinction, and not because I am proud of the fact, but because, like it or not, that's what I am. That's what I've been forced to become by the good folks down at Greenleaf/Phoenix/Embers/etc./etc., in San Diego. My reputation as a writer – whatever that may be – was established by what Greenleaf contemptuously calls "Fag-Hots," and in order to continue attempting to earn a decent living (without having to resort to selling toilets at Sears) I've had to continue along lines which they drew up for me.

[...]

Just step inside your Friendly Neighborhood Dirty Book Store and look around (or glance once again through that mailer you got last week). Is that truly the "New Gay Image" you see? Does it reflect in the slightest degree the humanized homosexual – or "homophile" – which so many have worked so damned hard to achieve? Can anyone believe for one minute that the battle for gay civil rights could be helped in the least by a display of titles such as *The Leather Queens, Pot & Pansies, Cocksure, Copsucker, The Mother Truckers, The Fag End, Mr. Fancy Panties*, etc., etc., *ad* absolute *nauseum* – with all of those grotesque drawings and snapshots on the covers (and now *inside* the novels as well)?

It well may be that the authors of the above-mentioned opuses have worked hard and long to include something of "redeeming social value." (I know I did.) They may have labored like hell to make their heroes believable human beings, working hard at their jobs, worrying about taxes, helping little old ladies across streets, loving dogs (besides poodles) and cats (besides Persians) in addition to being big-peckered truck drivers and farm hands. But what good has it done if the editors blue-pencil those heroes' humanity right out of existence? I wish I had space to detail all of the cuts GC's editor made in my novels – whole sections of exposition cut out, vital parts of the climaxes sheared off – and then all the "pulsating purple cockhead" *additions* he made to patch up the gaping holes – all without one word to me!

And those ridiculous titles; I myself wouldn't look twice at a book called *Who Killed Queen Tom?*! How much humanity can a writer sneak into a manuscript (praying the editor won't notice it), which must not, in most cases, go over 200 pages? (The length of an average "regular" novel [detective, science fiction, etc.] is around 300 double-spaced typewritten manuscript pages; a "modern/psychological" novel may run up to, or beyond, 500 manuscript pages. But not underground gay books! If they go past page 200, chances are excellent that they won't once the editor has spent fifteen minutes on them.)

[...]

Most authors published by the major houses spend from six months to several years working on a novel. But a gay writer working for an underground publisher can't afford to take even six *weeks* for his contribution to our literature. He can't afford it because (again I quote from a letter from GC): "Our usual sum for regular manuscripts is around $500. For our higher quality lines such as GL, which deals with homosexuality, we pay $600 and up... Our usual procedures to not involve royalties, however, unless the book is *extremely* exceptional." (*Song of the Loon* was exceptional enough to open the doors into gay book publication for Greenleaf Classics; it was exceptional enough to stay on the stands for *four years*; it was exceptional enough to be made into a nationally distributed motion picture; but it was not considered exceptional enough to pay its author any royalties.)

[...]

If a gay writer doesn't have a full-time "regular" job, isn't being kept, or doesn't have an inherited bank account, he is forced to put out one potboiler after another just to keep the rent money coming in. How the hell can he possibly keep up the quality of his writing, let alone waste his time worrying about "heavy" original plotting, at "$600 and up ..."? (The highest price I've ever heard of a Greenleaf writer receiving is $1,250 – which would just barely cover expenses for six weeks of full-time work.) With prices and schedules like that, the temptation to follow a pat formula has become too great to resist. Change the names of the characters, shift the scene from the suburbs to a Midwestern farm, and – Write It Again, Sam! But quickly! (Ever wonder why so many books sound the same?)

You may be wondering at this point why the writers do not simply change publishers, or stop working for underground houses altogether. It's simple. No other underground publisher has as wide a distribution as Greenleaf. No other will give contracts for royalties – unless, of course, the book is "exceptional" (I was fortunate that Frenchy's Gay Line considered my writing exceptional). And very few are willing to spend any money for advertising.

[...]

Let me quote from two manuscript reader reports which were forwarded to me when *The Leather Queens* was returned for rewriting (along with GC's offer of $750 for the book; it was later "completely re-evaluated" and they raised their offer to a mind-boggling $800): "Very hot fag stuff; well plotted in so far {sic} as story development or 'suspense' is concerned ... style is good, with considerable 'literary quality' and the content includes shock-type sado and maso, al la de Sade [sic] ... [The hero] gradually comes to realize he's fag. He goes to the limits of degradation in the fag world in the course of the story – really hot stuff." And the second report: "Starts well, but not with immed fag hots. A *good* novel feel to it... Appears to have adequate fag hots once it gets going."

It is my personal conviction that no matter how "offhanded" a man is when he calls me a "fag" (or my writing "fag hots"), that man is insulting me (*and* my work, *and* my readers). And the insult begins to grate very deeply when that man happens to be making money off my hard work. The term "fag" when used by a heterosexual (or even a homosexual for that matter) is not innocent, no matter how offhanded it seems; it reflects the same old condescending attitude, the same disgusting overtones of "queer" and "pervert" and "degenerate" by which "right-thinking" heterosexuals attempt to maintain their supposed superiority to homosexuals.

It is quite true that – although *The Leather Queens* would come off like *Pollyanna's Picnic* if compared to, say, *Naked Lunch* – some of the final scenes got pretty wild; but there was a purpose to the wildness beyond giving the reader a thrill: In the climax of the original manuscript, the hero goes to an S&M pot-orgy, where, high, drunk and angry/unhappy, he flips out and almost kills someone. Thereby he is shocked into realizing that his is not cut out for the S&M "games" – there is still too much repressed hostility in him; but one realization leads to another, and he is finally able to admit his love for another man, and thus to settle down with him. Unfortunately my editor, like his manuscript readers, missed the point entirely; he cut about five pages of that climactic scene (including the almost-killing – the whole damned point of the thing) and reduced the episode to what *he* thought it should be: Pointless "degradation" – which he equated with *"really hot fag stuff."*

His choice of the title was another blinding example of his attitude: In the book I made a definite point of the fact that the S&M crowd did not like to be called "Leather Queens," so of course it was published as *The Leather Queens!* The book, incidentally, became a bestseller for a while (until GC withdrew it for some unfathomable reason), but not because of sales to the S&Mers; most of those that I've talked to refused to even glance through the book because the title insulted them.

[...]

Let me just make it clear that I am no more against the sex novel (an out-and-out jackoff book) than I am against sex itself. The Scandinavians have proved – to any reasonable person's satisfaction – that pornography lowers rather than raises the sex-crime rate. I am convinced that jackoff books act as a safety valve and should be legally available to any *adult* (that's *a-d-u-l-t*) who wants to buy and read them. I do not believe, however, "erotic literature" needs to be the sniggering trash that it is in a sickening number of current gay novels; it *can* be well written, ans thereby even more erotic (and I don't mean artsy-fartsy writing; gutsy stuff can be well written).

From *The Advocate*, **August 19, 1970**
Plight of Gay Novelists: Who gauges market correctly, publishers or writers?
by Larry Townsend

San Francisco
On June 15, 1970, a meeting took place in the quarters of the Society for Individual Rights (SIR), which may herald the beginning of a new era for homosexual writers.

Those of us who are gay, who write stories about gay people, directed towards a basically gay readership, are rapidly approaching a new self-realization, as well as an equally new awareness of our own responsibilities.

As in any social movement, whether it be revolutionary or – like ours – an attempt to bring about necessary humanistic changes within the framework of our existing culture, writers must form an integral part of the movement's core. It was toward both these ends that SIR held its symposium.

On the panel were: Richard Amory (*Song of the Loon*), Dirk Vanden (*Leather Queens, I Want it All*), and Phil Andros (*My Brother, the Hustler*). In an attempt to bring the Los Angeles writers into their group as well, Vanden spoke to me on the phone a couple of weeks before the meeting and urged me to attend. I did so and was most cordially recognized and introduced from the audience. There were a little over 200 people present.

Writers who were not able to attend, but who had been contacted in an attempt to ascertain their views, included: Douglas Dean, Carl Driver and Peter T. Hughes, among others. Thus a majority of the better known West Coast contributors were either present or represented in spirit.

Forced Into 'Adult' Market

Under discussion was the future of the gay novel, and this involved an attempt to explore several ramifications of our present peculiar situation. Because of the difficulties in persuading standard publishers to produce books with frankly homosexual themes, most of us have been forced into the "adult" or "porno" market. None of us are overly pleased with this, as it restricts our range of expression. As Dirk Vanden noted, we are limited to an exposition of 50,000 to 65,000 words – too short for proper development of characters and plot, especially when it is necessary to devote approximately twenty per cent of our text to "hots" (sex).

The financial returns on these books are likewise insufficient to permit a professional writer – one who makes his living completely or almost completely from his writings – to spend the time he otherwise would on each effort. The net result is a series of stories with less literary merit than we want to see within the covers that bear our names.

Phil Andros gave quite a long, articulate statement on the writers of the past, where he noted the problems inherent when the reverse of the present situation was the norm. Back in the thirties, forties, and fifties, a gay writer might occasionally find his way into print with a story about homosexual protagonists. But he was then constrained to allude only delicately to sex that occurred between the men. Sometimes, he was even forced to mask his story by casting one of the lovers as a woman. Those who "knew" could read between the lines; anyone else would miss the point entirely.

When *Song of the Loon* hit the market in 1966, it revolutionized many previously held concepts. Because no serious governmental action interfered with its distribution, it opened the doors to what has now become a new "cultural standard." A rush of books, some of them quite tasteless and poorly written followed rapidly on the heels of the *Loon's* successful distribution.

But it did not take long for this previously thirsty market to become saturated. Readers were soon demanding books with stories and believable characters who did more than flop into the sack for page after page, *ad nauseum*. Emerging from this situation, we have our current assortment of stories and writers with whom many readers are familiar.

New Hope
Our problem now, and the problem we discussed in San Francisco, is: *Where do we go from here?* At the moment, the future seems a bit nebulous, although the hardcover publication of Gordon Merrick's *The Lord Won't Mind* would seem to offer a potential alternative. This book is now a best-seller, with sales approaching the 30,000 mark. It is distributed through the regular (non-porno) channels, although it is frankly homosexual and every bit as explicit as anything any of us have written. Just as *Loon* changed the market four years ago, this new book may open the doors which have continued to be closed. Let's hope it does.

Commercial considerations must always be a serious determinant of what is written and published. In this we must look to our fellow Gays for both support and guidance. Many of you enjoy a book designed for "one-handed" reading. Others prefer something to stimulate the higher centers as well. There is now a core of authors who are capable of giving the reader what he wants, once we solve the dilemma of publisher-distributor. To us as writers, however, remains the question: *How do we best serve our community?* Reverse communication is nearly impossible, because of the fearful attitudes on the part of our sequestered, closeted brethren.

How do we reach them to find out what they want? Once we've written it, how do we tell them it's out and waiting for them? Publications like *The Advocate* are a great help, but there are too many of our people scattered all across the country who are afraid to buy or subscribe to a gay newspaper. Many more don't know about it. And these are the very people who should be reached and inculcated into the "movement."

Want Improvement

At its meeting, SIR took a sampling of opinion and readership habits from the couple hundred people who attended. While this would be an inconclusive (because of size) and biased ("aware" group) sample, the results should still be interesting. By a show of hands, however, it was made very plain that the audience desired a general improvement in the quality of gay stories available to them. Is there a publisher with the courage and foresight to recognize this?

That is our dilemma. Perhaps the answer will come quickly, perhaps not. At the moment it is impossible to say.

What we produce in the future will depend on the buyers' responses, which in the end will prove the best – and only – true measure of what you want. Regardless how fast they come about, each subsequent stage in the development of the gay novel should prove very interesting indeed.

From *GAY* magazine, October 26, 1970
"Coming Together (The Beginning of ????)"
by Dirk Vanden

It may have been genius, or just plain dumb luck, or something somewhere between those extremes, which resulted in publication of *Song of the Loon*, back in 1966; Richard Amory insists it was pure luck, and I know both those who would argue with him and those who would agree. But whatever the reasons, *Song of the Loon* was the right book at the right time, and became almost an "overnight classic," and there are a great many gay writers, myself definitely among them, who owe Richard Amory a debt of some sort. Publication of *Song*, plus the other two books which make up *The Loon Trilogy* (*Song of Aaron*, and *Listen, the Loon Sings*) changed the whole ball game for underground publishers, gay books, and perhaps even gay life itself. Without doubt, it put its publisher, Greenleaf Classics, Inc., on the map as far as gay books are concerned. In the five years since the *Loon* books were published, Greenleaf Classics has grown like a weed, to the point where it now controls or influences a majority of all gay books published in the U.S. today; it is the pace-setter, the price-setter, the policy-setter, and if for no other reason than the tremendous number of gay books it publishes, the leader in the "Fag-Exploitation" game – but we'll get to that momentarily.

It was because I had read Richard's first three books (he has since published three more: *Longhorn Drive*, *Naked on Main Street*, and *Handsome Young Man with Class*) that I sent one of my own books to Greenleaf three years ago, not realizing I had confused the philosophy expressed in the *Loon* books with a certain "ethical understanding" on the part of the publisher. It took me a long, hellish, ulcerous year to understand my mistake, and by then I had written three more books for Greenleaf. Almost a year after I'd signed the all-rights release on the back of their check for $800, my first book appeared on the stands as *Who Killed Queen Tom?* bearing as little resemblance to the original story as the new title did to my *Tom, Tom, the Piper's Son*. The day I received my *two* "complimentary" copies of that travesty was the day I realized I'd been a trusting and credulous fool; that was also the day I stopped writing for Greenleaf. But through all my own problems with them – my futile battle to get contracts for royalties, or at least something more than $800 – $850 per manuscript; my discovery that my editor and his manuscript-readers referred to gay life as "the fag world" and to gay sex in the books as "fag hots," and so on, and so on – through all of this, it never occurred to me that Richard Amory might have fared as badly as I. His name, to me, at that time, was synonymous with Greenleaf; as I watched his new books appear on the stands, I imagined him getting richer and richer while I worked my ass off just making enough money to pay the rent.

Then in March of this year, a west-coast gay magazine published an interview with me in which I briefly mentioned just a few of my complaints against my ex-publisher. To my happy surprise, the first response I received was a letter from Richard Amory himself, beginning: "I read your interview yesterday ... and have been jangling ever since. To put it bluntly, I think some people ought to get together and *do* something about (our mutual editor) and Greenleaf Classics. I have had six novels published by them ... and my list of woes, all stemming from (that editor's) cute, old-style, essentially anti-sex attitudes, is going to sound very familiar ..."

We got together shortly afterward and I discovered that not only had Richard fared worse than I, but because of his complicated personal circumstances he was not even vaguely aware of his books' tremendous nationwide popularity. Inconceivable as that seems, it was true – and to an extent is still true; he still refuses to believe that, as Greenleaf so proudly proclaims, *Song of the Loon* has sold "more than 2,000,000 copies." In the five years since its publication, I was the first person to ask him to autograph the book which revolutionized underground publishing! Because of those personal circumstances, he had been almost completely out of the mainstream of gay life, so he'd had no way of knowing the impact his first three books had made on the gay public – and his editor hadn't bothered to tell him! As a matter of fact, Richard autographed my copy of *Song* only three days after discovering that his book had been made into a movie – and that was two weeks *after* its "World Premiere" in Los Angeles!

My friend and I took Richard to see "his" movie when it opened in San Francisco. (The theatre manager said "Oh," when I told him the author would be at the opening. So, like everyone else, Richard Amory stood in line for an hour in the bright glare of the streetlights and the marquee bearing his name, while people in the apartments opposite stared and pointed and giggled and cruised.) Then several days later, after he had stopped "jangling" enough to discuss things objectively, we got together to record this exclusive interview for *Gay*:

Vanden: How does it feel to be re-exploited on *Song of the Loon*?

Amory: About the same as it has all along. Shitty. I'm used to it. I should be, I guess, after five years with those people.

Vanden: Now that you've had a chance to calm down, how do you feel about the movie?

Amory: I'm only sure of one thing, Dirk, and that is that I want to publicly disclaim any and all responsibility for that thing. They're using my name and my title – and I can't stop them from that – but the movie has nothing whatever to do with my book.

Vanden: Why can't you stop them? Isn't there some way you could get an injunction, or sue …?

Amory: No way. They own all the rights to the first book, and you can't copyright a title, or a pseudonym for that matter. No, the only thing I can do is tell as many people as possible, "Don't waste your time or your money." And that's not sour grapes – it's a *bad* movie.

Vanden: There was something that hit me, mid-way through the picture – as you sat there cringing and muttering, "What are they *doing*? What the hell are they doing???" – and that was, at six bucks a head, there were enough people sitting in the theatre right then to have made up the entire amount Greenleaf paid you for the book – seven hundred and fifty dollars!

Amory: True. When I stop being angry, it's almost funny.

Vanden: Here the book has been on the stands for five years, has sold – according to Greenleaf – over two million copies, has been made into a – what they claim is a full-length motion picture – and all you got out of it was seven hundred and fifty dollars. When you talk about exploitation, that has to take some kind of prize!

Amory: You know, when I saw those ads and realized that the movie had already opened, I wondered why I hadn't been invited to the "Gala Premiere"; I think that hurt about as much as the exploitation thing. But I understand now – they were embarrassed. And they knew damned well what my reaction would be. They were probably worried that I'd ask Gay Lib to picket the theatre. Come to think of it, that's not such a bad idea.

Vanden: You didn't know about the movie until *after* it had already opened?

Amory: Nope! Oh, (my editor) had hinted about it, maybe a year before. On one of his letters he added a postscript – just one sentence saying something about some movie company wanting to do the book as a film. Naturally it excited me – even though I knew I wouldn't make a penny on the film. But, what the hell? *My book* as a movie – you know? So I asked him in my next letter: "What's going on?" He didn't answer. I kept asking him – over and over and over – but he still hasn't answered.

Vanden: I had the same editor, so I know what you mean. You write a dozen letters trying to find out something very important and you finally get a snotty little note saying, in effect, "Buzz off, Faggot, and stop bothering me!"

Amory: God, don't I know it! I wrote – at least five letters, and finally had to threaten legal action, just to pry loose a royal statement on *Aaron* and *Listen* – just a *statement*! And since then, not a word. I'm still trying to get them to send me a copy of the deal they made with Sawyer Productions on the movie.

Vanden: What good would that do if you sold the book outright?

Amory: That was *Loon*. I've got contracts on all the others – for all the good it's done me. In the ads for the movie, Sawyer claims to own the rights to the entire *Loon Trilogy*, and if it's true, I want to know about it. My contracts allow Greenleaf to act as my agent for things like foreign publication and movies, but they don't allow them to sign over my rights and not tell me – or not pay me. By now, of course, (my editor) knows I've written my last book for him, so he hasn't got anything to gain by placating me – which means simply telling me what's going on with my own books. I've put up with this same kind of shit for five years, but you get to a point where you say to yourself, "This is *my* self-respect that's involved here," and you have to make a decision – either stand up and fight, or sit back down in the horseshit and let it pile deeper and deeper. Well, I've reached that point. They've exploited me, they've fucked up all six of my novels, one way or another, and now I'm through with it! I'm through talking and writing letters and asking questions.

Vanden: It sounds like you're turning militant on us.

Amory: Goddamnit, you've got to! You can along kidding yourself that things are getting better, but, man, one day you wake up and you see that it just isn't so! You think, "Well, even if I am writing things to their formula, still I'm saying something important. Even if they cut this or add that, still it's something I wouldn't be able to say without them." But that's bullshit! It really is. Because once they put their trademark on something, that's it – the scarlet *A* right here on your forehead – it's ghettoized, underground crap!

Vanden: Except in this case, it's the scarlet F – for Faggots.

Amory: Right. Right. That's how they think of us.

Amory: The people at Greenleaf remind me of the classic dirty old men selling fuck-pictures in dark alleys. Sniggering out behind the outhouse about "queers and rears." They have no real knowledge of, *or* understanding of, *or* sensitivity to the gay person's needs or circumstances. What's more, they don't *want* to understand – even if they could, which is doubtful. Look at what they did with the movie. I don't know if the people who made it are gay or straight, but the end result is the same – there are gay exploiters who are every bit as bad as the straight ones – worse, in fact, because they know better!

Anyway, the whole point of the book was that the hero didn't *have* to die or commit suicide, that he could go on living with a male lover with whatever compromises they had to make in the relationship about infidelity and jealousy – but what happens? After this whole buildup of getting Ephraim to where he could accept Cyrus's love - BANG! – they kill him off! You wonder if they even looked at the book when they adapted it. I take that back – they obviously looked at it because they lifted a lot of the dialogue straight out of the book, out of context, without referents, without anything to make it make

245 Appendices | 245

sense. But I sure as hell didn't write that last line: "Oh, he died."
Shit!

Here's the thing: they've never got beyond the back-of-the-out-house mentality regarding sex, gay or straight. They really believe sex is funny, especially gay sex. They've discovered it brings them in potfulls of money, so they traffic in it, but they really believe that two guys making it is hilarious. And if you as a writer don't make it knee-slapping enough, they add or they cut so it comes out pointless or dirty – and funny as hell – *to them*. And that's what disturbs me. I mean, I'm not *that* funny, and my lovemaking isn't that funny. But as long as gay writers keep on writing for them, and as long as gay readers keep on buying from them, it will never occur to them that everyone isn't having a grand old time giggling about reading about cocks and assholes and sucking and fucking.

And, when you really start thinking about it, there is no way in the world to say something important when you have to work through such people. There is no way they can possibly comprehend the sort of attitude which has arisen, particularly among young people, since the early sixties. There's a beautiful sort of free-swinging, open acceptance of sex and love – which I think is so healthy and so beautiful! But to dirty old men, a young person with that sort of attitude automatically gets lumped with the queers – as a "hippie" – and then they slap their knees and giggle some more.

Vanden: Don't you feel that a lot of gay authors actually help perpetuate this attitude – by writing books that make gay people and gay sex appear to substantiate the "funny" or "sick" image?

Amory: Of course! There are still a great many gay people who feel that way about themselves. But they're dwindling. They're vanishing. There's a whole new thing happening. You talk to twenty-year-olds, the student generation – a fantastically bright and lovely bunch of people who are getting their priorities straight. You tell them you're gay and they say, "Who cares?" They may be predominantly straight, but they don't give a good god damn whether you suck cocks or not – as long as you don't try to hassle them into converting. If they like you and feel like making it with you, they will. No problems. No hang-ups. And, personally, I think that is healthy.

Vanden: If something were to happen – if you were able to write what you wanted to, and get it published, without interference from the dirty-old-men publishers – would you cut down on the sex scenes or what?

Amory: Good lord no! Our sexual orientation is the major difference between ourselves and the average guy on the street. And that's got to be reflected in the gay novels. We want to approach real sex honestly, so we've got to approach fictional sex honestly. Besides which – I like sex and I like writing about it. I think jackoff books have a valid place in our literature. But there's such a thing as overemphasizing sex, which is as bad as not emphasizing it at all. No, the thing I would change would be the social and political content of the books. I want to be able to make political comments without worrying that my publisher is going to take the bite out of it – or cut it out altogether.

Vanden: Do you feel that gay people generally should become more politically oriented?

Amory: We have *got* to! There's no question about it in my mind. Look, we're a hundred years behind the blacks as far as political action is concerned. In many respects I can really dig the Black Panthers. Those guys *know* what they're up against. They *know* that Whitey doesn't listen. The blacks have been talking sweet reason for four hundred years, and where has it got them? No – it's the people who have *stopped* talking who are making things happen. Putting on pressure. The Chicanos are finding it out. And the students. And Gay

Lib. They all know that talk doesn't mean a damn thing if you can't back it up with pressure of some sort – political, economic, whatever. That's how the establishment works, so that's what it understands best – *pressure!*

I feel very strongly that the minorities – all of us – sexual, racial, religious, the young – the minorities are going to be the salvation of this country. The direction of American society in the past hundred years – at least that, maybe more – has been in the hands of the gringos, the honkeys, the straights, the eighty-year-old judges and senators... And they've fucked it up. That's all you can say – *they've fucked it up!* And the minorities have got to become the conscience of this country. We've got to make the white heterosexual protestants realize what the Constitution is all about – what the Bill of Rights is all about – what Christianity itself is about! We've got to, or this whole mess is going to go right down the drain!

Vanden: So how are we going to start to accomplish all this?

Amory: The very first thing is to stop publishing through underground publishers like Greenleaf Classics – through any straight editor who thinks gay sex is funny or dirty. If we can possibly do it, we should set up a gay publishing house with gay writers, gay editors, gay copyboys, gay typesetters, gay proofreaders, gay lawyers – one hundred percent gay. Gay people have got to get together as the blacks have done, as the students have done, with our own *honest* literature, our own theatre, our own art – and we've got to decide who we are and what we want out of life. We've taken the first step with the underground novels and magazines, now we've got to go further. To step out, make ourselves heard and felt – come together. Then we'll have something really worthwhile. Something we can be proud of. It's that or sit back down in the horseshit and just wait 'til it smothers us.